holy hell

holy hell

A LILLIAN BYRD
CRIME STORY

ELIZABETH SIMS

alyson books
los angeles | new york

© 2002 BY ELIZABETH SIMS. ALL RIGHTS RESERVED.

MANUFACTURED IN THE UNITED STATES OF AMERICA.

THIS TRADE PAPERBACK ORIGINAL IS PUBLISHED BY ALYSON PUBLICATIONS,
P.O. BOX 4371, LOS ANGELES, CALIFORNIA 90078-4371.
DISTRIBUTION IN THE UNITED KINGDOM BY TURNAROUND PUBLISHER SERVICES LTD.,
UNIT 3, OLYMPIA TRADING ESTATE, COBURG ROAD, WOOD GREEN,
LONDON N22 6TZ ENGLAND.

FIRST EDITION: JANUARY 2002

05 06 07 08 09 **a** 14 13 12 11 10 9 8 7 6 5

ISBN 1-55583-653-4
ISBN-13 978-1-55583-653-5

LIBRARY OF CONGRESS CATALOGING-IN-PUBLICATION EATA
  SIMS, ELIZABETH, 1957–
    HOLY HELL : A LILLIAN BYRD CRIME STORY / BY ELIZABETH SIMS.—1ST ED.
    ISBN 1-55583-653-4; ISBN-13 978-1-55583-653-5
    1. WOMEN JOURNALISTS—FICTION. 2. LESBIANS—FICTION. I. TITLE.
  PS3619.I564 H65 2002
  813'.6—DC21   2001045821

CREDITS
COVER DESIGN BY MATT SAMS.
COVER PHOTOGRAPHY FROM PHOTODISC.

ACKNOWLEDGMENTS

Since a novel is more or less a manifestation of the innards of the author, and since no author is self-invented but is formed by, if not made up of, her experiences, I'd like to thank everyone I've ever met.

A handful in that group stands out:

My mother, Carolyn Sims Davis, whose reverence for books and authors set me to thinking, way too young, hell, you know, how hard could it be? My late father, Frank Sims, who gave of himself everything I ever asked. My loving brother David Sims, my beautiful sister Kathleen Cristman, and my steadfast uncle and aunt, Leonard and Tracy Romey.

Pauline Adams for humoring my grandiose ambitions. My special friends Maureen M. McClellan, Arlene-Marie, Brad Grube, Lucinda Reinas, Gesa Kirsch, Thom Powers, Jan Kimmel, Terry McKenzie, Cindi Forslund, Anne Kubek, Molly Sapp, Andrea Smith, and Philip Lenkowsky. Sue Brooks and Kay Solsbury, through whose door I found the community, and so much more. Tim Gable, Elaine Morse, and Don Powers, as holy a trinity of booksellers as ever lived. The uncommonly sensible Angela Brown.

And my beloved Marcia Burrows, who keeps believing that a best-seller is just around the corner.

1

A new chapter for me began on an average Monday at the offices of the *Eagle Eye,* when I abandoned diplomacy for mild violence, and it worked. Unfortunately, I also became suddenly and vividly unpopular with my boss, the publisher.

I liked Ed Rinkell because he let me report on anything I wanted as long as we didn't get sued. And he paid me a decent wage. He was a former ad man, however, and in the newspaper business, revenue from advertising makes the world go 'round, so naturally his values system put the look and quantity of our advertisements at the top. Since his son, Bucky, was in charge of advertising layout and I was combination reporter and editor for our tiny weekly paper, you can grasp the dynamics. When Bucky needed an assistant, he got one; when I needed a photographer, I got a camera. This is not to complain. I enjoyed taking pictures.

What burned my toast was when Bucky pawed me. Yeah. The first time he did it, I was so taken aback I almost doubted it happened.

I'd been working at the *Eye* for about four years when he came on board after losing his job as a bouncer at a strip club in Sterling Heights called Big Dick's. I don't know why the place shut down; it couldn't have been for lack of wit. We worked together in the composition room nearly every day, the Buckeroo manicuring ad layouts while I stripped down photos and copy, and wrote headlines to fit.

Mostly, Bucky was sullen, but when he was feeling festive he'd make sparkling comments. "Hey, Lillian," he'd say, above the loser-land strains of the Jimmy Buffett tapes he played over and over, "*thighs!* and *breasts!* are on sale! Sixty cents a pound at Kroger's. Think I oughta get some for dinner?"

Our typesetter, Nona, sometimes tried to interfere, touchingly, by replying, "That price isn't until tomorrow. Tomorrow is when they go on sale." Nona missed the point a lot. Usually I'd ignore him. Once in a while he'd get to me, and I'd respond with something droll like, "Well, you might as well—I doubt you'll get any other kind."

Bucky looked the ex–high school linebacker he was, thickly muscled but plumping up. He wore stretched-out polo shirts and Dockers, whose current ad campaign was saying it's OK to be a boring guy going to pot 'cause you're in good company. His face might have been handsome but for a distinctive dullness about the eyes, which I associated with poor study habits in his early years and too much beer later on. He covered his bald spot with some gimme cap at all times, indoors and out. That summer his favorite one was a purple tribute to the Gibraltar Trade Center, a gigantic and wondrous indoor flea market off I-75 south of Detroit.

Bucky admired Steve, his best friend, whose dad had gotten him an incredibly high-paying job as a welder right out of high school and who had totaled three Trans Ams before he was twenty-one. Bucky quoted that statistic with awe whenever Steve's name came up. There was something poetic about it to him. Bucky himself had recently gotten under payments on a brand-new Camaro with a custom blue-sparkle paint job. He loved the hell out of that car, you could tell, the way he talked about it and looked at it and rubbed invisible dust off the fender every time he parked it. He kept it immaculately tidy and waxed, which was the one thing I respected him for. I like a nice clean car.

Occasionally, he'd get disgusted with himself and go on Slim-Fast. He'd struggle along on coffee and cigarettes, and claim to be working out every day at the Y, but he couldn't keep it up. I felt sorry for him actually, knowing the women at the young-'n'-restless bars he frequented didn't give him much of a chance.

All this might make Bucky sound like a real shithead. I don't mean to be unfair. He had friends. He could make me laugh. I've known bigger shitheads.

To prevent wasted steps, the layout counters were set in rows close together, so we had to squeeze past each other as we moved from page to page. One day, after Bucky had been working at the *Eye* a few months, he squeezed past me and at the same time rubbed his crotch against my backside. It was one of those moments where maybe it was or maybe it wasn't, so I let it go.

But it happened again a couple of weeks later. I felt I'd done my bit putting up with the verbal crap, so I felt a tad pushed. But then, what did I expect? If I put up with crude comments, I was in effect saying they were OK with me. On the other hand, they sort of *were* OK. I mean, what the hell. Sometimes Bucky was funny, especially when he ridiculed his dad's hairpiece, which the rest of us couldn't get away with.

And I have to tell you, I loathe prissiness.

So, right or wrong, it took his dick against my thigh to get me good and revolted. After the third time, when I was sure it was no accident, I turned to him.

"Bucky," I said loudly, "you rubbed your crotch against my rear and touched my breast too this time. You've done it before. Don't do it again, goddamn it." Nona reeled in her swivel chair in front of the Compugraphic. Later she told me she also had received Bucky's creative attentions from time to time.

The normal buzz in the outer office ceased, and Archie, the circulation manager, poked his head through the door-way. Bucky retreated to the classified board and grinned uncertainly.

He left me alone for almost a month, then did it again. As his broad back moved away down the counter, he leered over his shoulder, and suddenly the X-Acto knife in my hand took on a whole new meaning. A slim, silvery wand with an inch-long blade, always close at hand—what a sudden little friend!

"Bucky," I said, this time in a low voice so only he could hear, "if you do that again, I'm going to carve your ass off with this blade." He laughed delightedly and scratched his back with a ruler.

Like the dolt I was, though, I thought I should try again for a peaceful resolution: I had a private talk with Bucky's father. Hey, the boss is the boss, right? He should take care of trouble, right?

I explained the situation, bouncing the heel of my penny loafer on the aorta-colored carpet in Ed Rinkell's office.

Rinkell looked mildly surprised, then chuckled indulgently. He promised to have a talk with his son. *That's my boy*, his face told me. I knew, I knew.

We come up to the ordinary Monday afternoon under discussion, actually a Midwest-style fireball July Monday afternoon, about a week after I'd complained to Rinkell. Our building wasn't air-conditioned, but it was built of cinder blocks so it usually stayed cool. This afternoon was an exception: The heat was turning the composition room into a sweat lodge; as a matter of fact, the weather was to stay murderous all week—an appropriate choice of word, you will see.

I was leaning on one perspiring forearm over the sports board, cropping a rare action photo of children's softball, when Bucky sidled over. Absorbed in trimming the shot, which showed a diving catch by an infielder, I didn't realize he was coming until I felt that flabby crotch.

He eased past, casually stroked my waist, and looked down at what I was doing. "Whoa!" he said. "Don't trim his little *head* off, Lil. Heh heh."

My adrenaline surged, and without thinking at all I turned as he passed and sank my blade up to the hilt into the left buttock of his stonewashed Dockers. I twisted it a little. The sharp blade moved easily in his soft flesh.

Looking back on it, I suppose it was one of the few real moments of truth in my life. Diplomacy can work, but you have to have common ground. There needs to be dialogue. Bucky Rinkell and I had no common ground until I stabbed him. Or maybe it was the heat.

The aftermath of the stabbing unfolded in slow motion. I drew the blade out, saw it coated with blood, and threw it into the trash can. Ignoring Bucky, I took up another blade and continued to trim the shot. His roaring filled my ears, but I couldn't quite make out what he was saying—my own blood was rushing around so. He stumbled into the men's room and stayed a long time. Rinkell didn't fire me on the spot, because he wasn't there. I think he would have, given how men—well, you know, how men can be sometimes.

As I finished the sports section, it occurred to me that my days at the paper could be numbered. Yet I'd acted in justifiable self-defense. I figured Bucky's butt would heal, he'd never touch me again, and everything should be fine.

I didn't really consider that when you don't bend to the powerful—or worse, when you humiliate the powerful, however briefly—they have ways of getting you. Subtle ways, instinctive ways. While Bucky Rinkell might not come across as a particularly powerful guy, circumstances gave him an edge over me. Blood is thicker, as we all know, and I had spilled his.

That afternoon when I crossed the street to the police station for my weekly check of the white sheets—the crime reports—I savored the moment in a state of high numbness. My heart was still pounding, though an hour had passed. Bucky's engorged face and Nona's pale, joyful one bobbed in my mind's eye; the bloated roar of Bucky's voice echoed in my ears.

I stabbed a guy, I affirmed dramatically as I crossed the shimmering street. True, it was only a one-inch blade plunged into surely more than an inch of extraneous butt tissue, but still. Before, I'd always believed the pen was mightier than the sword. Now, while you couldn't exactly say I was gripped by bloodlust, I was beginning to understand the efficacy of pure action.

Eagle is one of Detroit's older suburbs, one whose downtown is really a downtown, with a main drag and a business district, brick storefronts and a craggy city hall. The streets are lined with big old trees that cast thick, deep shade.

The Eagle Police Department occupied a venerable building with a great set of stone steps and massive iron lampposts on either side of its varnished double doors.

"Yo, Lillian," called Katzinger, the traffic sergeant, as I pushed through the doors. He got up from behind the counter and handed me the week's sheaf of reports on a clipboard. "Not much here this week."

The accident and DUI reports were usually small potatoes, though sometimes you'd come across a piquant statement ("As soon as I collided with the post office, the car just flipped over.") or an amazing circumstance ("Vehicle struck a refrigerator in right lane of northbound Elm.")

I always skimmed for names I recognized. Not that I'd necessarily make a point of reporting the drunk-driving bust of, say, a school board member, out of all the drunk-driving busts for the week, but it would be wise to have a note of it somewhere for future reference.

"Righto, Sarge," I said, flipping through the pages. I handed them back. "Thanks."

Upstairs was where the interesting white sheets were, in the detective division. "Hey, I was about to call you," said Tom Ciesla, the boss lieutenant, as my head poked up from the stairwell.

His family was descended from some Eastern European tribe; Tom had the dark, deep-eyed sturdiness of a rural priest. He once told me that most of his relatives changed Ciesla to the more pronounceable Chester, but he wanted to respect the old country, so he kept Ciesla. You pronounced it "Chessla."

"C'mere," he said. He smoothed a fresh yellow file folder open on his desk. "Old Lester Patchell found a body this morning on his property. Unidentified. It's a miracle the guy came across it, 'cause he doesn't get around so good anymore."

"What happened?" I asked, scanning page one.

"Homicide. The body was rolled up in a piece of carpet and stuffed into a big crack in the foundation of one of his barns."

"The one that's falling down? Back from the road?"

"Yeah. The great thing is, she was just dead, last night, and the night was cool. For a change. So there wasn't much decomposition."

"Great," I agreed. "No I.D., no nothing, huh?"

"Lester said he had a junk dealer coming to clean the place out, and he wanted to go through his stuff."

Not much in the way of murder happens in Eagle, though body dumpings occur on its outskirts now and then, the same as in other metropolitan Detroit suburbs. During the string of Oakland County child killings back in the '70s, owners of remote pieces of property found themselves taking long walks on weekends, poking around for something they didn't want to find.

"Any likely missing persons reports?" I asked as I read the description: dark-complected black female, five-foot-four to five-foot-five, slight build, short haircut. "She was shot?"

"No missing persons yet," Ciesla said. "Once in the back of the head. A .22, from the look of it. No obvious signs of sexual assault. The coroner's doing an autopsy, maybe today. He's had a slow week. But here's what we want—Erma, where're those Polaroids? We'd like you to run a drawing of her in the *Eye*. An artist from the sheriff's department's making a sketch of her now."

"You'll give it to the dailies too, right?"

"Yeah, but they might not run it, or maybe only way inside the paper, but you guys could run it on the front page, and at least people around here would see it."

"Think this one might be related to the Midnight Five?"

"I don't know. There's a body this time."

One by one over the past two years, five women in the metro Detroit area had inexplicably disappeared overnight. Since there had been no evidence of foul play and no bodies had turned up, the cops were stymied. No one knew whether any crime had, in fact, been committed. The papers were starting to call them the Midnight Five, as if the string of murders was over. There hadn't been one in a few months.

Det. Erma Porrocks handed me a Polaroid snapshot. Porrocks was a diminutive, graying institution at the Eagle P.D. Her feet never touched the floor from any of the man-size chairs there, but I once saw her subdue a rampaging drunken bastard three times her size when a brawl spilled from the Eagle Tap Room into the street.

The photograph, of the victim's face, had obviously been taken at the scene. It was blurry and off-colored, but legible enough. Most people think, from the movies, that if a person gets shot in the head, half the head explodes and the face disintegrates. With a shotgun or rifle, that's often the case, especially at close range. But with a small-caliber handgun there's usually just a little hole and some blood. Something about the photograph made me turn and hold it under Ciesla's desk lamp to get a better look.

What the written description in the file can never convey is the character of the face, the suggestion of its mobility, its grace: This dead face, upturned to the morning sun, had been intriguingly beautiful, with deep mahogany skin, a wide firm mouth and slightly crooked nose, and a brow high and strong like the prow of a ship. I say that, because I had been intrigued by it before, some little time ago.

"Do you know her?" Ciesla asked sharply.

He and I had gotten pretty friendly in the years I'd been reporting in Eagle. I liked the police department. Carefully, over time, I'd built a good rapport with the cops, especially Ciesla. He was the ideal cop in my opinion; he had common sense and a brain in his head. He actually read, would sometimes walk over to the library on his lunch hour and look at *Psychology Today, The New Yorker*—magazines most cops, face it, don't read. We'd discuss current events.

The phone rang, and Porrocks answered it.

"Ah, no, I don't," I said to Ciesla, composing myself, still looking at the picture. In fact, I didn't exactly know her, but I had seen her and talked with her in an attempt to get to know her, and it jolted me down to my socks that she was dead. I was trying to decide what to say or not say when Porrocks announced, "Southfield police. They got a positive I.D."

Ciesla and I turned.

"Yeah. Uh-huh," Porrocks said into the phone. "Ciesla and I'll probably come over. OK." She hung up. Cops never say "Goodbye" on the phone. They say "OK," or they just hang up.

"Name: Iris Lynn Macklin. M-A-C-K-L-I-N. Age: thirty-four. Address in that big apartment complex on Plaza Drive in Southfield. Her husband reported her missing at noon. He just ID'd her." She hitched up the waistband of her skirt.

"OK, let's go talk to him," Ciesla said. "Is that what you

said—he's at the coroner's now? Let's go." He turned back to me. "We won't need you to run that drawing, then."

"I'll talk to you when you get back."

I walked over to the window and gazed out at the street, at the *Eagle Eye* office, at the Eagle Tap Room next door. I looked down again at the picture in my hand. It was Jean, all right. Iris Macklin? What else did Porrocks say? Her husband identified her? *Husband*? This was news to me, news to the newswoman.

2

My mind traveled back a couple of Saturday nights to the Snapdragon. It was a melancholy night—everybody's melancholy when they're going through a breakup, right? Judy and I had been together about three years, three nice years. It was a joyful period for her, because she'd finally found someone who would accept her love as she wanted to give it: fierce, greedy, final. But it was a sweet-sad time for me, as I gradually came to know I'd have to leave her.

She was, to me, achingly beautiful. She would enfold me in her heavy warm body, presenting herself to me and at the same time claiming me, and I'd feel safe, safe, safe. Her face, framed by delicate golden tendrils, was high-boned and ruddy, her expression always questioning and hungry. What did I want? If she could give it, I would have it. She wanted to be my everything: lover, mother, child. A powerfully attractive combination. Except those roles don't mix, not really. Try to mix them and you're in for some long-term problems.

Ah, but she understood me, she loved me. She spoiled me. Love notes taped to my windshield, back rubs and breakfast in bed! That was the nurturing part of her—then there'd be the resentful child. The child jealous of my time away from her, the child who was always late—such a tiny but potent insult!—the child who had the shocking habit of undermining the friendships of others, if she felt excluded. And my faults? Why, my faults are legion, God and my friends know. Boy, do they know. But faults and fixes, well, they're not exactly the point here, are they? With patience you can cope with imperfection in others and yourself. You have to.

I would take her face in my hands and look into it, loving her and feeling sorry at the same time. She would see the love but not the sorrow; or rather, she would mistake the sorrow for a deeper love that wasn't there. That was my problem. I wanted to love her so much more than I did.

This wasn't destined to be a quick breakup, one tidy wrench and then over. I had to try to explain, to somehow justify myself. How do you say I just don't love you enough? Or, it's taken me a while to figure this out, but I think you're the wrong life partner for me? Or, I don't know why, but I simply need to leave? But I had to try to explain. So we talked. Oh God, did we talk. We talked until our throats were sore, until the air in our apartment filled up with sentences, exclamations, clauses, punctuation.

How can words do justice to the most mysterious of emotions? After a point it felt as though we were trying to dissect a moth with a chain saw.

There were tears, rivers of tears. Mostly hers. Some people say it's as painful to be the one to initiate a breakup as it is to be broken up on. Some self-serving wretches even

13

claim it's *more* painful to be the one to make the break. Well, if you've been on both ends, you and I both know it's easier to leave than be left. Sure, you suffer if you leave; it hurts like hell, the worst thing knowing you're causing pain to another human being. But at least you know you're doing the right thing for yourself—nay, the right thing for everybody in the long run. At least that's what you hope you're doing.

In a shower of words and tears, I moved out, along with Todd, my pet rabbit. We took an upper flat in a house in Eagle owned by an elderly couple who lived in the lower. But as I say, this wasn't to be a quick breakup. Judy and I continued to see each other on a reduced-intimacy basis, tapering off as it were, her hoping, I know, I'd change my mind. For me, the tapering off was a safety net: What if I *did* change my mind? I fooled myself into believing my chief motivation was the desire to be humane. Taper it off, she'll get used to it, we'll stay friends.

I was never much for the cruising scene, but loneliness can be a powerful influence. I mentioned a Saturday night at the Snapdragon. That afternoon had been a gorgeous one, balmy and sunny, just the kind of Saturday that Judy and I would've pounced on together, perhaps taking a road trip out to the country for a round of golf, or produce-buying, or just riding and dreaming.

Instead, I deep-cleaned my new flat, a satisfying enough activity. By deep-cleaning I mean working over every surface with water and a cleaning agent. By every surface I mean not just the tops of things, but the sides and innards.

For instance, you don't just wipe off the stove after you've cleaned the oven, you pull all the grates and burner pans up and wash them in the sink with a brush; you scour the edges of the oven door, and you pry off the knobs and soak them in ammonia water, and you take a toothbrush and a mini bucket of water with Spic and Span dissolved in it, and you brush the grime from around the oven handle, from the chrome trim, from around the clock face. You take hold of the stove and walk it away from the wall, and you take a rag and wipe out the greasy dust from the back of the stove and all under it. You deploy steel wool against the caked-on drips down the sides. Then you take a rag soaked in nothing but clean water, and you wipe down the whole thing. Reassemble.

I listened to some Scruggs-style banjo music while I did this—you know that Folkways record? Loud and fast.

I dusted the tops of all the doors and the baseboards with a piece of damp chamois leather, the kind people use on their cars. It's the best dust cloth there is. Once a speck of dust touches that chamois, it stays on it. I took down all the overhead light fixtures and washed them in soapy water and dusted the bulbs. I vacuumed, then spot-dusted again. The bathroom: scouring pad to the tile, sponge to the ceiling and walls, rag to the floor.

Back in the kitchen there was a little closet that must have been used as a garbage depot by previous tenants. I got in there with a bucket of water and Spic and Span. For about ten minutes I thought somebody had painted the baseboards black, but at last the grime gave way and pretty yellow paint showed through.

Then as the sun faded into a molten ball low over the rooftops of Eagle, I took a long hot shower and dressed up for the Snapdragon. I put on my least baggy jeans, a plain white linen blouse, and my newer oxblood Bass Weejuns in case I wound up hitting the timber. My sinuses were nice and clear from all the cleaning agents.

The Snapdragon bar was tucked between a rent-to-own shop and an abandoned gas station in northwest Detroit, on Livernois near Seven Mile, not far from my neighborhood in Eagle. The gas station had been boarded up for as long as I could remember, probably still is. Parking was tight, as always; I left my 1985 evergreen Chevrolet Caprice in the alley and gave the keys to the security guard, a relentlessly cheerful fellow named Emerald who jockeyed cars and watched the street life all night. He made a point of learning people's names. I lingered with him for a few minutes.

A breeze was sweeping off nearby Palmer Park, and the summer weeds were bustin' up from the cracked pavement. "Do you like Detroit, Emerald?"

"This is where I'm from," he said. He had a caterpillar mustache and kind eyes.

"But do you like it?"

"You are really white, you know? Lillian. Lily. Lily-white! 'Do you like where you live.' You gotta bloom where you're potted, baby."

I thought about that.

"You know I live right over there?" he said. "I walk to work. Yeah," he went on, "it's different from before. You'd think as time went by there'd be less bullshit, but there's more. People don't learn."

I don't suppose Detroit is the only city where bars like the Snapdragon have to worry about security, but the clandestine ritual of going in always made me feel like a bit player in some grungy drama.

The vestibule was a little wooden structure built onto the

back door, the front door being permanently barred. I stood in the dim, musty-smelling hut and positioned myself in front of the steel security door with its one-way glass window and pushed a white button, hearing it ring faintly inside.

You always had to wait for Sandra to put down her drink somewhere in the passageway and recognize you through the window and then buzz you in. She collected my dollar cover charge. Though the owner, Bonnie, invariably ignored me, her lackey Sandra gave me a friendly hello.

Bonnie had purchased the bar a couple of years before from a splendid aging queen and transformed it from a men's G-string joint to a quiet women's pub. The women of metro Detroit were grateful for this, as God knows in any burg the men's bars outnumber the women's by about a jillion to none. Bonnie got a softball league going, organized dances and talent shows, and in other ways drew women to her joint.

Nobody seemed to know her well, though. She was friendly only toward certain people. I could never figure out what her friendliness criteria were.

The Snap was busy but not packed. I liked it that way: plenty of potential dance partners, plus you had room to breathe. I noticed Bonnie hunkered in her usual spot at the center of the bar. I made respectful eye contact as I passed; she dropped her eyes to my clothes, then my shoes. I found a little table with a good view of the room and ordered a drink from Kevin, the mascot waiter.

Kevin was slim and handsome, with a strong jaw and a gorgeous head of dirty-blond hair. Thus, you would expect to find him on staff at one of the men's bars—Banjo's or even the old Stock Exchange where he could really shine—

but he was shy. Plus for about a year he'd been going with a possessive accountant who partially supported him. So Kevin watered the garden of women at the Snapdragon, where his personality, not his looks, got him the good tips.

Now, don't start with me about how *lesbians* and *good tips* can't be in the same sentence. I reject that. I tip well, and so do my friends, damn it.

"Kevin, is that a new blouse?" I asked. He beamed and turned so I could see the back. Delicate shirred fabric dropped in a cloud from his shoulders. "It's beautiful," I told him. "What're you doing wearing it to work? One of these brutal dykes could spill a drink on it."

"Oh, I like to look nice all the time." He had a lofty little way of talking. "Besides, Ralph's picking me up later."

When he brought my Dewar's and a splash—no ice, short glass—he said, "We haven't seen you in a while, Lillian." His face showed that undefinable level of concern that communicated the full sentence: *It's a Saturday night, and I see you're not with Judy—does this mean what I think it means?*

I admitted, "Yeah, Judy and I are about three-fourths split up. I moved out." Guiltily I gazed down at my drink. "I'm trying to extricate myself. I shouldn't go over there anymore."

"Is there someone else?"

"No." I looked up. "Just—it just doesn't feel right, it doesn't feel like I should stay with her anymore. I don't even have a clear idea of what I want. I'm just restless, I guess."

"Stop saying 'just' all the time, like you're an old dog dish. I know Judy, too, you know. I always thought she was too maternal for you."

"You think so?"

"Oh, yeah, way, way—everybody could see it. So you're trying to be responsible and end something before you get petrified into it. What's wrong with that?"

"That's what I keep telling myself. So why do I feel like such a shit?"

"Because, dear heart, without guilt to keep us going, we'd all die. We'd simply shrivel to bits." He made a weary spiral motion with his hand. Then he gave a little start. He closed his eyes for a moment, then blasted them at me. He bent down close and said, "Would you say you're on the prowl?"

"Oh, God, no. Well, not yet, anyway. I mean, I guess it depends. Why?"

He shot a glance over the top of my head. "The new DJ is why. I think she's your type, Lil. Just turn slowly."

Well, wowie, there was a hell of an angel behind the glass in the disc jockey booth. Looks aren't everything, I harshly reminded myself, then Kevin said, "She's really a dear. But cool and aloof! Oh, God, she's perfect for you. This is coming straight from my gut, you understand. Her name's Jean. Gotta go."

Jean. I couldn't say my heart stood still, but it sure, well, *paused*. The light that spilled into the DJ booth highlighted her close-trimmed jet-black hair, her high handsome forehead, her slender arms. She was wearing a scoop-neck T-shirt, black.

I scooted my chair slightly and, in the quiet luxury of darkness, observed. The dance floor stretched between me and the booth; women swam back and forth in my field of vision, hiding then revealing Jean. I found myself swaying slightly in opposing measure to their movements so that Jean would come into view a split-second earlier and go out of view a split-second later.

Jean had the coolest job at the bar: spinning tunes, conducting the emotions of the women on the dance floor, adjusting their heartbeats with tempo and lyrics. Unlike some DJs who are, oh, sort of egotistical, in love with being a bonbon under glass, Jean appeared matter-of-fact and professional.

Her hands moved expertly among the records and CDs, adjusting the controls with minimal gestures. From time to time she sipped from a red plastic thermos cup. Her face shifted smoothly between expressions, now focusing calmly in the middle distance, now smiling slightly at perhaps a line in a song.

What she played I couldn't tell you. Although I love to dance, I'm bored practically to suicide by bar music. I try and try to relate to that disco-beat café music, but I can't. Even most Women's Music, with those capital letters, leaves me needing oxygen. So dip me in shit. What do I like? Real rock 'n' roll. Bluegrass. Or classical, for God's sake. If I never have to try to dance to "Bette Davis Eyes" again, it'll be too soon.

Of course, I immediately assumed Jean was unavailable— the first line of defense when the heart is awakened to a new and uncertain possibility. *Get back to reality,* said the little voice of reason in my head. I say "little." I mean it.

I looked down at my drink and swirled it. My thoughts drifted. I wondered if I could hold off grocery shopping for another few days; I worried about Judy; I tried to come up with an idea for the coming week's editorial—maybe something about blooming where you're potted. Maybe I could relate it to recycling.

After a moment, still gazing into my drink, I became aware of a looming presence. My peripheral vision registered a sturdy leg encased in heavy blue denim. A work boot flew up from the floor and landed with a bang on the seat of the empty chair next to me. I didn't have to look up to know it was Lou.

But I did look up, out of reluctant politeness. I'm not short, but from my seated position it was a long way up from Lou's booted foot to the yawning crotch of her overalls to her loud plaid shirt to her column-like neck to her stern red face, tonight sporting an aggressive smile for me.

She leaned down and propped an elbow on her knee. She'd been letting her iron-streaked hair grow out, I noticed; she had it in a rather bouncy ponytail that took a few years off her. She was a Snapdragon regular.

"I was hoping you'd come in tonight, and you did," she said, a note of triumph in her scratchy voice.

Lou had liked me for a long time, way before the Snapdragon existed. I thought she was a nice-enough person, from a distance anyway. I have nothing against husky women in overalls who happen to be a little lacking in manners. I just didn't like Lou the way she liked me. Over the years at the Snap and other places—blind pigs and house parties—I'd managed to dodge her advances without hurting her feelings. But tonight she was especially intent.

"You and Judy," she said, and drew a finger across her throat.

"Well," I said, "not exactly. Um..."

She heaved her boot back to the floor, yanked out the chair, and straddled it. She appeared perfectly capable of devouring me in one bite. Her eyes locked into mine. "Are you or aren't you two together anymore?"

"Well, Lou, see—"

"Are you or aren't you?"

I stared back down at my drink.

"You look nice tonight, Lillian," she volunteered in what she must have intended to be a tender tone. "Have you done something new to your hair? The color?"

"No. It's naturally brown."

"You're cute. I've always thought you were very cute."

I am not cute. I'm homely. I'm a skinny, homely biscuit, and I know it. I once socked a boy in junior high school for calling me cute. We weren't little kids on the playground; we were fourteen and right in the library, but I just couldn't stand it.

I make the best of things with fastidious hygiene and simple good clothes. And I make a point of getting quality haircuts and dental work.

Lou bore down on me for a few more hellish minutes. After silently debating with myself, I decided on the honesty method.

"Look, Lou, I'm really not interested. OK?"

She pretended not to hear, so I had to repeat it, louder. Then she wanted to know why, and she wanted to argue with me about it. She wanted me to dance with her. She wanted me to acknowledge her qualities. She wanted me to appreciate her, goddamn it. The more I said, the worse it got. So I finally fell silent, forced into the rudeness method.

After a while she shambled sorrowfully back to the pool tables where the other regulars were hanging, watching. I heard muffled hoots.

I went back to scrutinizing Jean, whose beauty and charm were increasing by the minute. Yes, OK, she certainly gained by the contrast with Lou.

Eventually I got up with my drink, intending to move over to the bar. I was feeling mellower. The Snapdragon was a fine place, truly, I mused. Kevin came by: "Need another? I should think you do. I saw you squirming over there under Lou's, uh, attentions. But hey, what do you think of Jean?"

"Don't need another yet, thanks. Um, yeah, she seems nice."

"Plus she has good taste in music."

"Hmm."

He glanced over his shoulder. "I should probably inform you that Bonnie's got her eye on her too."

"Well, doesn't she put the moves on every DJ who comes in here? I mean, remember Lauren?"

"Oh, God, Lauren," he groaned. "Do you know the whole story of that? What happened when Lauren quit?"

"No, you know I'm not on the inside track of anything. Do tell." At that instant, we heard Bonnie's voice cut through the low din: "Kevin!"

"Can she hear us?" I said.

"She probably read my lips. I think she's got demonic powers."

"She must be a bitch at times, but aren't all bosses?" I finished my sentence hastily because Bonnie had uncoiled herself from her barstool and was making her way toward us. She had a thick body and frizzy orange-toned hair.

"I called you," she said, pushing her face into Kevin's.

He drew back a little. "I was coming."

"I want your ass covering this floor. I don't pay you to chit-chat." In the dimness her face looked pasty, yet I thought she was attractive in a full-lipped, overblown sort of way. "Gwen needs a hand with the Bloody Mary mix." Kevin hustled off, and Bonnie cast me a fishy look. I refrained from saying, "How come you've got such a nice joint here, yet you yourself are so disagreeable?"

Right then Bonnie's look shifted, as if some invisible person had whispered something in her ear. Some nasty gossip about me, perhaps. Her eyes widened, and she looked at me hard and deep. I held her gaze out of self-defense, wondering what she was thinking. Then her eyes softened and dropped. I felt relieved without knowing why.

"You're a prize, aren't you?" she said, looking at my loafers.

"I've been called worse."

Abruptly, she turned and waded through the crowd back to her place at the bar. What the fuck that little comment meant, I didn't know.

Saturday night was now in full bloom, and the Snap was getting more crowded. The air-conditioning was going full blast, but there were so many people smoking that the air was blue. I hung at the outskirts of the bar for a while, talking with acquaintances, then danced a few steps with a chipper schoolteacher I knew. I do love to dance. I kept glancing over at the DJ booth.

There was a pause in the music, and Jean put on a tape and slipped out of the booth. She moved smoothly through the crowd to the restroom. I sidled over to intercept her as she came out. What the hell, I thought.

After clearing the door, she almost bumped my chest with her nose. As she looked up, I saw her eyes deciding whether to be irritated or interested.

"Get you a drink?" I asked quickly.

She smiled a cool little smile and tipped her head back to see me better. I tried to look wonderful.

To my utter delight, she took my arm.

3

We carved our way through the haze to the tiny table next to her booth. A red candle pot flickered on it.

"I'm Lillian Byrd," I said as we sat down.

"I'm Jean."

I waited.

A smile. "Just Jean."

You know the old saying that you're really getting to know a gay woman when you're on a last-name basis with her? I smiled back.

Kevin, ever alert, appeared, and she ordered an orange juice. I made it two.

"I don't drink liquor while I'm working," she explained. "I drink coffee in the booth."

Up close she appeared less confident than she had in the DJ booth. The tape was playing some thumpy song, and the background noise was probably as loud as it ever got, but I thought I detected a quaver in her voice.

"I was admiring you from over there," I said, "and I thought it'd be nice to talk for a few minutes."

"You're very nice."

"Well. It's nice to be nice."

The crook of my arm was still vibrating where her hand had nestled in it. Her skin was flawless, and I saw large, even teeth when she smiled. I noticed a sideways jog at the bridge of her nose. *A perfect imperfection*, I thought. Her eyes sort of swerved around my face without coming in, though.

"Were you a DJ someplace else before here?"

"Not really. But I told Bonnie I was experienced, that I spun tunes back in my hometown."

"Which was?"

She looked at me. Our orange juices came.

"To your health," I toasted. We sipped. "Well," I said, "I might as well ask you this very extremely important question that's been on my mind for minutes now."

Her eyebrows dived.

"Do you like terrific food?"

She laughed, relaxing a fraction. "Of course."

"Well, there's a great all-night deli up on John R Street where we could grab a sandwich later. They bake their own rye bread—it's out of this world."

She considered that. I watched a muscle in her smooth cheek twitch. She held her body gracefully; you could tell it was resilient and strong. I yearned to get her out on the dance floor.

She picked up the candle pot and cradled it in her hands, making the hot wax run up the sides. The wick flared. Her nail beds glowed pink, like tiny rosebuds.

"I'm in a relationship now," she finally said.

"Oh."

"But I'd like to get out of it."

"Oh!"

She set the candle pot down. "This—this person is not a bad person, but there's not the—involvement." Then she looked me right in the eye. "There's not the passion."

"I see."

"I used to be a good little girl. Now I want to break loose."

"What's stopping you?"

"You're intelligent."

I couldn't tell whether this was sarcastic. My reporter instincts were churning. I wanted to ask her a hundred questions—learn where she lived, what she did during the daytime, how her nose got crooked, what she liked besides good food, what she hated.

I love learning what people hate.

But I held back: Her manner informed me that she'd bolt if I tried to learn too much too fast.

Her back was to the bar. I saw Bonnie watching us. Jean saw my glance, followed it over her shoulder, and gazed at Bonnie for a long moment. When she turned back she wore a soft smile.

"Are you and Bonnie—?"

"Oh! No!" Jean said. "But she's nice."

"I don't think so." I ironed my cocktail napkin with my palm.

"You have to get to know her, that's all. She's nice to talk to."

"Hmm."

She curled her hands around her glass. "What do you do, Lillian Byrd?"

She seemed to want to warm up to me, yet there was this

moat of nervous reserve around her. I sought a drawbridge.

"You mean for a living? I'm a reporter for—"

"A reporter!"

The moat widened into a chasm, just like that.

"Well, yeah, for the *Eagle Eye*. You know Eagle? The *Eye*'s just a weekly town paper. What's wrong? Are you, like, some kind of undercover—"

"I have to get back to work. I'm sorry. There's nothing the matter with you being a reporter. I guess I must seem jittery."

"Yeah!"

"It's just that—" she stopped. Her eyes appeared to glaze over, then she said something under her breath. I didn't hear her clearly, but it sounded like, "I don't know what I'm doing here." She might have said, "I don't know what I'm mourning here." Her gaze fell to the tabletop. "I'm sorry," she said again.

I gave it one last shot. "Sandwich later?"

"No."

"All right."

She covered my hand with hers for an instant. "Thanks for talking."

"Sure. See you."

Hoo boy, I thought as I wended my way back to the bar. *That's one conflicted chick.* One gorgeous, fascinating, conflicted chick. Comfortable enough behind the glass, but not quite ready to come out and play.

I left soon after, bringing a Coke out to Emerald in the parking lot. My car was where I'd left it near the mouth of the alley. Some stuff on the ground caught my eye. You know how you can tell one kind of trash from another, even if it's smashed or dirty—McDonald's box, six-pack ring, vodka bottle? The little objects near my car didn't fit any normal category, so I bent down and looked closer: a couple of plastic syringes, one with a needle, one without.

"Hey, Emerald, you gotta watch out for these homeless doctors around here," I called.

He looked over and laughed. "I *try* to run a clean parking lot!"

I swung my foot back to kick the syringes aside, when he said, "Wait, I'd best pick those up. Kids ride their bikes through here sometimes."

Then I noticed something else. In the dirty light filtering down from the one tall pole overlooking the parking lot, something gleamed softly. I thought maybe someone had lost an earring; it looked like a pearl or an opal. I squatted and picked it up. Slowly straightening up, I rolled it over in my hand. It was small and beautiful, a God-made thing of simplicity and valuable function, but when I realized what it was, I flung it away from me.

It was a tooth. An incisor, I judged, from either a dog or a really big rat. Some dried blood clung to the root. I heard it *pink* on the concrete somewhere in a shadow.

I peered down the alley, cluttered with Dumpsters, boxes, piles of aging refuse. Urban alleys, like deserts, teem with life not always visible, life sustained by strange means. Emerald bent down and carefully picked up the syringes. A few drops of blood were coagulating inside one. In his wrinkled palm the needle looked terrifyingly sharp. He shook his head. Traffic flashed by on Livernois.

4

So. I'd seen, spoken with, and touched this woman, this murdered woman. It'd been a little more than a week since Kevin had pointed her out to me, and now she was a corpse in a Polaroid. Still holding the picture, looking out the window from the upper floor of the police department, I felt queasy. *God. Dead. A woman with a husband and a fake name working at the Snapdragon. Was she or wasn't she?* It'd be damn unusual for a straight woman to apply for a DJ job at a women's bar. On the other hand, many a married woman discovers the lesbian in herself and explores it before letting go of the man. I know I felt *something* stirring in Jean—well, now Iris—that night.

I studied the picture more closely. A thin stream of dried blood ran from one ear, the lips were closed, the mouth looked bruised and swollen. Had she been beaten up first? I'd learn more when Ciesla and Porrocks got back from the morgue. I shook my shoulders to bring the blood back up to my face, then sat down at Ciesla's desk to copy the information from the white sheet into my notebook. When I was done I should've left the photo on the desk next to the file, but I looked over at Porrocks's desk and saw a few more shots that looked identical. I slipped the photograph into my notebook. The other cops were busy, and no one noticed.

Why did I take it? I didn't rightly know. I sat for a minute, thinking. My old taboo of not talking about my private life on the job was rearing a new, surprisingly ugly head. For of course, if I told Ciesla about seeing Iris Macklin at the Snapdragon, I'd essentially be coming out to the whole police department. A daunting thought at the moment, because believe me, there's something to the generalization that cops tend to be homophobic. The ones in Eagle, anyway. I'd heard the edge of anxiety in their voices as they swapped fag jokes in the squad room.

But that wasn't all of it, couldn't be, because in a case of murder, so what? "Oh, I *had* to lie to stay in the closet!" No. There was something else, a feeling I had about this woman and her death. It had to do with privacy, her privacy, a strange and dangerous privacy. That was my vague thought at the moment.

As I crossed back to the office through the oppressive street air, I figured if those cops are cops, they'll find out about Iris's job at the Snapdragon soon enough, and that was about all I'd be able to tell them anyway. They already knew more about her than I had after talking with her for ten minutes. Who knew whether her connection at the Snap had anything to do with her death in the first place? It occurred to me that perhaps the Detroit dailies would get a photo of Iris from her husband and run that along with a story on her murder. Then maybe somebody else from the bar would recognize her and say something, if the husband didn't know or wouldn't tell.

To my relief, Bucky's sparkle-blue Camaro was gone from the curb in front of the *Eye*. Inside, everyone had been feasting on the day's big event. As I passed through the outer office, Archie turned from his carrier lists. "Lillian, admit it, you were trying to emasculate him, weren't you?"

"Yeah," I agreed. "My aim was lousy, that's all." I left the door to my office open as usual, and went to work editing a pile of filler copy. It was Monday and we published on Wednesdays, so the Detroit dailies would break the news of the murder first, on Tuesday. I'd wait to begin writing my story on it until Tuesday, when doubtless more facts would be available. Not that the daily papers made too terribly much of murders, plain old murders: People got murdered every week—every day, it seemed—in Detroit.

Ed Rinkell stuck his head, topped with its dead-hamster hairpiece, into my doorway. "Got a minute?"

"Sure, Ed." He came in and lowered himself into my side chair. He was an indoor mountain of a man, thick-necked and full-bellied. He liked his shirts tight and his ties wild and woolly.

"Bucky's at the hospital," he said. His face was grave beneath its thatch of Dynel.

"You're kidding."

"He needed stitches."

"You have absolutely got to be kidding." If I were Bucky, the last thing I'd have done would be to go to the hospital and get stitches in my butt. I'd have let it bleed.

"They, uh, they said he'd have a big scar if he didn't get stitches."

I laughed. "I'm sorry for laughing, Ed, but jeez. How big could it be? How many stitches?" I imagined Bucky explaining a jumbo old scar to some brainless girlfriend someday.

"Four."

Unbrightly, I laughed again. "I hope he lives."

"Bucky would love to see me fire you."

"I'm sure he would. Ed, man, look. I don't hate Bucky. We've all gotten along pretty well here, except for one thing. I just wanted him to keep his hands off me."

He blew out his breath impatiently. "Lillian, read between the lines here. You're one of the best things that's ever happened to this paper. You're a great worker, and everybody likes you." Inwardly I cringed. Somebody every-body likes is usually a mealymouthed loser. "Even Bucky liked you." Past tense, hooray.

"Maybe he did. I don't think Bucky actually likes many women, but that's another topic."

"I know Bucky. Hell." Rinkell paused. "He's a young dog."

"He's twenty-three years old, and somebody ought to teach him how to behave. This is an office, Ed, not a fucking stag party."

He knew Bucky got what was coming to him, but he couldn't admit it. "Maybe if you apologized—"

"Absolutely not."

"Lillian, you stabbed the kid! What's wrong with you? You're usually so reasonable. What the hell's your problem?"

"I just got sick of the bullshit. Ed, this doesn't have to be a big deal. You didn't handle things, so I did. That's all there is to it."

"I don't want to fire you."

"Good, I think Bucky's the one you should consider firing."

Rinkell popped out of the chair and gave off a sound like a blast furnace.

I backpedaled. "Forget it, forget it. This is not the hill I want to die on. Hey, have you talked to any cops today? Somebody dumped a body last night on old man Patchell's property. Woman from Southfield."

"What was her name?"

"Iris Macklin."

"Don't know the name."

"I'll call and see if Ciesla's back from the coroner's yet."

Rinkell turned to go, then turned back. "Do you think your job's secure? It's not."

I shrugged. "Guess it's out of my hands."

"Goddamn it." He went out without saying anything else.

Ciesla and Porrocks hadn't gotten back, so I kept at my work until six o'clock. They were either still at the morgue or gone on to somewhere else, so I went home.

5

My usual through-the-door routine consisted of greeting Todd and doing a cursory check for Todd-damage, then getting my bra off as fast as possible and putting on a T-shirt.

Todd was my truest friend, ever since I lifted him out of his cage at the state fair the year before and he bit my left index finger almost in half.

I'd gone into the rabbit building for the hell of it, having split off from a group of friends. I fell in love with every bunny in the place, except the longhaired ones, which scared me, like stuffed toys come to life. I knew my ardor would fade as soon as I left the building. But toward the end of a row, so close to the doors that I could smell the horses next door, a compelling scene was unfolding.

An old man stood next to a rabbit cage, looking furiously over the shoulder of a judge who had just set a rabbit back in the cage. I looked over the judge's other shoulder and watched as he wrote on a card attached to the cage,

"You have not even sexed this rabbit correctly. It is a male. DISQUALIFIED."

The judge moved on dispassionately to the next row. The old man's eyes met mine. "Shit," he said, making it into two syllables: "Shee-it." He looked and sounded like Walter Brennan in the old TV show *The Real McCoys*. If you can remember drinking Tang, thinking it tasted good, and watching *The Real McCoys*, simultaneously, you're about my age.

"I ain't made that mistake in a long time," he said in a voice that suggested a rusty privy hinge moving back and forth. He scratched the pit of his chest. "I don't need no more males this year."

I regarded the rabbit. It was a young standard-style one with short brown fur, looking unusually dignified, I thought, for having just had its private parts pushed around. "Want a rabbit, lady?" the old man said. "We'll likely eat him otherwise."

I'm not the kind of person who falls for animals. The only pet I'd ever owned was in childhood, a sorry little turtle that lived beneath a tiny plastic palm tree on a tiny plastic island in the middle of a tiny water-filled plastic dish. When I lost interest in it, it disappeared, and I was given to understand that it had run away. I didn't question.

The rabbit ignored me. I put my face down to his and gave him a once-over. "What's his name?"

"We just call him dubba-you forty-six." I could picture the missus and the kids and grandkids all sitting on the porch listening to the radio back home in Fowlerville or someplace. I scooped up W-46 from the rear; that's when he turned and bit me.

The rabbit needed a name, he needed me. The old man

tore a strip of cloth from the exhibit table skirt. I wrapped up my finger and left with Todd in a box.

Over the months, I learned a lot about rabbits, most of which should bore you unless you're a pet person. In a nutshell, Todd liked to chew, and he liked his back to be stroked. He liked to eat in moderation, and he liked to thump his hindquarters forcefully, for urgent reasons known only to him, down on the floor now and then. I don't know why I named him Todd. It seemed like a good idea at the time.

As I said, I'd always say hi to him when I got home (he'd hop right over to me) and do a visual baseboard sweep. He'd gotten pretty good about not chewing wood and electrical cords. Of course, I kept most of the cords blocked off by furniture. He settled into our new flat nicely. He had the run of the place and the good sense not to blow it.

A drink was in order. Straight off, I should tell you that I am the daughter of tavern-keepers. My father and mother ran a bar in our neighborhood on Detroit's south side for years and years. I grew up toddling around barstools and pool cues; the regulars called me—affectionately, I like to think—"the little bitch." Perhaps you've noticed my demure vocabulary. Nature or nurture? The question lingers.

My friends find it disconcerting, but I'm far more comfortable walking into a dim little shot-and-a-beer joint with old guys sitting around coughing than one of those cute places with frothy names. And somehow the old-timers in such dim places seem comfortable with me too. I guess it's something in your blood.

Even though I appreciate good mixology, my home liquor supply consists of only one bottle, and it's Scotch. I switch brands every few years or so. That year it was Dewar's. One part cool spring water and three parts whisky, and you've got yourself a fine drink. A lemon twist if you want to be fancy. I took the drink outside to my little balcony over the street and flopped into my yellow plastic lounge chair. The light was softening and slanting through the trees, the air starting to lose its hot slap.

"Here's to you, Bucky, you bastard," I said, and toasted him. "And here's to you, Iris, rest in peace. Whatever the hell happened to you?" I tipped my head back and closed my eyes, thinking of Iris and the police station and the Snapdragon. My arms became heavy. I set my glass down and dozed for a while.

I woke to one of Todd's thumps, which reverberated along the floor like the single beat of a Kodo drum. It jarred me even on the balcony. I came to thinking of Iris, rolled up in a carpet and lying all night next to Lester Patchell's barn.

The sky was purple and the air cooler and clearer. My neck was stiff. I went back inside and found the Polaroid in my notebook. I looked at it for a while, then put it back. Not a good way to remember somebody. The terrible dignity of death. I pulled myself together and drove over to the Snapdragon.

"Lovely evening," Emerald greeted me. He was sitting on a parking bumper eating something out of a box.

"Wow, is that sushi?" I asked as I came up to him.

"Um, yeah," he said in his measured way. "I like it. It's different."

"It's also expensive. Where do you get it?"

"That place right up on, you know, Fourteen Mile?" He

gestured northeasterly. "It's not so very costly. I only get it once in a while. Want one?"

"No, thanks. You enjoy it."

He popped a jewel-like disc into his mouth and waved as I stepped into the vestibule.

It was early, maybe only nine o'clock, so not much was going on yet. Plus it was a weeknight. Sandra was at her usual post near the door. "Hi, dear, how ya doing?" she said.

"Thanks," I said absently. My eyes immediately went to the DJ booth. It was dark. The atmosphere seemed palpably different—something in the air. Tension? Relief? My imagination? I took a seat at the bar, next to a half-finished drink and a smoldering cigarette.

I scanned the room casually, dreading making eye contact with Lou. Fortunately, she wasn't there. My answering machine had recorded three hang-ups the prior week, and I had the sinking certainty they were her.

The Snapdragon was large and busy enough to support a DJ every night, though evidently there would be no substitute this evening. The bartender was a twenty-something-ish woman I'd never seen before. She came over, smiling tentatively. "Dewar's, right?"

"Huh, how'd you know?"

"I remember you from a couple weeks ago." She had a pixie face.

"But I didn't sit at the bar."

"No, you sat over there, and Kevin served you. I remember the drink: Dewar's and a splash, up, short glass."

"You remember everybody's drink like that?"

"No." She fixed me with a steady eye. I gave a short, stupid chuckle.

"Actually," I said, "tonight I'll just have a ginger ale."

A huge blast of music made me leap in my seat. I spun around, half-expecting to see Iris in the blazing booth, the dance floor seething with bodies—but no. It was the jukebox, blaring like mad, and Bonnie rising from a squat behind it where the volume control was.

She started across the empty dance floor, her face flashing purple for an instant, reflecting the jukebox lights. Up until recently my main mental image of her was a dim, crabby figure crouched perpetually on a barstool. As she moved across the floor to the bar, I looked her over more carefully. Her body was solid but seemed quite flexible. She moved fluidly, almost elegantly across the floor. I saw how, under the right circumstances, she could be appealing.

Her outfit, however, an orange smock-like top over a pair of black Lycra tights, plus her frizzed-out orange hair, made her look off-kilter: ridiculous, the Great Pumpkin. She came over to the bar and sat down in front of the drink and cigarette.

I met her eye and nodded. She nodded back and kept her eye on me. It struck me that she seriously lacked imagination in her self-presentation. She wore a faux-Native American amulet on a thong around her neck. It was a shield-like disc of wood, inset with bits of seashell. I imagined she had a dream-catcher hanging over her bed.

"Hi," I said brightly.

"How ya doin'," she said in a low voice. Her lips curled into a little smile, and she turned her head away as if to keep me from seeing it.

Even before I'd gotten home that day, I started speculating about Bonnie: How much did she know about Iris? Was she the last to see her alive?

Her eyes began to wander distractedly, back and forth

among the bottles facing us. I watched her in the mirror. Her complexion was smooth but not firm, her frizzy hair cut in sort of an old-style pageboy that looked to be growing out unevenly. She peered from beneath fluffy bangs. The bangs did something for her, actually, as her features were crowded together at the bottom of her face.

Still looking at the bottles, she said, "I've been thinking about you."

"Oh?"

"You're very dorky."

"Oh, yes, I know."

"I like that." She met my eyes in the mirror.

My stomach flipped when I saw her expression: It was intense, like the other night, unblinking, almost hard, but overlaid with a certain sweet dreaminess, like a starving kitten thinking about a saucer of milk.

I wanted to nip this shit in the bud. "So!" I exclaimed, upbeat, "No DJ tonight!" I heard her take in her breath. "Got the jukebox instead, huh?"

"Yeah." She took a drag off her cigarette, rescuing it, as it were, from slow death in the ashtray. I glanced at the pack next to the ashtray: Carltons. I always say, if you're going to smoke, smoke something you can taste, like Camel filters or Marlboros. She probably drank diet pop too, I guessed.

"So how come?" I pattered on, trying to make my tone still more airy and innocent until I realized it must be verging on idiotic. "How come no DJ tonight?"

Bonnie turned her stool square to me. Suddenly her eyes were hot and narrow. Big long pause. "She quit."

"Oh, no kidding," I said in elaborate disappointment. "I liked her. Huh. Didn't she only work here for a few weeks?

Huh?" The owner of the glass I was drinking ginger ale from picked up her drink and cigarettes and eased off her barstool. I put my hand out. "Didn't she only work here for a few weeks? When did she quit?"

Bonnie turned back to me with acid impatience. "Today."

"Today? *Today?*" I felt my body temperature drop about nine degrees. Bonnie jerked as if someone had punched her between the shoulder blades. She closed her eyes and ducked her head just for an instant, then came back up, flat and cool. I can't say what my face must have told her, except I know I had that "oh, shit" expression for at least the length of time she had her eyes closed. Shit.

"After closing last night," she said finally.

"That would be today," I agreed. "Her name was Jean, wasn't it?" I asked. All of a sudden I realized both Bonnie and I were too scared to keep talking.

She replied only, "Yeah."

Were her hands trembling? My courage returned somewhat.

"Jean what?" I pressed. "Do you know where I might get a hold of her? Jean what?"

"You'll have to ask her."

"Yeah, but how will I get a hold of her? If she's gone?" My heart was pounding like bongos.

Bonnie's eyes appeared to go completely bloodshot in one second. She leaned close to me and parted her lips, and I thought she was about to whisper something, when she seized the back of my neck. Instinctively, I jerked away, but she gripped me tight with both hands. I felt her thumbs pressing vertically into the sides of my throat. I smelled her: an odd mixture of something sweet—English lavender, I supposed it was—and something off, a gluey sort of smell. Her face was inches from mine. I saw an eyelash that had fallen onto her right cheek.

Then she planted her mouth over mine in a forceful kiss. It was like being slapped, hard.

She flung her hands apart just as my arms were driving upward to break her hold, grabbed her cigarettes, and walked off, leaving her drink. She moved deliberately across the empty dance floor and disappeared down the back hall. The bartender, having backed away and busied herself washing glasses, didn't look up as I left.

6

I drove up Livernois to Eight Mile on autopilot, my mind in suspension, then suddenly realized I wasn't heading home. Damn it to hell.

Me: You're headed for Judy's, aren't you?

Me: Ah. Well.

Me: You're headed for Judy's because you're weak. You're weak because you're scared. You've had a hell of a day and you should just go home to bed.

Me: But Judy'd be glad to see me. It'd be nice for her.

Me: That's a cop-out.

Me: Well, she would.

Me: I didn't say it was a lie—I said it was a cop-out.

Eight Mile Road is a major east-west channel along the northern boundary of Detroit. Here you find entrepreneurial America in its purest form: The commercial property that borders it is cheap; thus there's a dazzling array of business ventures from the brilliant to the dim, from the honest to the rotten.

Mixed among the fast-food outlets and small manu-facturing shops are party stores, check-cashing places, used-furniture shops, bakery outlets, heavily fortified bank branches, radiator shops, pawn shops, more go-go joints than you can count, as well as a host of ventures that defy categorization.

What do you make of Mike's Demolition Studio, House of Scarves, Crazy Nancy's Nails 'n' Knees, and Touch Me There? (Well, we can guess on that one.)

Vacant, decaying storefronts become raw material for the dreams of future tycoons. Virtually all the architec-ture is shed-like, with heavy emphasis on signage. Speeding along at night in a car, you're a space traveler, the clusters of lighted signs swooping past you like mete-or showers.

Some do-gooders label this corridor blighted and whine for it to be redeveloped, replanned, prettied up. All I know is, I'm proud to live in a country where if someone wakes up on fire with a business vision combining vitamins, work shoes, and a karate school all under one roof, there's a place for it to happen.

I returned to my argument, rubbing my lips yet again, trying to erase the feeling of Bonnie's wet sucking mouth.

Me: So I'm going in the direction of Judy's, so what? I'm not there yet. It doesn't mean I'm going to turn down her street.

Me: If you went over there, it'd give her false hope, and she'd wind up hurt.

Me: Hey, she's a big girl, and it's a free country. I know I'm trying to make this breakup permanent. But God, I'd just like to see her, talk with her...hold her.

Me: That's what I'm talking about.

Me: Hey, I'm human too!

Me: Do not go over to Judy's.

All the while, I'm driving along Eight Mile toward the apartment we used to share and in which she now lived alone.

I felt like Mrs. Tannin, in the next apartment, who had a food-dependency problem. I'd run into her sometimes at the 7-Eleven on Nine Mile, where I'd observe her knobby shoulders stooped inside her old fuzzy coat, her arms laden with Hostess cakes, Klondike bars, and Mystic Mints, her face ravaged by some sad inner strife. It was obvious she fought with herself every time.

Even as I was ringing the bell, I felt I still had an out: Judy might not be home. But she *was* home, and my heart leaped. As soon as I saw her, I knew I was done for the night. "Come on in, sweetheart," she said, taking my arm and pulling gently.

She stood in her long nightgown in the soft light from a rose-shaded lamp, a fair-haired plump angel ready to enfold me with her wings. She'd been sitting next to the lamp rereading *The Mists of Avalon*. The dog-eared paperback was splayed facedown on the coffee table.

A trace of concern crossed her face, but it was concern for me, not herself, as would have been wiser. Her face shone with complete trust, total faith in the rightness of this surprise. For all I could tell, she'd been expecting me all evening.

"What is it?" she said, snuggling down next to me on the couch.

I told her about stabbing Bucky and about the body being discovered and having seen the woman at the Snapdragon, leaving out my feelings of attraction. I told her about my conversation with Bonnie at the bar, including the kiss.

A little V formed between her eyebrows. "I don't want anybody kissing on you but me."

"Well, it wasn't that kind of kiss."

"Be that as it may." There was a silence. Then she said, "What can I get you? Food? Something to drink? I have some Dewar's."

"It's all right," I said. "I'm all right with it. Yeah, I'll have a drink." She fixed one for each of us. She kept a jug of spring water in the icebox. I rubbed my lips with the liquor to disinfect them.

"Are you going to tell Ciesla about this? I mean, my God." She stroked my hair, my shoulders. Her hands were in continuous motion, gesturing, touching, roving.

Suddenly I was very thirsty. I drained my drink. She fixed me another, then rejoined me on the couch. Her hands smoothed my aura, so to speak, while her gentle voice soothed my soul: She knew me so well. I sank my head into her shoulder.

"I miss you," she said softly.

"I miss you too," I admitted. "But…"

"But what?"

"It's hell."

She nodded, her chin moving up and down on top of my head. "It's hell when we're apart. Thank the Goddess you're here now."

What I meant was, going through with a breakup is hell, but I found myself unable to articulate it. However, I forced myself to say, "I'm not coming back." I could feel her tearing inside—she gave a little moan. She held me tighter.

"You're here now," she repeated.

"Yes." I had no explanation. She began kissing the top of my head, hard firm kisses I could feel through my skull. I twisted in her arms like a porpoise and turned up my face. The same kisses pelted my lips like hailstones. In unison we stopped for air, and I kissed her in return.

There was something new about her, something in this forcefulness, something hard. Strength? Yes, strength, but beyond that. Anger? Ah. Before tonight I hadn't known anger had aphrodisiacal properties. After unresolved fights, our anger would spoil any attempt at lovemaking. When we made up, everything was fine again.

But this anger seemed to come from a different place. It was new to Judy too; I saw in her eyes a kind of fierce bafflement. I rejoiced, for without being able to put my finger on it, I'd known something was wrong all along with her reaction to my leaving. There'd been plenty of sadness, confusion, even self-pity. But anger and the power that comes with it had been missing.

Moments later we were horizontal on the couch. Judy transformed herself from a nurturing angel to a fiery one. We wrestled for position. Her hands careened over me, as if to find their way through clothes and skin and flesh to bone.

We moved to the bedroom without further words, where she continued to excavate new nuggets of emotion, using our bodies as pick and shovel. I believe I more or less ceased to exist for her; this night she made love to herself. It was as though she needed to tell herself something.

I felt her wrench away from me like a ship breaking its moorings. I sensed this separation, though physically we remained glued together. Suddenly I felt needier than ever and wanted to be next to her all night, wanted to be there in the morning. She held me tightly, a little too tight for comfort, in fact, and her hot breath chuffing into my neck was the last thing I remembered before sleep.

7

In the morning, I stopped at home to shower and change, making it to work at the *Eye* at eight o'clock. I half-expected Bucky to take the day off to recuperate, but he was there, working in the composition room when I went back to get a cup of coffee. He glared at me but didn't speak. They'd be playing for the Stanley Cup in hell before I was going to apologize. Waves of resentment rose from him like steam from a wet dog.

The elder Rinkell checked in briefly to meet with me on our front-page stories. I reminded him about the body dumping and promised a story for tomorrow's edition. The subject of Bucky didn't come up. He took off in his gigantic leased Oldsmobile to call on some advertising accounts.

I got right on the phone to Ciesla. "Anything more on that homicide yesterday?"

"Yeah. Time of death between one and four A.M., no sexual assault, no signs of struggle, one .22 slug in the head, uh, uh…" He stopped, slightly flustered. Out of character for him.

"Yeah?" I said encouragingly.

He went on in a different direction, "Address in Southfield. Married, no kids, no connection with drugs—we talked to the husband yesterday, you know. We're working with the Southfield police on this. Um, and she worked for O'Connor Services."

"The temps?"

"Yeah, temporary service. She did clerical stuff, word processing. The last assignment she had was at Monolyne."

"What's that?"

"A plastics company in Troy."

Nothing about the Snapdragon. "Anything else on the circumstances of death?"

"That's pretty much it." Only because I knew Tom Ciesla so well could I detect a slight note in his voice, something a little too official. I was sure there was more.

"Any theories? You've ruled out suicide?"

"Oh, yeah. That shot was right in the back of the head. And she was dumped for sure."

"Will you be talking more to the husband? Any suspicion on him?"

" 'Course, we always check out the guy. He seems clean right now."

"How was he at the morgue?"

"Oh, the usual. Traumatized but not hysterical. There's no obvious motive for him. He had a pine-box insurance policy on her. No other money involved."

"Love triangle?"

"So far no evidence of that."

"History of abuse?"

"Nothing there either. All he says is, she was gone when he got up in the morning. When she didn't come home by noon, he called it in. They didn't write up a report, 'cause it hadn't been twenty-four hours. But the desk guy saw our message and remembered the call."

I toyed with the space bar on my IBM Selectric. When it came to publishing technology, we at the *Eagle Eye* were still snorting around in the Stone Age. Rinkell had shelled out big bucks for a used CompuGraphic, but we weren't composing pages on it. Nona was too afraid of its forbidding console to learn anything more than how to make it spit out columns.

That was all right. I preferred to work at my typewriter, to hammer down my words onto nice white paper instead of a flickering screen. Plus I enjoyed composition-room work, at least until Bucky had started his shenanigans.

"Her car?" I asked. "Is that missing?"

"Yeah. We haven't found it yet."

"Seems like maybe robbery, then? Car theft, then they kill her?"

"Well, you'd figure, if it was a carjacking, a professional job, that'd explain why we haven't found the car, but why the execution and dumping? And then some psycho, or somebody who knew her and wanted to kill her, they wouldn't necessarily have a way to dispose of a car. You'd figure they'd have left it somewhere and we would've found it by now. Maybe it'll turn up this week."

"Some psycho?" I repeated. Once again Ciesla seemed to go over a bump with a quick silence.

"Or the car could be out of state now," he said doubtfully. "The missing car I don't get. The fact that we don't have a crime scene yet might make this one a bitch to solve."

"No crime scene?"

"Yeah, in this case the place where the body was found wasn't where the crime was committed. The actual crime scene can tell you—well, practically everything. The dump site isn't giving us much to go on."

"Oh. Did she have friends who could tell you more?"

"You're pretty interested in this," Ciesla said with a sudden edge.

Yikes. "Aw, I'm just trying to think like a cop." I swallowed a nervous laugh.

"As a matter of fact, the Macklins have only been in town a few months. He's an executive for Hastings Benevolex. Got a transfer here to work on a Chrysler project. They've moved around. Their last address was in Cleveland." Hastings Benevolex, a hugely successful data-processing company, made news every so often because of its ultraconservative policies and fascist dress code. Ciesla continued, "We'll be talking with her coworkers today."

I decided to cool it on the questions. "I'll stop over later to get the last few specifics—DOB, family details..."

"OK. If I'm not here, Porrocks'll have the file. Lillian?"

"Yeah."

"You sure you didn't know her? You really looked at that picture."

"I didn't know her. Ah, to tell you the truth, she did look a little familiar at first, but—no."

"Where from, familiar?"

"I just really can't place her. I—it was just a momentary thing."

"OK." He hung up.

8

Christine, our receptionist, popped into my office with the *News* and the *Free Press,* the two dailies, refolded from Rinkell's desk. I assumed they'd have the basic facts on the murder, nothing more, but I was wrong. As soon as I laid flat the front pages, a heavy, dark feeling ran through me.

Both papers had run a small story on page one below the fold, with the immediate info from the white sheets, including the victim's name and address, so they must have called back after Iris was identified. But in addition, the *Free Press* must have paid a visit to her husband at home the previous night, because they ran a small, grainy, dark photo next to the story.

It was an old picture. Iris was younger, her hair much longer—it was straightened and done in a big winglike style—and she was wearing thick glasses. Was this the best picture they could find? I'd been betting I wouldn't have to come forward with information about Iris's night job because someone else would. But no one who knew her as Jean would recognize her.

9

I worked on other projects for about an hour, until I thought Ciesla would be out questioning Iris's coworkers. I finished my editorial for the week, "Recycling: Let's Bloom Where We're Potted." Porrocks, I hoped, would be out too, but when I arrived at the detective division she was at her desk doing paperwork. Sitting behind the police-issue gray desk, with her slight build and longish plain face, she looked like a kid forced to do Sunday-school homework.

There aren't that many female senior detectives out there, but somehow Porrocks fit in: the result of unwavering professionalism, phenomenal patience, the guts of a rhino, and pure longevity. She was about fifty.

"Too bad you can't be out right now playing cops and robbers," I said with a smile.

She looked up briskly. "It's too damn hot out there anyway."

"Is that the file, on Ciesla's desk? For the murder thing?"

She nodded and rose quickly as I moved for the file.

"Wait, I'll get it for you." She reached it first and pulled out a few pages. They were the white sheets and the notes Ciesla had made after talking with the husband at the morgue. The missing car was a maroon Escort, and her husband's name was Gerald Macklin. What I really wanted to see, of course, was the autopsy report. They cranked them out like pancakes when they felt like it. Sitting at Ciesla's desk, I took notes slowly from the pages Porrocks handed me. The file now lay on her desk next to her elbow.

As a child I'd had a touch of asthma and so had a fair amount of experience with coughing fits. I began coughing quietly, then built to a small crescendo. Porrocks looked up, but I met her eye and shook my head with a reassuring smile. She bent to her paperwork again.

I scribbled in my pad, then suddenly took a sharp breath, let it catch halfway, then began cranking out big, steady, chesty coughs. Porrocks looked up again anxiously. As my body began to jerk spasmodically, I pantomimed drinking and mouthed "water." She jumped up, hesitated over the file (at which point I dropped my head helplessly), then dashed out of the office.

Still coughing, I moved quickly to the file and flipped it open. The autopsy report was on top. It looked long, but I knew the important stuff would be at the beginning. The upper floor of the cop shop had no water cooler, so Porrocks had to either run downstairs to the squad room cooler or find somebody's coffee cup and take it to the washroom to fill up.

My eyes skimmed over the description of the body, then the measurements and characteristics of the bullet wound. The payoff, halfway down: "...lips and oral tissues slightly swollen. Examining the mouth now...observe...all teeth except several molars have been extracted. Extraction likely occurred postmortem...absence of massive bleeding and swelling. Teeth missing are numbers four through fourteen inclusive and nineteen through thirty-two inclusive."

Holy hell, somebody yanked her teeth out. The report went on, but I closed the folder, listening for Porrocks's running feet. I coughed some more and was about to turn back to Ciesla's desk when, to my surprise, Ciesla himself strode in. I would've beaten Porrocks, but Ciesla caught it: my hand flashing backward from the file folder, my guilty look.

"Whoa, Lillian Byrd," he said, and walked around the desk to me.

Porrocks swooped in with a paper cup and stopped short. "What?" she said.

"Um," I said.

"You shouldn't snoop," Ciesla said cheerfully, throwing his sport coat across his desk. "Did you look at it?"

I coughed weakly and Porrocks handed me the water. "Yeah," I admitted.

"So," he said, "you've checked the autopsy information when you knew we didn't want you to and you've stolen a picture of her. Tell us what's going on." Ciesla indicated a side chair for me, and took his chair at his desk. Porrocks perched on the edge of her desk.

"How'd you know I took the picture?"

Porrocks said, "I shot nine pictures at the scene. The sheriff's artist took the two best ones. You had one in your hand when we left the office. When I came back there were six."

"I didn't think you were that meticulous, Erma." She gave me a wounded look. I took a deep breath. "Well, what do you want to know?"

Ciesla said, "The question is, what do *you* want to know?"

"Hey, I'm naturally curious. I haven't covered a murder lately. I'd like to beat the dailies on something for once." I swallowed and folded my arms.

"You knew her, didn't you?" Porrocks asked.

"I might have."

"Well?"

"Can you guys actually *make* me talk? I mean, what if I don't want to tell you?"

"For God's sake, Lillian," Ciesla said, "you stole the picture from us. You were caught attempting to steal a police document. What do you expect here? Come on, come on."

I sat there trying to think of a way out, my eyes focused on Ciesla's shirt front. Ciesla liked to look sharp. He bought good clothes, tailored to fit his massive neck and short waist. Nothing fancy, just good. As most energetic men are, however, he was hard on his clothes. In and out of the car, shouldering through courthouse crowds, taking down the occasional suspect, grabbing a fast hamburger. You could usually spot a button on him ready to fall off, an abraded elbow, a hastily rubbed mustard stain. Today I noticed a small ravel at the cuff of his otherwise perfect blue broadcloth shirt.

We sat in silence. Cops can sit in silence longer than Trappist monks. Finally, I said, "OK. I saw this woman at a bar. Her name was Jean, somebody told me. OK? That's it. I saw her one time. I barely even talked to her."

"What did you talk about?" Ciesla fingered his raveled cuff.

"As I remember, it was a brief conversation about orange juice and rye bread."

Porrocks said, "That's it?" Ciesla made a note.

"Well, what bar?" Ciesla asked. He and Porrocks stayed tuned in, their expressions neutral. However, the air molecules in the office started zinging around, as if the air pressure within the room had increased.

"Goddamn it," I said. "The Snapdragon."

Their faces were blank. Then Porrocks crunched her eyebrows. "Where is it?" she asked.

"Livernois, down the street from Baker's, near here."

Ciesla said, "How come we don't know that bar?"

I hollered, "Oh, goddamn it!"

They waited.

I clenched my teeth and growled, "It's a lesbian bar."

"For women?" Ciesla said. He and Porrocks nodded and exchanged glances, Friday-and-Gannon style.

They granted me a split second to work with. I said, "Oh, guys, grow up." They exhaled together and regarded me solemnly. The air pressure returned to normal.

Ciesla asked, "Are you sure that was the woman you saw at the bar?" I told him I was pretty sure.

"Because you just saw her that once, right?" Porrocks said.

"That's right, just that once. But there's a difference between just noticing someone and sort of being hit between the eyes by someone." Ciesla nodded in his guy way, his head and neck moving as one unit. "Of course, I could be wrong. I figure you guys'll find that out. But I don't think I am."

I told them some more facts I thought they'd want to know. After a few minutes Ciesla started zeroing in.

"Now, this woman who owns the bar," he said, "her name's Bonnie, Bonnie what?"

"I don't know. I've never heard anyone say her last name."

"And you think she might have killed Ms. Macklin?"

"I think she might know something about it. I can't say whether she killed her. *Why* she might have done it, I don't know. All I'm saying is, you should check her out. She about took my eyebrows off when we talked. I think it's also interesting that the husband didn't say anything about Iris having a night job. At least I'm assuming he didn't. You guys didn't say anything about it."

"That's right," Ciesla said.

"Maybe he didn't know about it," Porrocks said.

"Macklin let us look through her things at the apartment," Ciesla told me.

"And you didn't come up with any check stubs or anything?" I said.

The three of us looked at each other and said in unison, "Paid under the table."

Ciesla questioned me more about the Snapdragon and the people I knew there. I told him about Sandra, Bonnie's sidekick, and Kevin, the waiter. "Lots of other people work there, though. But this isn't about them—it's about Bonnie."

Ciesla said, "What this is, Lillian, is an investigation. You try to get the big picture. You do that in your reporting."

"The kind of reporting I do around here is pretty surfacey. But I know what you mean." I tended to take at face value anything anybody told me, even if my gut said it was wrong. But I was learning fast, you bet.

"Trusting your gut's important," Ciesla said, reading my mind. I smiled. "For example, I knew right away you knew more about Ms. Macklin than you admitted. You gotta trust yourself to read people."

"Thanks, I'll work on that."

"And you gotta know they're trying to read you," Porrocks chimed in.

"OK, Erm. Well, now the both of you know what I know. Now tell me, what the hell was that stuff about her teeth being extracted?"

Ciesla said, "Well, somebody put a boot on her chest and pried them out. No clue yet as to why."

Porrocks said, "We didn't realize it at the scene—it just looked like her mouth was bloody."

"But why would somebody do that?"

The two cops shrugged.

"There's a lot more psychos out there than you think," said Porrocks. "Actually, I believe there are other cases on record where people had their teeth pulled out after they were dead."

"Really? Where?"

"Well, I don't know." She looked a little sheepish. "It just seems like I've heard about this kind of thing before."

"To me it seems either really vicious or really ritualistic," I said.

"Both," Ciesla said. "Lillian, we have to ask you not to print that detail. It's something we can use when we finally get a suspect, or if we get a confession, to verify it."

"I'll keep quiet about it. Are you guys running tests on that piece of carpet she was wrapped in?"

Important stuff could be determined, I knew, from forensic tests on evidence like that. As a child I developed an interest in extreme crime—murders, kidnappings. I read the few books about such things in the library over and over, eventually convincing myself, when I was about twelve, that in a prior life I'd been a murder victim, dismembered and hidden under the floorboards somewhere.

One of my favorite books was about serial murders, except they called them mass murders then, not distinguishing between a bunch of people killed all at once and a bunch of people killed one at a time. I read about a guy who killed two children and got nailed because the handkerchiefs he used to strangle them had a defective weave. They found the third handkerchief from the set of three in his dresser, looked at it under a microscope, then told him what they found. He confessed.

Porrocks said, "Yeah, the lab's doing all the forensic tests. It'll be a while before they can give us a report."

"We'll check out this Snapdragon thing," Ciesla said.

"Discreetly?" I asked. My anxiety over Bonnie blossomed at the thought of her connecting my nosy visit with the cops coming.

"Don't worry," said Ciesla. Detectives, who carry loaded guns under their armpits everywhere they go, say "Don't worry" easier than other people say "Hold the mayo."

"OK, I'm outta here," I said, grabbing my notebook. There was this story to write, plus layout and headlines for tomorrow.

Ciesla got up quickly and came around his desk. "Lillian," he said, taking my arm lightly, "there's a difference between reporting on an investigation and meddling in it. You're going to stay out of this, right?"

"Sure—God, yeah, Tom. I leave the tough stuff to you."

I was only too glad to leave it to them.

10

The ax started its descent when I walked into the *Eye* offices. The familiar surroundings of cheap walnut paneling and matted carpet tiles felt strangely inhospitable. I looked around for a second, trying to tell if something was different. Nobody in the outer office met my eye.

"Lillian?" said Ed Rinkell from his doorway.

I followed him in. "This is gonna be serious, right?" I asked as he closed the door. "Lemme get a cup of coffee at least."

"Sure," he said through tight lips.

I ducked into my office for my mug, a thick white diner one Judy had found at one of her flea markets, and headed for the back. There were only a few dregs in the pot. I got out a filter and the coffee can from the cupboard, then took the pot and headed for the darkroom, where we drew coffee water from the big sink.

The door stood ajar and the fluorescent light was on. As

I pushed into the room, I suddenly smelled coffee, a different smell than my nose was expecting: The darkroom always reeked of chemicals. The room was tiny, maybe six feet by eight. By the time my brain said "coffee," it was also receiving signals from the back of my neck that said "Someone else is in here."

Momentum took my legs the three steps to the sink. I was turning to see who was behind me, when the light went out and the heavy door swung shut.

When that happens in a darkroom, it becomes, well, really dark. No pinhole, no crack under the door, nothing.

I stood with my back to the sink, the glass coffeepot in my hand, my mouth instantly metallic with the taste of fear.

Bucky Rinkell's voice jumped at me from a spot near the door. "Hey, Lillian, whatcha doing?" The disembodied voice was the perfect aural replica of Bucky: insinuating, clumsy, inane. In a microsecond my fear disappeared and anger took over—anger that Bucky Rinkell could cause me a moment of such fear.

"Whaddaya want?" I said.

"You made a big mistake. You're gonna get it, Lillian."

I half-laughed; he sounded so much like a ten-year-old pretending to be a tough guy. "For what?" I said. "Poking you with my blade? You deserved it, for God's sake."

I could almost hear his head swinging bovinely from side to side. Then a coffee-slurping sound.

I felt along the countertop for the redlight switch. I snapped it, and there we were in that backstage sort of glow. Bucky stood with his back angled against the door, holding his he-man coffee mug, filled to the brim with extra cream and sugar. I stood ready to smash the pot against the counter and threaten him with the jagged handle.

"Nobody does that shit to me, Lillian—"

I snorted.

"—and gets away with it."

"Buck, when I talked to you about keeping your hands off me, you didn't get it, did you? You had to be a pain in the ass about it. You didn't *want* to get it." His expression was stony. "You play at being a nice funny guy, but deep down you're an arrogant, contemptuous fucker, aren't you? What did you expect me to do? Or Nona? If some *guy* grabbed your balls, you'd beat the shit out of him."

"Suck my dick."

I laughed again, he was being so predictably awful. He was wearing his Gibraltar Trade Center cap backwards, the plastic pop-strap tight across his forehead. Keeping his brains secure. I watched his chubby hands flex open and closed.

"I know you know how to behave," I said.

And he did. One spring day a year before, he'd invited the staff over to his apartment for a cookout. He lived in a building on the west side of Eagle, one of those places with microscopic balconies carpeted in plastic grass, and little storage closets in the basement. He had set up a hibachi on the balcony and took us all on a grand tour of the place just as nicely as Jackie in the White House: "And this is where I keep my camping stuff and my car stuff. My carport's around back. Anybody hungry yet?"

Unfortunately, he had placed the hibachi right down on the plastic grass, which by the time we returned was melting and smoking. Nona thought fast and turned over the ice chest on it. Then we phoned out for pizza. I'd never seen him as nice as on that day.

"You don't want to learn anything, Bucky. You don't

want to admit you behaved badly. So you keep digging yourself in deeper by blaming me. An apology would be nice. How 'bout it, man?"

His face contorted as if I'd thrown acid in it. I turned my back to him and opened the water tap at the sink. The rushing water created a sudden matter-of-fact atmosphere. The chrome handle felt nice and cool. I filled the pot and turned off the water, then turned back to him.

"OK, how 'bout this?" I ventured. "If I forgive you for pawing me, will you forgive me for stabbing you?"

"I didn't do shit to you."

"Then how 'bout getting out of my way?"

He pushed himself off the door. "You think you're something special," he said. "You'll see."

"Daddy's gonna whup my ass, right?" I said.

"You'll see." He walked out, slamming the door.

Ed Rinkell was hunkered behind his desk when I returned. His swivel chair was in its full upright and locked position, and he looked uncomfortable in it. He beat around the bush for about ten minutes.

"Honestly, Lillian, I don't know how I would've kept this paper going without you." He twiddled his letter opener.

"You've always been good to me, Ed."

"It's like this," he finally began. Whenever somebody says, "Well, you see it's like this," you can be sure they're not going to follow it up with, "You've been promoted."

"Bucky's my son."

"Uh-huh."

"And you're not."

"Uh-huh."

"I need to ask you to resign."

"Sorry, no."

"Then I need to let you go."

The words hung in the air. I breathed shallowly, feeling the force of the moment. I'd come all this way with the newspaper just to let that goddamn prick ruin it for me? I said nothing.

Rinkell ran his hand over his hairpiece, sighed heavily, and shifted in his chair as if someone had strewn gravel under his meaty thighs.

"You're usually so controlled," he said, "so—together. Now...I'm not sure I can trust you anymore."

"Hah!"

"I hate to do it, Lillian, but I have no choice."

"I don't quite see it."

He sighed again and turned his head slightly so that his eyes aimed over my shoulder. "This is the situation: Bucky's deeply upset. The doctors say he might have permanent nerve damage."

"Permanent nerve damage?"

"There's an area of skin where he might not have feeling anymore."

"Well, how big is it?"

"A few inches."

"On his butt, right?"

"Yeah. This is a bad situation," he repeated, "and I need to run this paper. I can't change Bucky, but I can change editors. Bucky says if I don't fire you, he'll press assault charges against you."

I was speechless.

"I don't see how I can get around it." He was whining now. "Would you want him to do that?"

I could imagine Bucky trundling across the street and telling his story to the cops. They'd laugh in his face, but if he persisted, they'd have to take a complaint. If the question was, did I stab him, well, yes, I did. Nona had even witnessed it.

I chewed my coffee and thought some more. If Bucky pressed charges, this could wind up in a courtroom. But there was provocation: He was taking liberties with my body. Nona could back me up there.

Was I willing to deal with it? Any judge with a speck of sense would throw it out of court. But maybe not. Assault with a deadly weapon, which is what you *could* call those blades: a serious charge. If found guilty, I'd probably come out of it with only a mild penalty, but also with some kind of record. Let alone all the legal hassle and expense. Oh, fuck me.

"The point is, Lillian, it's not up to you to decide whether you're leaving. I won't have two of my staff at each other's throats. Bucky doesn't even want me to let you quit, but I'm offering you that choice."

"Big fucking deal, Eddie," I said. "I choose the boot."

"So you'll get no job reference, no nothing?"

I snorted. "*Ed,* Christ almighty. In the regular world, they ask for job references. In our business they ask for clips. Right?"

"True."

"So you can take your reference and crumple it into a tight little ball and stick it—"

"OK!"

"You're handling things like a moron."

"I was forced into it. If only you hadn't stabbed the kid."

"He's not a kid, and if I hadn't stabbed him, he'd still be pawing me and I'd be contemplating something worse."

"All right." He patted his hands on his fake-wood desktop, the signet ring he wore on one pinky clacking unpleasantly. He looked down at his hands, then up at me. "Will you stay and finish tomorrow's issue? I'll get Bucky out of here for the rest of the day. I'll do his work myself," he offered. His face was the picture of belief.

I stared at him, making sure I'd heard him right. Then I walked out. He gave a little puff and looked mournful.

I shut the door to my office and quickly pulled out some files and collected my odds and ends. I made sure to get all my notes for the Macklin story.

Archie and Christine watched silently as I carried my stuff to my car through the outer office. Then I returned and made for the back. Bucky, a triumphant smile wreathing his lips, was sitting on a table swinging his legs. I looked through him. I found Nona clicking away at the CompuGraphic. She swiveled around.

"You're really leaving?" she said.

"If that's the rumor, it must be true. Hey, Nona, take care. You know what this was about."

"Yeah. What will you do?"

"Don't know."

She stood up and gave me a hug. "I'll miss you."

"Good luck," I said, casting a glance toward you-know-who. I walked out past him, as he gloried in what had to have been the most satisfying moment of his sorry bastard life, and back to the outer office. Christine and Archie made regretful noises.

Nobody, however, said anything like "Gee, you sure got screwed, and I'm going to tell Rinkell what I think." When you work for somebody else, there's always that Ritz cracker ready to fall Cheez Whiz–side down if you don't watch it.

It was still hot, but an easy breeze had sprung up, and suddenly nothing about the world seemed oppressive to me anymore. The sunlight felt great on my shoulders as I stepped onto the street. The gigantic maples in the neighborhood behind the office looked as majestic as ever, their branches arching and tossing over the buildings on Main Street. I felt lighter. Stronger. I rolled down the windows of the Caprice and peeled out. After a swing through the A&W on the corner for a cold root beer, I aimed the hood for I-75 and a nice long run through the countryside of Oakland County.

11

The car knew where I wanted to go, even if I didn't exactly. I-75 north of Pontiac is, midday, pretty serene. You get up out of the flat floodplain of Detroit into rolling green land, small hills left over from Ice Age glaciers. Maple, oak, and beech make up most of the woods. In the fields and clearings along the highways, you get plenty of sumac and shrubby cedars, and all through the summer the goldenrod and asters shoot their pollen into the world. May through August, I'm never without one or two Benadryl pills in my pocket.

Before I knew Judy, I dated a woman who was into natural healing; we were two bugs making love in the spring, and my allergies were our constant companion. She seized the opportunity to test her gifts. First she took me off my wonderful pink Benadryls. "Those things are poison! They dehydrate your cells," she said, twisting her hands in the folds of her parachute pants. "Allergies can be healed naturally. Completely!"

The spiritual name she had chosen for herself was Sky. Somehow it was even on her driver's license. I never learned what her real name was. Organic vitamin C, she prescribed at first. I swallowed copious quantities of the dry, sour tablets every day.

When that didn't work, she got some herbs from a metaphysical pharmaceutical center. I ate them, drank them, and inhaled steam from them. She even made poultices and applied them to my feet and the small of my back.

I tried to suppress the sneezes; I bathed my eyes in cool water. God knows I wanted it to work, for her sake as much as mine. I could always revert to drugs, but who knew what Sky would come up with next.

As the weeks rolled by and the empty Kleenex boxes piled up, she gradually lapsed into discouragement. She told me she felt inadequate. I sensed trouble coming fast. First she blamed the vitamin C and the herbs. Next she blamed herself. Then she blamed me.

"I've discovered," she announced one day with an ominous toss of her crystal earrings, "that allergies aren't real. It's your body being out of tune with your emotions." She showed me a book that listed various ailments, from abdominal pain to warts, and assigned correct blame to various departments of the sufferer's inner child.

"You are trying to control your love in a self-serving way," she read aloud.

I gave her a kiss and ran to the drugstore to buy a fresh box of Benadryl. When I got home, I opened it deliberately in front of her, savoring the tiny pop of the bubble packaging. She shook her head with a hostile smile. I tossed a pill back with some Vernor's and awaited relief, while she gathered up her herbs and left for good.

As the afternoon heated up and I drove farther into the countryside, I could almost see the clouds of pollen blanketing the landscape, like fallout over Los Alamos. I popped a Benadryl and washed it down with the dregs of the root beer, and shortly thoughts of pollen disappeared. I turned off the expressway onto a two-lane road and headed west into the lake-dotted area beyond Mount Holly.

There's a nature preserve surrounding an aging swamp, miles from nowhere out there, wedged between county land and a railroad right-of-way. Few people go there—I guess because there's no nature center, toilet, or canoe rental. All that's there is untamed quiet and massive populations of plants and animals. Det. Erma Porrocks, a closet birder, gave me directions to it once.

I turned down the little access lane, shut off the motor, and coasted to a stop. It was quiet at first, very. But then I gradually heard the little sharp music of tanagers and titmice, the percussions of a woodpecker, and the soft, foamy sound of treetops leaning and turning in the wind. The air smelled heavy and clean.

I stretched over and popped open the glove compartment for my hand lens and compass. After standing by the car for a few minutes, listening to the natural sounds overtaking the ticking of the cooling engine block, I set off down the path.

Bull thistles and jewelweed, marsh marigolds and all the varieties of asters were in bloom—well, all the summer flowers were doing what they were supposed to be doing. The high old-growth canopy closed over my head, and I became the biggest animal in this full-blown, furiously green swamp in summer.

I walked along the springy trail, stepping carefully over

rivulets and rotten logs. To my right lay the bog itself, with the heads of snapping turtles poking up here and there from the black water, clear-black, as good swamp water is. To my left, the maple-beech forest. I twisted a twig from a spice-bush and chewed it. The sharp taste mixed with the moist air my lungs were taking in and made me feel good.

Much as I would have enjoyed not thinking for the rest of the day, thoughts did come. So this is what it's like— one step out of line and they've got you. I'd taken a risk. Rinkell, of course, had his own place in the pecking order, below people who held power over him: creditors, adver- tisers. The game goes round and round.

However, those who don't have the concrete, idiot-proof kind of power that money and influence confer, have the power of choice, if not cleverness, on their side.

During my years at the *Eye,* I'd come to understand that a successful journalist possesses two important characteris- tics. One is the ability to be an asshole at will; the other is having the killer instinct.

Being able to turn asshole at the drop of a hat is essen- tial when, for instance, you're told to get quotes from peo- ple whose mobile homes just got flattened by a tornado, or when you're assigned to cover the Eagle Garden Club's spring fashion show.

To break it down further, those two examples represent separate dimensions of being an asshole.

In the tornado case you can pretty much just say to the people, "Talking to some asshole like me has got to be the last thing you want to do right now, but I'm supposed to ask you how you feel."

Amazingly, lots of people will warm right up, open their guts right up to you, a complete stranger. "We've lost everything. Look. I can't find my Hummels. I can't find none of my mementos. That door didn't used to have that post through it. My Danny? I guess God's looking after my Danny now. Let me tell you how Danny saved a little blind girl's life, back when the winters were a lot colder..."

The other type of situation, the Garden Club's spring fashion show, is a lot harder, because you find yourself in the middle of a Byzantine ritual that everyone takes extremely seriously. You cannot acknowledge being an asshole, because of its implication for your subject.

You've put on your simple wrap skirt, following the rule of dressing "at" or "below" the level of the people you'll be reporting on, and you watch and listen seriously, and you take account of the spectacle carefully, in all its gentle pastel gorgeosity, even though your teeth are hurting from all the sugary salads and what you really want to do is run away screaming. For your account will be clipped out and dissected at the next regular meeting—and you will hear of any inaccuracies, small or large—and take my word for it, all are large.

The other characteristic necessary for success in journalism, the killer instinct, is simple. All you have to do is shove everybody else aside to get the story first, or more of it.

But the problem is, most stories are pretty cut-and-dried. I mean, how much can you do with a traffic study that concludes all the town's stoplights are exactly where they should be? You want your scrap of a story to be special!

So you find some weirdo who hates the cops and the traffic commission and claims that the streets will soon be littered with the corpses of children killed by speeding cars unless the duration of the amber signal is lengthened. How do you find such people? They find you, of course. All you have to do is return their calls.

If you're covering public officials, you must pounce on the slightest conceivable suggestion of scandal, ready to cold-bloodedly destroy any sorry son of a bitch you've gotten to know. Dirt sells.

Most reporters choose to think of such behavior as honest and noble. I haven't met a reporter yet who isn't convinced she's going to heaven.

Walking along, I resolved to never be on somebody's payroll again. I'd always saved money; the Caprice was paid for; my habits were inexpensive. Therefore, I was in shape to think about a change.

I never had any trouble being an asshole when I needed to, but I didn't know about the killer instinct. Working on a local weekly, you get plenty of opportunities to be dirty and cheap, but it's not as if you're fighting for a Pulitzer. Burying somebody, I mean actually destroying a career, even getting somebody sent to jail, for the sake of *your* career—that's different. As a freelancer perhaps I'd find out whether I could do it.

Perhaps more importantly, I could find out whether I could *avoid* doing it and still make a living.

I knew the *Motor City Journal,* a slick monthly, was always looking for good features and dishy crime coverage. Yes, I'd promised Ciesla I'd leave the Macklin story alone, except for what I'd learn through him.

But if the *Journal* wanted a feature story, given the extra angle I had on it, business would be business: I'd have to do more investigating. Before, when I first saw the police shot of the murdered Iris, I'd felt that odd sense of protectiveness, even secretiveness. *Well,* I thought in a more pragmatic light, *she's a dead woman and doesn't need any protection, does she? What she needs is justice.*

I hiked the five-mile trail through the swamp. I didn't see any new birds, but I have to admit to being a pretty oblivious birder in spite of my last name. Near the end of the loop, I squatted with my hand lens to study a tiny brown toad that hopped once in my path, then stood still. The size of my thumbnail, its little sides heaving, it eyed the large clear disk of glass poised above it.

A minuscule beetle, the size of a flea, stumbled over a grain in the loam at the toad's front feet. We both noticed it at the same moment. The toad dipped its head slightly; the beetle was gone.

"It's all relative, ain't it, kiddo?" I said to the toad.

12

The next day I called up Ricky Rosenthal, editor of the *Motor City Journal,* and gave him enough information on the case to let him know I was onto something unusual. Oh, yes indeed, he said, he'd be interested in a nice juicy crime story. I was willing to write it on spec, which meant I'd get paid for it only after Ricky had read it, liked it, and published it.

There you have the downside of the freelance biz: total uncertainty. I told him juiciness wasn't my aim, just a good solid story. If part of the reason Iris Macklin died was that she had felt a slice of her life should be secret, an honest account could make a difference to somebody.

"It'll be juicy," Ricky said happily.

I organized my notes and figured my next steps should involve the Snapdragon, Bonnie, and the husband, Gerald Macklin. Knowing that Ciesla and Porrocks would probably talk to Bonnie that day, I puttered at home until mid afternoon, washing and waxing the Caprice, and taking Todd out for a romp in the grass.

I'd bought my car at a police auction for two thousand dollars; it had been an unmarked detective car and was showing the kind of rough edges a city vehicle gets after four years of hard service. It was a dependable car, and I liked everything about it, especially the shotgun brackets in the trunk and the extra map pocket screwed into the driver's door. The first time I thoroughly cleaned it, I found almost nine dollars in spilled change in the seat cracks. The engine and exterior were in good shape. I liked to keep it shiny. My green machine.

Todd grazed on grass blades as much as he could, then zigzagged around, slowly at first, then with greater momentum so that I had to work to keep heading him off.

Mr. McVittie, my landlord, trumped up a reason to come outside and chat. "You're prob'ly wondering when I'm gonna get those branches trimmed," he yelled, pointing up at the horse chestnut tree that shaded my balcony.

"Think they need it?" I yelled back. We were about four feet apart, but he was nearing old age and almost deaf. Mrs. McVittie, who had just torn her seventieth birthday off the calendar, couldn't get him to wear his hearing aids—no way, no how.

"Hell yes, they need it! If one a them boughs blows through your window, you're gonna know it!" He squinted at the tree, whose upper branches looked fine to me.

He was white-haired and a bit stooped but strong as a donkey and spry too. Everything he needed done he did himself, whether he had to lay new vinyl in the kitchens, repaint his station wagon, or clamber up a ladder with a saw and a bucket of pitch to do some tree-doctoring. "I'll get up there tomorrow!"

He picked up Todd, whom I'd corralled inside the coiled garden hose, and held him tightly in the crook of his arm. He stroked his nose with his thumb.

"Mildred's up in Marquette!" he shouted.

"Oh?"

"Her sister's having brain surgery!"

"Oh, my!"

"Neurological problem!"

"Oh!"

"I'm having candy for lunch!" When his wife was away, Mr. McVittie indulged in his favorite foods and television programs. He liked *Baywatch* and all the police shows.

We shouted back and forth for a while, until he wandered back inside. I finished rubbing out the Caprice's hood, then gave Todd a fragment of a Pecan Sandy, for being so good as to not bite our landlord.

I watched him nibble the cookie, his little tusks rattling. Then I remembered the tooth I'd found on the ground behind the Snap. Shit! I hadn't given it a minute's thought until now. Well, it wasn't Iris's; that was the night I'd met her. It probably belonged to an animal, just as I'd thought at the time. But I wondered anew about the Midnight Five—the missing women from around the area. Could any of them have been connected to the Snapdragon, to that dirty back alley?

I called Ciesla a little later. He and Porrocks had just returned from the Snapdragon, where they'd found Bonnie in the back office doing paperwork.

"Yeah, we asked her some questions," Ciesla said. "She couldn't tell us much."

"What do you mean?"

"She said Iris Macklin had been working there less than two months and she didn't know her very well."

"You believe that? Did she seem sincere?"

"Mmmph." He made a rumbly sound. "Actually, Lillian, I could see how you could be suspicious of her. I didn't get a very good feeling from her."

"Well, she's not all that likable. You must have gotten something more out of her, though."

"We asked her about Sunday night. She told us Ms. Macklin stayed late after closing to help with some chores, then left by herself. We're trying to corroborate that."

"Check with Emerald, the parking lot guy."

"She didn't say anything about a security guard."

"Why am I not surprised?"

"She admitted to paying her under the table, so we were all correct on that point. She said Ms. Macklin kept to herself, just showed up for work and left without doing much socializing."

"How did Iris get the job?"

"She must have seen an ad Ms. Creighter ran in a magazine, um, *The Triangle* magazine—"

"Who's Ms. Crater?"

"Bonnie Creighter," and he spelled it. "That's her last name."

"Oh. *The Triangle*'s the local gay rag. Do you know it?"

"Yeah, Ms. Macklin must have picked it up somewhere, maybe another bar."

"Or one of the bookshops or coffee shops, you know. Counterculture nation," I said.

"Yeah. Look, I gotta run."

"Wait, Tom. Did you by any chance take a walk down the back alley?"

"We did. Why?"

I told him about finding the tooth.

"Well, we didn't see anything out of the ordinary. It couldn't have been Ms. Macklin's anyway, right? You're sure which night it was?"

"Yeah. To me it looked like an animal tooth."

"How come?"

"Well, I guess—I don't know why I thought that. I mean, who'd expect to find a human tooth just lying on the ground like that?"

"Where did you put it?"

"I threw it. I was grossed out. I don't even know which way my hand was going."

He paused. I could hear him silently trying to justify sending an officer out to look for it. "Well," he said, "try to find it, OK?"

My turn to pause. "OK."

I asked him if he'd seen a copy of the *Eye* yet.

"No, they usually deliver around five o'clock. Why? Something special about your article on this?"

I snorted. "Naw, I got fired. God knows what the article's gonna look like, if there is one. Didn't Ed call you yesterday? To get the basic info?" I told him about Bucky, the blade, and the boot.

"I always thought you were too good for that paper."

"Thank you and God bless, Tom. I'll be on my own now—I'm going freelance. Putting something together for the *Motor City Journal* on this."

"Go for it. But be careful, and remember what you promised. Anything I can do to help, let me know."

"Tom, if I can just count on you to tell me what's happening with this case as it moves along, that'd be great."

"I'll give you as much information as I can. You have to understand that I won't be able to tell you everything."

"I know. Thanks. So you're really not into Bonnie Creighter as a suspect?"

"We need to do more work on it, but there's nothing emerging right now. Ms. Macklin could have been abducted outside the bar, or she could have gone somewhere to meet somebody—who knows? We'll talk to the husband again before the week's out. I want to get a better handle on him."

When I got off the phone, I jogged downstairs to see if the paper had arrived, and it had. For the Macklin story, Ed had simply plagiarized verbatim from the *News* and *Free Press* stories the day before. The rest of the paper looked all right; I'd already edited almost all the copy and written the editorial. He added a few stock summertime photos to fill up the front page: kids eating hot dogs at last year's Parks and Rec picnic. "Huh," I said sarcastically to Todd.

The phone rang, and I thought it might be Ciesla calling back.

" 'Lo."

"Lillian."

I didn't recognize the voice.

"Yes?"

There was a long sigh, then, "Oh, Lillian, I'm so glad you answered."

I knew the voice now: the scratchy tone, the professional-wrestler enunciation. I sighed too. "Hi, Lou."

"I really need to talk to you."

"Well. What, uh, what's on your mind?"

"You."

"Oh, Jesus." I swung into my big orange armchair and set the phone on the floor, keeping the handset to my ear.

Though it caused me no end of inconvenience, I still used a rotary dial phone. In plain black. Ah, the innocent, unhurried pace of yesteryear.

She went on, "When we talked at the bar that night, I didn't really tell you how I felt about you—how strong I feel about you."

"I thought you came on plenty strong."

Todd hopped over to me, and I reached down to pet him.

"I've been thinking about you a lot. All the time." Lou's voice was like rocks grinding together along a fault line. "I can't seem to get you out of my mind, no matter what I do. It's even—it's even hard for me to concentrate on my work. I got bit twice yesterday."

Lou was an animal control officer for the city of Detroit.

"Gee, Lou, I'm sorry but—"

"And that tells me I need to see you again." I heard a little hiccup of emotion. "Lillian, please go out with—please—me. I'll take you anywhere you—we can do anything you—I just really need to see you."

I kneaded the upholstered arm of the chair. It was a deep comfy one, covered in nubby fabric the color of solar flares. I like bright colors in my home.

I took a deep breath. "Lou, you're a nice person. A good person. A well-liked person. And it isn't that I *don't* like you. But I don't want to go out with you. I wish—"

"Your wish is my command!"

"Lou." I stood up, to add authority to my voice. "Listen to me—"

"No! You listen to me. Are you listening? I love you."

"Oh, Jesus. That's not possible. You—"

"It is!"

"You barely *know* me, Lou. I don't want to talk anymore.

I appreciate your asking me out, but no thanks. No. All right?"

"Not all right. Lillian?"

"C'mon, Lou. Goodbye."

I went into the kitchen and put on a pot of coffee. Stovetop percolators are coming back, I hear; well, I've always liked the smell and the sound of them. While the coffee perked, I leaned against the counter and tried to shake the Lou-ness away. I wondered how much, being a regular at the Snapdragon, she knew about Iris, or whether she knew Bonnie very well. I would have asked her a few questions, but I didn't want to prolong the conversation, and I didn't trust that she wouldn't run and say something to Bonnie. And Bonnie was the last person I wanted to spook.

My guess was I'd hear from Lou a few more times. I felt sorry for her, but people get over these things.

13

Since the afternoon was wearing on and Bonnie was at the Snap, I decided to wait until early the next morning to return to the alley to look for the tooth. Nobody'd be around at daybreak.

I was disappointed that Ciesla and Porrocks hadn't found anything dramatic yet, but I guessed that was my cue. As suspicious as I was of Bonnie Creighter, I really needed to give Iris's husband equal time. I located Gerald Macklin's number in my notes.

"Mr. Macklin, my name is Lillian Byrd, and I'm reporting on Ms. Macklin's case for the *Motor City Journal*. I want to extend my sympathies to you."

"Uh-huh." His voice sounded youngish and tired.

"I know the last thing you may want to do is talk to a reporter, but I was wondering if you'd be willing to meet with me, at your convenience, maybe for just fifteen minutes."

"No." Click.

I fired up the Caprice and drove out to the apartment complex. It was one of those big expensive ones, with a pool, a clubhouse, berms, and cedar fencing around the Dumpsters.

I was standing in the vestibule of Macklin's building debating whether to buzz him, when a couple of tykes in bathing suits scampered out. I grabbed the door and made my way through thickly carpeted corridors to the apartment. The door opened a moment after my knock.

"Mr. Macklin, I really think it's important we talk."

He was on the tall side of short, with an interesting narrow face, light-skinned, glasses. He would have been the latte to Iris's espresso.

Startled, he moved to heave the door shut, but I said, "I knew your wife."

He took a step backward, his expression tightening. He looked me up and down. "Come in for a minute."

He was alone, wearing khaki slacks with a blue webbed belt, a green alligator shirt, and Timberland loafers with no socks. Throwback yuppie style. He stood rigidly in the center of the room. White carpeting and white soft furniture magnified the sunlight bouncing in through a patio doorwall.

Though his voice had sounded quite young on the phone, he was closer to middle age. His hair, which showed a little gray at the temples, was conked and slicked back.

"What do you want?"

"Well, uh, it's that—" I broke off and sat down on a marshmallowy couch. "Can we sit down and talk for a few minutes? Come on, man."

He sat opposite me on the edge of a matching couch, on the far side of a glass-topped coffee table. Arranged diagonally on the table were a large vase of white silk calla lilies and an Ansel Adams photography book.

"First of all," I began, "were you aware of Iris's other job?"

His mouth shifted from side to side. "Uh-huh."

"I saw her a couple of times there, over at the—"

"That bar."

"Yeah, the Snapdragon." He did know. "Well, did she talk about it much?"

"No. I didn't want to hear anything about it. Suppose you talk about it. Who are you?"

"My name is Lillian Byrd. Until yesterday I was a reporter for the *Eagle Eye*. The newspaper. The—Iris was found in Eagle, you know." His flat-eyed expression didn't change. "Anyway," I went on, "I'm continuing to look into the case as a freelancer. I saw Iris at the bar, and—I don't know, man—she made an impression on me. OK?"

Macklin said nothing.

"Frankly," I went on, "I find it pretty unusual that one half of a married couple would have a night job like that. She was killed after working that night, do you know that? How come you didn't tell the police about that job?" I realized I was stepping way into cop territory, but it was too late. I was pretty stupid.

He finally opened his mouth. "I don't know that I need to tell you anything."

"You don't. But don't you want to know what the hell happened? Don't you want to know who killed your wife? I do. This night life of hers might hold some clues, don't you think?"

"I've dealt with the press before," he murmured, as if talking to himself. Then he evaluated me with his eyes once again and said, "I'm going to tell you something off the record, all right?"

I waited.

"All right?"

I knew enough not to respond.

He pursed his lips in annoyance, then went ahead. "Iris's second job was her business. She had a—an unconventional streak in her. Well, it was a wild streak, to name it right. The girl was wild. But instead of trying to break her, I decided to let her go, you know? Take her chances, as long as she didn't interfere with mine. Do you know where I work and what I do?"

"You work for Hastings Benevolex. I don't know what you do there. Or what that's got to do with anything."

He leaned forward and said, "I'm vice president in charge of special projects. You know anything about Hastings Benevolex?"

"Well, it's a high-tech company—computers. They subcontract with the car companies..."

"Yes. And it's a very conservative company."

"I've heard that too."

The place, owned by some fundamentalist idiot-savant, had a ten-page dress code and an unwritten series of personal conduct laws that rivaled Nazi Germany's. A copy of the dress code had found its way to a reporter on one of the Detroit dailies, which printed parts of it, causing much public derision. Hastings Benevolex's stock price, however, was unaffected by anything but its ever-surging profits.

It was a gigantic employer, and like Amway, everybody knew somebody who was involved with it. The few gay people I knew who worked there were a well-paid but sorry lot, heavily closeted and doomed in most cases to stagnant careers, the best promotions going to white men with families. I'd never met any person of color who worked there.

"Somebody murdered Iris," Macklin said. "All right. I can't do anything to bring her back. She probably got mixed up in something over her head. That was a bad part of town. It could've been a random thing. Those things happen, don't they?"

His voice accelerated. "The publicity's been bad enough already. I don't want it in the papers or anywhere that my wife moonlighted as a DJ at a goddamned lesbian bar. I *do not* want that! In about six months I expect to be considered for senior vice president. Ingersoll is retiring." He touched his temples.

"I'm going to get it. Nothing's going to stop me. I've worked for this company for thirteen years. I started out in Memphis. I walked into Memphis with nothing! Then Indianapolis, then Cleveland, then here. I don't want anything more about Iris in the news. My God—I'd be out of there like shit through a goose."

He looked at me fiercely. "I know what you're thinking. Well, I'm not."

"Not what?"

"A token! I am not a token!"

The thought hadn't occurred to me. "Mr. Macklin, I'm really not interested in your career. Could we get back to—"

"I've worked like a dog for what I've got!" His voice jumped at me from across the coffee table. "You don't know how hard I've worked!" He clenched and unclenched his fists.

"Do you miss your wife?"

His face crumpled. He threw back his head and let out a long, keening sob. Then more sobs. After a few minutes he began to choke out words.

"I loved her. I did. Oh, damn!" He punched himself in the head. I'd never seen anyone do that. "But she, she—I was losing her. She said she wasn't sure she wanted to be married anymore. I thought if I gave her some slack, you know, she'd go off on her little adventures—*whatever,* and then—then come back to me a hundred and ten percent. Was that wrong?" He looked at me, his eyes streaming.

Taken aback by the force of his emotion, I couldn't speak.

He choked on, "And now this. You don't know what it's like. To be a black man. You can watch all the PBS specials in the world, but you have no idea. To gut it out every day, every day. The pain of trying to make it in an industry that ought to be color-blind. It ought to be! But it's not." The muscles of his cheeks gleamed with tears and sweat. "I've had to deliver three times more than any white man, and I've had to eat ten times the shit. Lady, I don't know *why* I'm telling you this."

He pulled out a handkerchief and rubbed his face roughly. Then his voice softened. "To make it into the inner circle, onto the top rung. Lady, do you realize I'm almost there? Can you begin to imagine what I've gone through and how bad I want it? I want it *so bad.*" His face twisted in anguish. "I don't care what you say. The Lord will be the judge of me."

He stopped, and we sat in silence for a few minutes. I looked at the sky beyond the doorwall while he used his handkerchief again. He cleared his throat. "What's done is done. I'm burying her tomorrow. I don't want any more publicity about Iris. I don't want you telling the police about her and that bar. Do you understand?"

"Maybe you're misjudging the guys you work for."

"I'm not."

I didn't tell him I'd already connected Iris to the Snapdragon for the police. I made him no promises. I just said, "Well, even if you're not interested in justice for your wife, the police are. And I am."

"Get out."

As I walked to my car, I reflected on Gerald Macklin and his obsession, and realized that there were, and always would be, things in this world beyond my understanding.

14

Shitsville. I'd been hoping for either a shocked, grief-stricken nice guy who'd become my ally in uncovering the facts, or a sinister bastard who'd murdered his wife. Macklin's indifference to anything but his career baffled me, but I found myself more determined than ever to see justice done. *Somebody* had to give a good goddamn about Iris Macklin.

The Caprice mixed and mingled with traffic on Woodward Avenue, and I found myself thinking about cars. *The* car, Iris's car, the maroon Escort. If somehow a professional ring had got hold of it, goodbye, but that didn't seem likely. It must be somewhere.

When I got home I consulted the phone book and found a Carl Creighter on Salem Street in northwest Detroit. I remembered Kevin or somebody saying Bonnie lived with her mother; likely, her father was dead. Perhaps, as many widows do, Mrs. Creighter let the phone listing stand. I dialed the number and got a sixtyish sounding female hello.

Once in a while reporters do things to confirm information or hunches that they don't teach in journalism school, not that I ever went to one. I could do a passable Swedish accent, and used it at that moment. It's all in the up-and-down rhythm and intonation. "May I speak to Mrs. Creighter, please?"

"Uh, speaking." Most Americans are caught off-guard by Northern European accents; their first impulse is to listen carefully and respond clearly, which leads to a cooperative feeling.

"This is Mrs. Olsen from the Northern European Life Insurance Group. Your late husband had a policy with us. Were you aware of it?"

"Why no, no, I wasn't." Mrs. Creighter's voice took on a suspicious yet hopeful tone. "European Life? Mr. Creighter has been dead for six years. European Life?"

"Yes, in the amount of fifty thousand U.S. dollars. There was a delay. We need to send you some paperwork for your signature. Let me see, you have one daughter, Bonnie, and our records show no other children, and no one else residing at your address. Is that correct?"

"Yes, no other living children. But wait, is this something he got at work or what? I never knew—"

The important thing is to interrupt and go fast. "You are still residing on Salem Street in Detroit? Yes, fine, we'll send this information along. Thank you very much and goodbye, Mrs. Creighter."

I put down some food for Todd and changed into a black T-shirt with my jeans, and my black Chuck Taylor basketball sneakers.

My thought was, I'd just drive by the house and have a look.

The Caprice was on the street beneath my balcony. As I approached it with my keys, a van with the Detroit city shield on the door pulled over across the street. As soon as I saw it, my heart sank and sweat sprang out on my hands. Lou climbed out, in her uniform and equipment belt. The way she got out of a vehicle was to grab the roof and swing herself out. She rushed toward me.

I was so startled that I ran around to the other side of my car. I stood, panicked, on the curb on the passenger side.

"I was in the neighborhood and thought I'd stop by!" she cried, planting her hands on the Caprice's roof. Her left wrist was bandaged. Her eyes were hectic. A miserable low howl issued from the rear of the van.

"Lou, you're scaring me." I looked up and down the sun-dappled street. Other than a couple of kids playing catch in the distance, nobody was around.

"*Scaring* you?" The look in her eyes changed to wonder. "*Scaring* you?"

I nodded emphatically. "Yeah."

"But I'm a very loving person, Lillian. I just had to see you for a minute." Her shoulders were rolling from side to side as she shifted her weight rhythmically and rapidly from boot to boot. Her face was extremely red. I sensed she was at the very edge of self-control.

Her vehement, raspy voice bounced at me across the car's roof. "I know I probably shouldn't be doing this," she went on, "but it's like—it's like I can't help it. It's like I had to come here."

"Get a hold of yourself," I said. "Where the hell did this come from? What can you possibly want from me? I can't be your girlfriend." I heard pleading in my voice. "Why don't you leave me alone?"

She looked down at her boots, then up at me. Suddenly her body language calmed down. "It's terrible, I know it," she said quietly. "I didn't ask for this to happen. Before, you were always in some damn relationship. Don't I have any chance with you? You are *so* cute."

Clamping my tongue between my teeth, I shook my head. "I'm sorry."

"But how do you know you wouldn't love me if you don't ever give me a chance?"

Her hands were moving on the Caprice's clean roof, leaving trails of perspiration. It bugged me, but I noted with satisfaction that the sweat was beading up: proof of a good wax job.

Lou's fingers were oddly slim, ending in ragged nails. She noticed me looking at her hands. "Do you have a problem with bull dykes? Do you have a problem with butches?"

"Oh, God, Lou. No! No! OK? But I do have a problem with *you*!"

"If only," she said, "you'd give me one chance. One date. That's all I ask."

"No, Lou. You're really pushing it here, and the more you push, the more you're not going to get what you want."

"You mean if I back off, you'll go out with me?"

"No!"

We just stood there for a moment.

"Then I guess I have to try to—" She made a chopping motion with her hand. "I don't cry in the daytime. I cry at night. I don't sleep good. I'm not sure what I might do."

"What?" I looked at her narrowly.

"I just mean, I'm not sure what I'm going to do."

I didn't like the sound of that, but I believed she would, in fact, get over it, and pretty quickly too. I couldn't imagine anyone obsessing over me for more than a week.

"Do you have someone to talk to, Lou?"

She grunted and squinched her eyebrows together. "You're the only one I want to talk to. But I know what you mean. I don't know. I guess I could see someone."

"I'd encourage you to do that."

The radio on her belt squawked.

"Hadn't you better get back to work?"

"I gotta go over to the zoo and then back to the shelter before six. Well. Bye," she said.

"Bye."

She gave me a long, deep look, then backed off to her van.

After she drove away I sat down on the curb for a while. The insane thought occurred to me that if I actually went out with Lou once, then turned her down, she'd somehow be satisfied and go away. Hah. But I had to admit a date with Lou could be an interesting experience. A crow flapped swiftly by, chased by a pair of screaming blue jays. They disappeared over the rooftops.

I got into my car and drove to the Creighter residence on Salem Street.

Late-afternoon light angled through the trees. The neighborhood was quiet. I cruised slowly past the address and noticed a red Fiero in the driveway. The white-on-blue license was a vanity plate that read BC-1. Check. The house was a basic brick two-story job, with white-and-green metal awnings, '50s-style. The driveway terminated in a small wood-frame garage set far back on the lot, with no window on its large metal door. I circled the block and drove by a second time, noticing the front door standing open behind a screen door, and a fan running in a window.

From the side door, which opened onto the driveway, a woman appeared, toting a large plastic trash bag. I rolled to a stop and slouched in my seat. She was heavy and old, unmistakably Bonnie's mom, wearing a sleeveless, flower-print housedress and wooden-soled Dr. Scholl's exercise sandals.

She walked stiff-legged to the garage, jingling a grapefruit-size clump of keys in her other hand. Together with the clacking of her sandals, the keys created a sort of samba rhythm. A tall maple in the backyard cast a broad mottled shadow that swallowed her up momentarily. She emerged from the shadow at the side of the garage where there was a regular door, glanced over her shoulder, inserted a key, leaned inside, and swung the trash bag in.

For a moment all I could see of her was her sizable printed rump and her stocky legs, knees locked. Her upper body reappeared minus the trash bag, and she carefully relocked the door. I slumped all the way down as she turned to make the trip back to the house. After a few minutes I peeked up and drove away.

I went over to Café Yokey-Dokey in Ferndale, which despite its name was a serious coffeehouse, run by a couple of earnest guys who believed in the city's potential. For a while downtown Ferndale was a lot like Lincoln Park, a tired business district far gone to wig shops and Laundromats, but lately a regeneration was happening. Citizens groups had forced the porno theater out of business, and shoestring entrepreneurs were making a go of it here and there.

I ordered a regular coffee and took a seat. The place had been appropriated by avant-garde teenagers. They're nice to share space with, because they're so far into themselves they don't even glance at other people. I listened to a little of their conversation. Every fourth word was "basically." The latest modifier.

I looked at a few magazines, then wrote a letter to my best friend Truby in California. We'd been classmates at Wayne State. Her degree was in French, mine in English; we were faces in the liberal arts mob. I'd been keeping her posted on the Bucky situation, so I filled her in on the latest. I also told her about the murder. "I'm about to trespass for the first time in pursuit of truth, justice, and economic freedom (mine)," I wrote. The sun drew low through Café Yokey-Dokey's streaked storefront window. I watched it set on my first day as independent journalist and professional asshole.

I hung out for a few hours, drinking too many refills while trying to deaden my nerves through self-hypnosis. "I am not nervous. It's normal to be nervous. But I am not actually nervous."

Then I left and cruised the Detroit expressways for another few hours, using up some of the caffeine. I gassed up the Caprice and checked the oil. Finally, I stopped at a 7-Eleven and bought new batteries for the little penlight I kept in the glove compartment. My hands trembled as I tapped out the old batteries. Then I swung by the Snapdragon and saw the red Fiero in the first spot by the door. Check.

The Caprice and I returned to the Salem neighborhood. I parked two blocks down and two over, took the penlight and a deep breath and climbed out. Affecting nonchalance in case anybody saw me, which no one did, I sauntered down the street behind Salem, then cut into the backyard of the house right behind Bonnie's. The house was dark. No sign of dogs in either yard. My Chuck Taylors made no sound on the concrete driveway nor then in the grass.

A sliver of moon hung over the treetops, its shine augmented by streetlights filtering down here and there. There was just enough of a gleam to see by, yet I felt pretty well-concealed. In case anyone discovered me, I was prepared to explain that I thought I'd seen an owl and was trying to get a better look. A birder could wind up anywhere.

I hugged the garage wall past a couple of sour garbage cans and followed it to the back fence. Like all fences in those neighborhoods, it was chain-link, a little high, but fortunately with the top wires turned over. I managed it in a boost-and-roost move, my foot kicking the links just a little. The whole fence rattled slightly as I dropped to the other side in a crouch.

The tough part about sneaking around in summer, I remembered from being a kid, was that open doors and windows made people more likely to hear you. I waited a couple of minutes, then moved forward. A few feet later I was touching the Creighters' garage. Same vintage as the house. But the paint was peeling; it seemed the garage hadn't been taken care of as well as the house over the years.

Light poured from the windows at the rear of the Creighter residence. The sashes were heaved up—no central air. I could see yellow walls and china bric-a-brac, the kitchen. I inched along to the side garage door. The grass grew right up to the garage. A few tall weeds pressed up at the foundation, having escaped mowing. The door was wooden with a large window, which was covered from the inside with aluminum foil. That was not so very unusual; lots of homeowners cover their garage windows, windows in garages having been in style before opportunistic neighborhood crime, or fear of it, made things different. I tried the knob for the heck of it: locked, of course.

Suddenly I heard voices close by. I darted for a shadow back along the garage wall and froze. A teenage couple passed on the sidewalk, murmuring. As I pressed against the wood covering the garage, I got a better sense of its age; it really felt weak. Chips of paint flaked off when I moved my arm. I scooted around the back by the fence again. In the dark I tested the boards with my hands: One, knee-high, was loose.

Kneeling in the weeds, I forced the middle of the board inward as far as I could, about three inches, then flashed my light for just a second. Tar paper or something covered the inside.

Out came my pocketknife, a little Case knife I always carry in the back pocket of my jeans. It's got rounded nickel bolsters and a black handle. At the paper I used it every day for cutting open packages, jimmying the lock on the paper-towel dispenser whenever we lost the key, etc. At the swamp I could pry an interesting stone out of the mud. Carrying the knife got to be a habit.

Holding the knife bayonet-style with two fingers, I cut away a strip of the tar paper. Then I got my eye close to the hole, stuck my flashlight in, and looked.

15

Yowza, there it was. A maroon Escort, the Ford logo on the grille staring me in the face. I flicked the light around for a second to confirm the color. For decades now, Michigan hasn't required a front license plate, so I was out of luck there. To identify the thing for sure I'd have to see and memorize the vehicle identification number.

Maybe the car actually belonged to Bonnie or her mother; Ford sure built them by the zillion. I fiddled with other boards, thinking to quietly pry away a big enough space so I could slip in. But none was loose enough. I'd have needed more tools and would have made lots more noise. My heart started to pound. Half on my hands I skirted to the front of the garage, hesitating at the large front metal garage door. It was a one-piece. No way could I pry a peek into that. To try the handle I'd have to expose myself to the street, plus even clicking the handle could create a noise, one of those unmistakable metal booms that say garage door.

So I moved fast from the corner of the garage to the corner of the house, a distance of about twenty-five feet. There was a concrete patio with a couple of aluminum-frame garden chairs and a little wrought-iron table. The shadows were deep there, so I crept along the side of the house, feeling with my hands and feet for sprinklers, hoses, whatnot.

Below the kitchen window I took a short breather, then lifted my head and looked in.

The yellow walls were done in high-gloss paint, brilliantly illuminated by two overhead fluorescent ring fixtures, old-style, one above the sink and one dead center. The sudden brightness was so much I had to squint.

Mrs. Creighter sat in profile to me at the kitchen table, a lighted cigarette between her fingers. The room, I noticed, was hazy toward the ceiling, even though a large pink plastic fan was oscillating in the corner. At the moment, she was exhaling a stream of smoke directly at the tabletop. She was hunched over rows of cards, playing solitaire. Her expression was distrustful. The deck nestled in her pudgy hand; she waggled it. *Nobody sits with a deck of cards and plays solitaire anymore,* I thought, *except convicts whose television privileges have been revoked.*

Mrs. Creighter regarded her cards with a steady expression of suspicion, sorting through them methodically, then laying one carefully down. Suddenly the ambient sound level increased, and she lifted her eyes.

I ducked, but she wasn't looking at me; I peeked again and saw a color television set tucked in a corner on the countertop. It was a commercial that caused the volume to jump, as commercials always do. Mrs. Creighter watched the commercial, a local one for a chain of sporting goods stores.

Then another commercial came on, and she watched

that one too. Taco Bell, being very aggressive. One more shortie, for a car. Some sports car. The program, *Cheers,* came back on, and she went back to her cards.

I looked hard at everything, hoping to see something sinister. Bloodstains? It was a real retrograde kitchen, with great old yellow-and-black countertop tile with serious grouting, ancient but shiny yellow tile on the floor; it was one yellow kitchen, you bet. Even the table was an oldie, one of those red-and-white enameled metal jobs with big square wooden legs painted yellow.

There were a few magazines and a pile of junk mail on the countertop next to the TV. A wall-mounted white princess phone completed the tableau. A darkened archway led to what looked like the living room. The kitchen was so big I guessed they didn't need a dining room. Other than how unusual everything looked, nothing looked unusual.

I watched Mrs. Creighter. Her pattern was to play solitaire when the program was on and watch the commercials when they came on. She was a large woman, but her head and neck were exceptionally outsized. When she moved her head she looked like a massive animal, ponderous and confident. The movements of her chubby hands, however, were subtle and delicate. She picked up her cards and laid them down with careful grace. She continued to smoke, pausing between cigarettes and cocking her head as if waiting for a letdown. Now and then she sipped from a sweating glass stamped with white and gold daisies; iced tea, it looked like.

I became conscious of a feeling of affection for her, mainly because of the kitchen—how did they keep that linoleum from wearing out?—when I noticed that her brand of cigarettes was Camel Filters, a contrast to her daughter's Carltons. Now this was an old broad who knew something about the small pleasures of a hot summer night: iced tea, solitaire, Camels. I forgave her the television, because she was ignoring one of the most insipid shows ever invented.

I bored my eyes into Mrs. Creighter's head, trying to read her mind. She didn't sense me.

How did her husband die? I wondered. I could try to check on that.

Eventually, she grabbed for the Camel Filters again, shook the pack upside down, caught the last cigarette, and balled up the pack. Twisting slightly in her chair, she shot the pack at a flip-top trash can with its lid propped up against the wall. The pack banked off the high plastic and went in. Aloud she said, "Shit." Then she exerted great force with her hands against the edge of the table.

Most people, if they did that with that heavy table, their chair would slide back, but with Mrs. Creighter it was the table that moved with a big shuddering moan. She rose slowly, crouching at first and edging her way out from beneath it, then slowly straightening. Having forgotten what she looked like on two feet, it struck me that in the upright position she looked unnatural, as a water buffalo would appear on two legs.

She heaved a sigh and settled onto her feet. Her eyes swung toward a high stool next to the telephone, her head followed, then her feet moved her to it. She led with her eyes. People lead with different body parts, I've noticed. Some people lead with their hips. If they do, you can guess they study yoga, and you wouldn't be wrong often. Most people lead with their eyes, though.

A boxy straw purse perched on the stool; she grabbed it along with her huge set of keys. I saw several rings linked together, along with colored plastic tags and charms. Mrs.

Creighter looked back once, and for an instant I thought she saw me, but no, she was just checking the TV. No commercial.

Leaving everything on, she exited. The screen door fell shut behind her. The inside door remained propped open with a doorstop.

My ears adjusted around the corner, where her Dr. Scholl's footsteps clacked on the driveway. *Shit, what if she comes to the garage?* But I knew she wouldn't. The footsteps faded down toward the curb. A car door slammed, an engine started; rubber tires, soft from the heat, made a watery sound down the street.

I was familiar with the neighborhood from having dated a woman who lived a few blocks over. Assuming the liquor store on nearby Beech-Daly Road would be her destination on this cigarette run, she'd be gone for about ten minutes. Not enough time to bother to shut and lock all the doors. Of course, she could be going farther, but I had to figure not. My watch said 11:55. I ran to the garage and tried the big door; it boomed and didn't budge.

OK, says I, walking quickly to the house. The screen-door latch opened quietly, and I stepped inside. I couldn't pass up this opportunity to look around.

Except for the kitchen the house was dark, so I flipped my penlight on and off quickly to get my bearings. Once when I was riding for a day with the cops on a feature story, we responded to a burglary call. It was morning, and the intruder was long gone; while the officer wrote in her notebook, I noticed a series of burned matches lying on the living room rug. They formed a trail to other rooms in the house.

The cop explained that one of the commonest burglary tools is a book of matches. The burglar lights them one at a time, dropping them when they burn down, thus making an informed tour of the premises while not interrupting the darkness for very long. The swerving glow of a flashlight through the window of a darkened house is suspicious; the flare of a match isn't, plus it isn't as noticeable. I hoped the short bursts from my tiny flashlight would look the same to any neighbor or passerby.

I'd seen the kitchen, so I checked the living room first. A long couch, a large Hammond organ, two upholstered chairs. What is chintz? I think there was chintz. I noticed a large cross on the wall over the organ, and a Bible open on top. I thought the cross and Bible were a bit incongruous. I mean, I didn't know anybody who made a show of old-fashioned Christian religion anymore, except my horrible gossip-mongering great-aunt, Alberta, who thought it threw people off from realizing how horrible she was.

Maybe Mrs. Creighter was the religious one.

The living room walls were covered in an odd wallpaper, sort of a geometric rectangular print. My light was so poor I couldn't tell what color it was. There were end tables, and towering on top of them were extremely tall lamps, complicated in design.

One lamp was particularly memorable, a large fish standing on its curled tail, such as you might see in a city fountain, made of plaster or ceramic finished in a dark pebbled glaze, as if cinders had been pressed into it. It looked like a leaping coelacanth trying to throw the lampshade from its head. A frothy doily at its base suggested the white foam of the sea.

My eyes hunted over everything, looking for something incriminating. Would they pile up evidence in the parlor?

As quickly as I could, I poked through other rooms on the first floor: bedroom, bathroom, bedroom. In the bedrooms I opened drawers and pushed stuff around a little to see the bottoms. I envisioned a little container of teeth, maybe a witchcraft-type altar. A gun. I almost forgot Iris had been shot. I didn't know squat about black magic and voodoo, except for hearing about devil-worshipping rings in Detroit that reportedly used pit bulls to sacrifice stolen German shepherds and Dobermans. I figured something as bizarre as teeth-pulling and execution had to have occult roots.

The bedrooms stayed true to the decor of the rest of the house. A cross loomed above each bed. The room I judged to be Mrs. Creighter's was a replica of Ozzie and Harriet's, though there was a double bed instead of twins. The dressers and nightstands were blond wood, very impressive. Well-cared-for. A white chenille bedspread! My liking for the old girl increased by the moment.

Bonnie's room was a bit of a shock. In the center of the not-very-large room was a short white four-poster bed, with a fluffy organdy bedspread with a frilled skirt all around. Every flat surface, including the bed, was covered with stuffed animals. I discerned a common theme of white plush. The furniture looked like plastic, but it must have been wood painted white with gold trim in that pseudo-French vanity style. There was a small desk and chair as well as dressers. An island of stuffed animals next to the desk turned out to be a two-drawer file cabinet. It was a Barbie-doll room. No dream catchers. No crystals, none of that crap.

I rolled open the top drawer and found it packed with papers that looked like bills, old receipts—*God, maybe there are tons of clues nestled here between the family tax records.* No time for a close look, though. I needed something plainly incriminating. Hastily I opened the sliding closet door and flicked my light again: just Bonnie's clothes. I recognized the orange number she wore the other night.

But boy, nothing. With the exception of the file cabinet, the room looked as if a little kid from the '50s had died and the parents had kept everything just as it was. The whole house looked that way, frozen in time. The color TV was the only anachronism. I began to feel pretty stupid as well as uptight. My watch said midnight, five minutes gone, five to go. I hesitated between basement and upstairs—I had to choose one or the other; there wasn't time for both. I moved quickly back toward the kitchen.

Before plunging down the stairway, I noticed out of the corner of my eye the stack of mail and magazines on the kitchen counter. I flipped through what was there. Electric bill, Domino's Pizza, One-Hour Martinizing. A magazine or catalog lay at the bottom. It caught my eye because something about the cover made it look different from a regular magazine. I slipped it out.

A posed shot of a handsome silver-haired man reclining in a chair with a pretty young woman bending over him, attending to him, made me gasp. The woman wore a smock and surgical mask, and held a power dental implement. The man, smiling brightly, wore a paper napkin clipped around his neck. The caption: "Equipment Roundup: Less Vibration Means Fewer Repetitive Strain Injuries!" The magazine: *North American Dental Hygiene Professional*.

Could I add two plus two? You bet I could. But would it play at the cop shop? I needed more. I bounced down into the basement like an over-inflated bicycle tire. A light bulb burned in the center, illuminating the belly of the beast.

It was the cleanest basement I'd ever seen. The tile floor gleamed white under the bare bulb. I became aware of a loud hum; the lighted corner was the laundry area and the dryer was on, must have been on a long cycle. The washtub was white fiberglass and spotless. It looked as if no one had ever so much as cleaned a fish anywhere near it.

The floor seemed to stretch for acres. There was no clutter. No boxes to poke into, no piles of old trunks to shove around.

I saw a little work station of some kind, in a corner. There was a work bench, a padded stool, a Tensor lamp, a swing-arm magnifier. Stamp collecting, maybe? I noted little tools, tweezers, paintbrushes with bristles so fine you could hardly see them. There was a bottle of black Quink ink, a small can of Minwax wood stain (mahogany), and an unmarked bottle of clear liquid. I opened it and lifted it to my nose; the septum-piercing fumes of hydrochloric acid scorched my airway. Did you take chemistry in school? Remember that smell?

What was the hobby here? There was no balsa wood, no paper, no etched copper, nothing. Then I saw a little drawer built into the bench. It was locked. I whipped out my knife to jimmy it but couldn't fit the blade in far enough.

My watch said 12:03. I had to get out. Now I had only questionable findings to report to Ciesla and Porrocks. If the car turned out to be Iris's, I'd be a heroine; if not, I'd have nothing to do but endure the contempt and future cold shoulders of Ciesla and Porrocks.

I hurried up the stairs. As the laundry light faded behind me, I looked up and saw the beautiful black rectangle of the screen door and the night behind it.

My ears hunted for the measured clacking footsteps that would indicate Mrs. Creighter's return. Nothing. I forced myself not to rush out. Quietly, I turned the screen door latch and stepped out into the night. I looked both ways and saw a pair of Dr. Scholl's sandals I hadn't noticed before on the driveway next to the door. Maybe they belonged to Bonnie or were just a spare pair for working outside. Something.

I crept backwards around the corner of the house, intending to leave the way I'd come. As I plastered myself against the bricks near the kitchen window, a feeling of intense relief swept through me, even though I was still on enemy turf. I'd proved I possessed plenty of foolish guts. Fresh, cool blood flooded my arms and legs.

I rested for a moment, deciding whether to scuttle back over the fence before Mrs. Creighter came back, or after. It was low-risk either way. I thought I'd maybe even stay and watch her a little more. Who knew what she might do, enlivened by fresh cigarettes and another cold drink? Who knew what I might see? I blew my breath out quietly.

There are some sounds that are loud but sound small, like a gunshot far in the distance. Then there are sounds that are small but sound very, very loud, such as the click of a gun's safety next to your neck.

Mrs. Creighter did that and then whispered deafeningly, "Nice night, huh?"

16

Over the years, I'd received quite a bit of covert operations instruction, unfortunately all of it from the movies and TV. Old TV series from when I watched a lot of TV, before I knew better. Remember *Mannix*? You probably don't. No matter what the plot, at some point in every show the detective Mannix would get hit on the head by a bad guy. That is just exactly how stupid I was.

Now, stupidity is not the same as ignorance—I think we all can agree on that. Stupidity is actually a complex blend of intelligence and poor judgment. I had the market cornered on that deadly combo that hot July night on Salem Street in Detroit.

So Mrs. Creighter whispers, "Nice night, huh?" My mind stopped cold while I ascertained I could still hear and that my heart had not, after all, exploded. When my mind came back on, all it said was *OH, FUCK* once or twice. Mrs. Creighter and I stood like that for a while, the echoes of her whisper dying against the side of the house where she had planted herself awaiting my return. I finally slid my eyes sideways and glimpsed her pale thick face floating inches from mine. I didn't dare turn my head enough to see the gun. "Inside," she growled.

Don't show fear, I commanded myself, the same as if she were a feral dog. We marched inside. Her footsteps made no sound; she slipped back into her sandals at the door. I started for the well-lighted kitchen, but she said, "No." We veered to the living room. As I stood stiffly in the middle of the room, she edged over and drew the drapes closed, then turned on the leaping coelacanth.

We faced each other by its golden light. I was still clutching my flashlight. My knife, I remembered, was in my pocket, but I couldn't see how I might put it to use.

Cooperate, say anything to get her to let you go, was my first thought. My second thought was, *I might be able to somehow break free and get away even if she shoots me.* I'd have to move fast and hope she wasn't a very good shot.

"Who are you and what do you want?" she demanded in an ugly voice. She held the gun at waist level, pointed at me gangster-style. It was a small semi-automatic, like the one that killed Iris. Her eyes were heavy-lidded, and she raised her eyebrows to gaze at me.

I shook my head as if to clear it and pretended to come to my senses. "Lady, please," I said. "I thought I saw an owl on your roof. I was trying to get a better look. Why do you have that gun?" My voice sounded as genuine as Diet Pepsi.

Mrs. Creighter twisted her mouth contemptuously. "I said, what do you want?"

"I don't know whatcher talking about. You want to call the police and have me arrested for trespassing?"

Mrs. Creighter stalked over to me. She put her chubby hand on my shoulder and stuck the gun barrel up under the soft part of my jaw. Thrusting it upward so that my head jerked back, she said, "Talk to me."

"OK," I gurgled. She released me and my knees buckled. I vomited all over the coffee table.

"You dirty pig!" I heard her say as I finished my coughing. I picked up a doily that had escaped the flow and wiped my mouth with it, then dropped it on the carpet.

She emitted incoherent cries of disgust. "Aogh! Aogh!"

"I know it," I said. I eased backward and sat on the couch. Snapshots crowded under the glass of the coffee table: picnics, birthday parties. "I'm an asshole, actually, and I was poking around here because I'm investigating Iris Macklin's murder."

Her eyes never left the mess on the table. I could tell she was dying to go get a towel to clean it up. "Yes, well," she said.

"I know you've got her car in your garage."

Her eyes flew wide open. She muttered something under her breath. I waited.

She stared again at the coffee table. She pointed the gun at the mess as if to shoot it.

She turned her face upward, as if searching for something on the ceiling, then remembered she ought to keep her eyes on me. She locked her eyes into mine and started up a conversation with somebody who wasn't me.

"Yes, but," she said, "I'm perfectly capable of understanding—" She appeared to listen, her head cocking slowly off to one side. "You don't have to spell it out for me. I'm just—" Pause. "Yes." Pause. "Yes." Pause. "No, never. Glory isn't what counts: I know that. The prideful find no rest." Pause. "*Your* glory, my goodness!"

I realized she was talking to God.

Finally, she said, "We'll go upstairs." I climbed the carpeted stairs, my back feeling the tiny black maw of the gun.

"In there," she said, giving me a shove. She snapped on an overhead light. We were in a small bare room, a rag rug on the floor, shade pulled down over a little window, no furniture at all except another small file cabinet.

"So you think you're pretty smart," she said. "Did you think I didn't see you?"

"That's what I thought," I responded politely.

"Well, I didn't actually see you, but I knew you were there. I knew somebody was there."

"Yep." I had nothing to do but watch her and the door, which was growing smaller by the second, behind her. It occurred to me to make a grab for the gun, but I was afraid. I didn't know how to do it with any measure of safety. As she was taking a breath to speak again, we heard something downstairs.

"That's Bonnie!" Mrs. Creighter said, her eyes sparking. "Bonnie!" she called. "Come here!"

"Ma, wait," Bonnie's voice came irritably up the stairs. "I'm bringing some stuff in. Ugh! What the—what happened! Who got sick all over the—"

"Right now, right now, *right now,*" Mrs. Creighter bellowed. Bonnie thundered up the stairs.

You should have seen her face when she barged in.

"You!" Then turning to her mother, "What-what-what?"

Mrs. Creighter said, "She was sneaking around. She was hiding. I've got to calm down." She took a big breath, stopped, and let it out slowly. "My heart. I've got to calm down. I don't want to have another H.A."

"You're not gonna have another heart attack! What's going on?"

Mrs. Creighter handed her the gun (which Bonnie instinctively aimed at me), then put her right index finger on her left wrist and felt the pulse. Evidently satisfied, she patted her wrist, retrieved the gun, and said, "I could tell someone was watching me in the kitchen. So I pretended to go get cigarettes. I left, but I parked down the street and walked back, and I caught her!" She threw back her head as if she were a big game hunter and I a runty trophy animal at her feet.

I took the opportunity to ask, "How did you know I was going to go back around to the rear of the house?"

"Because you would have. You did." She projected a curious blend of overexcitement and deep cunning.

To her daughter she said, "She saw the car. She saw your music person's car. But I caught her. She was the one you were talking about. She was"—her volume increased again—"she was the one who called on the phone today! Remember I told you about the life insurance!" Amazement and pure pleasure flooded her countenance. She poked the gun in my direction as if touching me with a ten-foot pole. "You called me today, didn't you?"

I couldn't believe the situation I'd gotten myself into. "Go to hell," I muttered.

"You know what I mean!" she screamed.

She approached me and again shoved the gun under my jaw. "She threw up before when I did this. Now. Talk Scandinavian." An evil smile stretched her lips tight. Her teeth were like Bonnie's: smallish and rounded with spaces in between.

Her expression was echoed in Bonnie's face, hanging over her shoulder.

I jerked my head away. "Go to hell."

"Ma, hold on," Bonnie said. A moment of silence filled the air between the three of us. Mother and daughter locked eyes. A quietness came over them.

Only then did my heart begin to understand terror. For they appeared to come out of themselves in a way, and communicate silently with each other. Their bodies relaxed, their shoulders, formerly high with tension, dropped. Their faces relaxed too, the savage muscles of rage and excitement falling into repose.

Across the two calm faces spread genuine smiles, light and confident. Their eyes shone. Mother and daughter nodded to each other and sighed lightly, as people do in anticipation of a pleasant, satisfying meal. Simultaneously they turned toward me.

17

These, obviously, weren't first-timers: They were experienced terror artists. I didn't catch them; they caught me, and they intended to kill me.

As I stood there, I thought of the Midnight Five, the string of missing women in the Detroit area over the past couple of years. If they were murdered, they were all killed expertly and without a trace of evidence. I felt I was about to join the victim club unless I did something drastic pretty soon.

Mrs. Creighter murmured, " 'And the king's servants said unto the king, Behold, thy servants are ready to do whatever my Lord the king shall appoint.' "

Bonnie nodded thoughtfully.

Her mother said, "Should we stay here or go over to the place?"

Bonnie put a finger to her lips and blew on it, as if deciding how thin to roll a piecrust, and finally said firmly,

"We'll stay here. We'd have to wait too long. It's not even, what, twelve-thirty yet. Do you want to wait that long until after closing? Sandra'll close up. Plus we'd have to get her over there. It's too risky."

Mrs. Creighter agreed. "We've got enough of everything here anyway."

"Yeah, Ma, will you go get the rope? Gimme that," Bonnie said, taking the gun. "Let's just get her tied up. I'll feel better." Mrs. Creighter exited, patting her heart.

Bonnie held the gun and her gaze on my stomach. "Lillian," she said, licking her lips. I hadn't known until now whether she even knew my name.

"Thought you were pretty hot shit there for a while, didn't you?" she said. I didn't reply. I decided that as soon as Mrs. Creighter came back with the rope and one of them got close to me, I'd shove her into the other and bolt. I'd blown tons of chances to run earlier.

"So you saw the car in the garage," Bonnie went on, excited and angry. "What, did Ma forget to lock it again? I can't believe her. What else did you see? Open up those file cabinets? Get an eyeful? Or no?"

I didn't answer.

"Well, you know what?" she said. "You are rather exceptional. Have you been thinking about me?"

"Yes."

Licking her lips once more, she got that horrible dreamy look again. She lifted her free hand to the amulet around her neck, the shield-shaped pendant made of wood and shell, and fondled it. She took a breath to speak again when Mrs. Creighter returned empty-handed. "I couldn't find it."

"Oh, Ma! You didn't look. Hey, 'seek and ye shall find,' you know? There's some right by the canned stuff. Still in the wrapper. Ugh! You couldn't find your butt with both hands."

Mrs. Creighter ignored this insult.

"I have to do everything," Bonnie said.

"Shouldn't we ask for guidance together first?"

"Guidance! We don't need any more goddamn guidance! This one's a no-brainer, Ma!"

"Cancel that blasphemy. Let us pray."

"Later, Ma."

Bonnie looked back to me with sudden suspicion, and I must have shown a break-and-run light in my eyes.

"Hell," she said, and I could see the gears of her mind working briefly, making a judgment. "You got the key to this door anyway?"

"Yeah."

"Gimme."

Mrs. Creighter rumbled down the stairs and back up again. She held out her giant key clump by one key. Bonnie, jabbing in my direction with the gun, herded her mother out, backing out behind her. The key turned in the lock and I saw the bolt slide into the doorjamb.

"Just stay here and keep this pointed at the door," I heard her say. Then, louder, she said, "Shoot through it if the knob even rattles." She took off down the stairs, and I turned instantly to the window. It was small, yes, but wide enough for me.

I snapped up the window shade, flipped the latch, and gave the sash a shove upward. It didn't budge. I looked closer and saw that the frame was painted shut. I yanked out a drawer of the file cabinet, thinking to smash through the glass with it. It rolled out heavily, jammed full of papers and photographs. The photos were all Polaroids, stacked in a few packs bound with rubber bands. Women—my eyes flashed over them too quickly to notice much except that.

The papers looked familiar. They were pages of bleached newsprint torn from a periodical of some kind—there was something I sort of recognized about them. But I was almost blind with panic and didn't have time to make sense of them.

I pulled, but somehow the drawer was latched into the cabinet and wouldn't come out, so I took another try on the sash. I squatted deeply and braced my arms. For the sake of my young life, I thought *Up!* and called forth my mightiest burst of strength. The window frame gave out a sharp crack and flew open. At the same moment I grunted, involuntarily, loudly, from the pit of my stomach.

Mrs. Creighter's panicked voice came from the other side of the door. "Bonnie! Hurry! She's getting out!" As I suspected, she didn't want to shoot because of all the open windows in the neighborhood. A single shot for my execution, muffled with a pillow, would escape notice, but not a fusillade into a wooden door. Especially now that I'd gotten the window open.

I pushed at the screen, but my arms were like rubber, rebounding from the effort of breaking the paint. I pulled out my pocketknife and ripped a slit in the screen, then tore it the rest of the way with my hands. Bonnie's footsteps pounded up the stairs, shaking the floor. I boosted myself up and got my left leg and upper body through the window. Outside—wow, no sill, no porch roof, nothing. I was at the front of the house, facing the warm silence of the neighborhood.

I saw Bonnie's Fiero in the driveway, the trunk and driver's door open. I remembered she said she'd been bringing something in. She'd forgotten about the car. I looked down. It was about sixteen feet—a clear, sharp drop. Below, shadows; I couldn't tell whether I was going to hit grass, bushes, lawn furniture, bayonets.

Keys jingled frantically on the other side of the door; Bonnie and her mother were jabbering like giant chipmunks. I scrabbled to get both feet on the window frame, crouched tightly, then with the cries of the damned raging closer, jumped.

18

I closed my eyes on impact. Something prickly flew up my nose: a twig from the low yew shrub I landed on. I felt the jolt in my spine, but it wasn't too bad. Then I was up, untangling my feet from the low branches, running.

Be smart, be smart, said my head, and my legs propelled me over the lawn toward Bonnie's car. Mrs. Creighter stuck her head out the window and said in a low terrible voice as I took off, "You are mine." The keys, thank God, were in the trunk lock. I slammed it down, jumped in and started the thing up.

As the engine caught and I rammed it into reverse, the front door of the house flew open and Bonnie rocketed out. I floored it, watching only Bonnie, until I judged I was in the street, then threw it into drive. As in a nightmare, the car didn't seem to have any pickup. Bonnie's face, a mask of desperate purpose, zoomed closer.

But unlike in a nightmare, where the monster actually

rips the car door off and grabs your throat and you wake up screaming, Bonnie fell away by one car length, then two. I didn't even glance back as I steered the tiny car down Salem to Seven Mile.

My heart clapped in my neck; all I could think of was getting to an expressway and putting some miles between me and the Creighters. *But don't get stopped for speeding,* I thought. Mrs. Creighter's car had to be at least a block away from the house.

I headed for the concrete canyon of the Southfield expressway and ate up a few miles. The little sports car felt odd and insubstantial compared to my stolid Caprice with its heavy-duty police suspension. I switched over to the Jeffries, then merged onto the Fisher downtown and continued south. It took only moments to fly across the Rouge River overpass beyond the city limits, then down past the Detroiter truck stop in Woodhaven.

I drove in a trancelike state for a while—that's the only way I can describe it. The kind of state you drive in when you realize you've had too much to drink but you need to get home. You concentrate on the road and other drivers and, being careful, check the rearview mirror every five seconds.

Eventually I came to my senses and looked at my watch: one-thirty. A lot more time had passed than should have. Ciesla needed to know about Iris's car in the Creighters' garage right away.

I turned around outside of Toledo and headed back north. My I.D. and money were back in my car. As I drove I rummaged in the console and dash for change. I found a quarter, five dimes, and a penny in the bottom of the console. I kept driving into the city, made the swerve onto the Lodge, and pushed it until I figured I was within the Eagle phone zone again so that I'd have enough change for the two calls I needed to make.

I exited at Caniff and found a phone under a streetlight at a gas station. Ciesla's home number had easily stuck in my memory; it was just two digits different from mine. He answered on the second ring.

"Tom!" I yelled.

"What." He was sleepy and guarded.

"Bonnie Creighter and her mother have Iris Macklin's car in their garage," I said rapidly. "They killed her—they practically said so—and they've got file cabinets with pictures of women in them—their victims. It's all in their house."

"How do you know?"

"Well, um—" I took a great big breath, "I was there tonight, just a little while ago—OK, I snooped. I know I shouldn't have, but I did. It was only because I'm doing this story for the *Journal,* I swear to God." I was talking as fast as my mouth could move, to forestall his groan, or tirade, or whatever was coming.

"I swear to God, Tom, I know I told you I was gonna let you guys do the work, but—but it's not that I lied at the moment, but it turned out not to be the truth—I know. They caught me, and they were going to *kill me,* but I escaped. Bonnie's after me, they're after me. You gotta get over there or send somebody over there, to find the car. Plus there's other stuff in the house, probably other evidence, too, God almighty!"

I heard a dry sound through the receiver, the sound of a hand rubbing a stubbly face. "Where are you now?"

"Someplace on Caniff at a phone booth. You gotta lock 'em up! You gotta apprehend 'em! I'm in danger," I added unnecessarily. I left out the fact that I'd stolen Bonnie's car.

"Lillian, I can't believe you. We were going to bring in Bonnie tomorrow morning for more questioning. If you're telling me the truth, you could have just fucked us right up the ass. How are we gonna get a search warrant on the basis of what you've told me? On the basis of a B&E?"

"Well, I didn't exactly B, but I E'd."

"Did you see the license plate or VIN?"

"No."

"Then how do you know it's the right car?"

"Oh, come on, Tom. They said—they admitted it was."

"What time were you there, exactly?"

"Ah, well, about midnight. 'Bout twelve-thirty. I'm on the lam, man, they're after me. I know I should have gotten to a phone earlier, but I was terrified and just kept driving."

"It's almost two. Right now they're probably getting rid of that evidence faster than you can say jack shit. *If* it is evidence. That car's halfway out of state or in Canada by now. *If* it is that car. Shit."

Anyone watching would have seen an underweight dyke fidgeting around under the streetlight, tethered by the head to the phone pole, like a moth on amphetamines.

"No!" My heart quaked anew. "They've got to still be there! You've got to go over and catch them." Can you believe how ignorant I was? Can you believe it?

"Lillian, listen." Ciesla's voice remained steady. "I'm not going over anywhere. OK? I'm not going anywhere. As long as you're all right. Go home and stay home. Porrocks and I'll go over to the house in the morning." He hung up in my face.

I could absofuckinglutely not believe it. This was not how it was supposed to work.

"Hunh, whoa," I said into the dead phone. Ignorance of police procedure was no excuse. Now, what the hell.

I dropped the phone and scurried back to the Fiero. I wound around the neighborhoods until I found myself on Warren, a street lined with gray little businesses, careworn neighborhoods stretching away on either side. I ducked down a side street, then turned into a back alley, and parked the Fiero in a shadow.

Stepping carefully in case a rat was lurking ready to sink its fangs into my ankle, I wiped off practically the whole car with the hem of my T-shirt: the steering wheel, shift lever, console, headlight knob and door handles, plus the top of the trunk, as I knew smart people did in the movies. Surely, when the car was found, the cops wouldn't bother dusting for fingerprints, but extra care couldn't hurt.

I left the alley and walked along Warren for a while, then called a taxi from a Lebanese all-night diner. It was cooler out now. I leaned against the rough brick of the building, feeling the stored heat of the day seeping out.

When the cab arrived, it was an appropriately awful one, the driver a surly white man who watched me in the rearview mirror. The seat cushions stank. I directed him to Bonnie's neighborhood, my eyes straining sideways at every passing driver. I didn't know what Mrs. Creighter's car looked like. It had to have been parked out front when I first cruised by the house, but I had no reason to take note of it then.

I got out at my car. Thank God the Creighters hadn't gotten around to searching me and taking my keys. I made a fast reconnaissance down Salem.

Ciesla was right: The Creighters had been busy. The house was completely dark. The garage door gaped open, and I didn't have to squint very hard to see it was empty. If the file cabinets had contained documentation of the

Creighters' activities, their contents could have quickly been transferred to the car and the car driven away anywhere. Sure, the cops were on the alert for it, but after one o'clock on a weeknight, it wasn't terribly likely a patrol officer would see it. For all I knew, the Creighters had obscured the license plate or changed it.

After being the hunter, then the captured prey, now I was the hunter again. But I was no longer hunting unsuspecting game; I had exposed myself, stepped out too early from behind the blind, missed with my first shot, and no longer had an advantage. A fine lesson, but costly.

I turned the Caprice homeward, driving in a disgraced funk. What were the Creighters doing right now? What would they do next?

Self-preservation had to be tops on their list. Once they'd lost me, they'd turned immediately to the incriminating evidence, working as an efficient team. They'd packed up the photos and anything else, thrown them in the car and fled. Or maybe only one of them fled while the other stayed behind to keep up a semblance of normalcy. Once they'd covered their butts for the immediate moment, they'd turn to the task of covering their butts permanently. That would involve getting rid of me.

Or would it? Would the fact that they'd be able to stymie the cops—who could search to hell and gone and find no hard evidence, who could question the neighbors and find not one, perhaps, who noticed the minor commotion outside the Creighters' house one hot night, cars being jockeyed around—be enough? I didn't think it would be. Killers who kill for pleasure, or for whatever the hell twisted reason, wouldn't hesitate to kill for security. For contingency. They had revealed themselves to me out of bloodlust and bravado, thinking I wouldn't live to act against them, and now they must follow through.

First they'd have to find out where I lived. (My address wasn't listed in the phone book.) Then they'd have to develop a killing plan for me, one that would allow them to get away with it and cast no suspicion on themselves. This would take a little time, overnight at least.

I drove straight home, parked a little way down the street, and scampered up the stairs to my flat in the dark. When I got in I didn't turn a light on. Todd bumped up to sniff my shoes.

By the light of the refrigerator I checked his water dish, then poured myself a tall glass of water, drank it down, then added a shot of Dewar's to the next one. I sat on the living room floor, my back against the couch. It was a long turquoise leather couch, from the waiting room of a famous plastic surgeon in Grosse Pointe, according to the guy at the secondhand shop. Todd nudged his head onto my thigh, and I patted him while I sipped my drink.

In the dark my heart and nerves slowed down. Goddamn it to hell, I began to think of Judy. I wanted her to comfort me, to marvel at my exploits, to fear for me, to insist, above all, that I come and stay with her until the danger was over.

Ciesla and Porrocks would interview Bonnie tomorrow. While it was possible that she might somehow crack under questioning or make a misstep with her facts, I doubted it. The Creighters could come for me now. I had to figure it would be soon. Everlasting hell. My head swung toward the phone. One of my self-debates started up.

Me: Call her. You need someplace safe. You need a safe harbor. In the storm. You need her.

Me: I have other friends.

Me: You need her.

Me: I know I do. I do, but—

Me: But what? What's there to discuss? This is life and death. You need somewhere to stay. Maybe not just a night or two, but longer. It'd work out. She'd love to have you. She'd understand.

Me: She would, once she'd gotten me to say "I love you" again. I'd be a phony. I'd be using her.

Me: You love her. You know you do.

Me: I do. Yeah, I guess I do.

In the dark my eyes strained toward the phone. Then it rang. I swear to God, it rang right then. Todd and I both jumped about a foot off the rug. It must have been about three o'clock.

Once in a while, though I know she resisted doing it, Judy would call in the middle of the night. Just out of loneliness—you know, how people do. But what if…? I hoisted Todd by his nape and nestled him on my shoulder. The ringing deafened us, as it does when you're alone in the dark. Todd's ears quivered against my neck. After eleven rings it stopped. I went over and switched on the answering machine.

I didn't know about Todd, but my ears needed soothing. I picked my mandolin from its hook in the dining room and checked the tuning. One of the D strings was flat, but the others were right on.

My mandolin is a little old flat-top I'd traded my extra set of golf clubs for a few years back. I liked to play a little bluegrass on it, and I was learning some Irish stuff. I believed that Todd's favorite tune was "Wildwood Flower," because he'd stretch out and go extremely relaxed whenever I played it.

So I nudged up the D string and played it softly, just picking out the skeleton of the tune. I played it through a few times, adding a little bit of ornamentation each time and a little volume too. Before long I was playing it out full with all the hammer-ons and slides. It felt good. I omitted my traditional "shave and a haircut" tag, just letting the last chord die.

Not liking the silence that followed, I played "Cripple Creek," then "Red-Haired Boy," then a snatch of "Carnival of Venice," to work on the old tremolo a little bit.

After a while I quit playing and just sat there. Finally, I looked at my watch, leaning over to a spot of streetlight coming through the bamboo blinds: three-thirty. I got to my feet creakily. My hips ached from the jump, and a knee and an elbow felt raw. In my bedroom I groped in the back of my closet until I found a piece of two-by-four some former tenant had left behind. I shoved it under the front doorknob, angling the other end into the carpet pile. Todd hopped back and forth under it a few times.

I brewed half a pot of coffee in my stovetop percolator and remembered I'd left my good coffee mug on Ed Rinkell's desk, when we had our last conversation. That seemed a long time ago. I was afraid to go to sleep. I drank the coffee sitting in the same spot in the living room. Exhaustion crept up anyway, and I wound up dozing on the couch. The night was staying just a little cool.

I came partly awake with the confused hope that the night hadn't been fully real. Light was building on the other side of the blinds. Todd, I saw, was sleeping several feet away from the couch, having made a little nest out of my socks and shoes. I was surprised he hadn't gone off to sleep on his bed of old towels in a corner of my bedroom.

"Hey," I said. He roused a little, meeting my eye in his usual calm way.

In the bathroom I flossed and brushed, looking like a zombie in the mirror. I took a quick, dribbling shower, not wanting to turn the water on full blast so I could hear someone breaking in and coming to stab me to death. I began to understand the overpowering paranoia shared by all fugitives.

With the gathering light I began to feel better. I decided to gather my courage and go to the alley behind the Snap and look for that tooth. My watch said five-twenty. I fortified myself with some toast and an orange.

19

Most city alleys are the same: filthy, stinking, chock-full of stuff that archaeologists might or might not give a damn about in the year 10,000. Of course, everything organic would be fossilized or something, so it wouldn't smell. And nothing would move because nothing would be alive. Therefore the alley, gradually exposed by little flicks of their dust brushes, would be a much safer and more pleasant place to be than it was now.

We may betray one another in our homes and work-places, we may bite one another in the streets, but in the alleys we do our worst. Here are the useful dump bins for all things unwanted. Here are the packing cases called home by rats and people. Here are the syringes, the blood and the sickness and the babies. Here are the barrels of grease and garbage, the gutter waste that sluices out the back door.

This particular alley, behind the Snapdragon, ran the

length of a long block. Tattered scraps covered the grimy pavement like leaf litter in the forest. There was a paint-spattered broken chair behind the rent-to-own shop. It wouldn't be there long.

I saw no one. The only sounds I heard were a few car doors slamming in the neighborhood, working people heading out for the early shift. That, plus a hardy handful of songbirds. Traffic on Livernois was sparse.

I gave the alley a cursory walk-through, then went to the place where I was standing when I had thrown the tooth away. I walked in vectors from the spot, looking hard. I got down on my hands and knees and peered beneath the Dumpster. I peered *into* the Dumpster. It was full to the top with bulging plastic garbage bags and flattened cardboard cartons. As I scuttled around, the light changed from gray to pink.

Here is what I found in that alley: assorted crumpled newspaper sections and advertising inserts, a wedge-shaped piece of plastic snow fence, a wadded-up disposable diaper, a small pile of what looked like sawdust, innumerable empty malt liquor cans (various brands), innumerable empties both broken and intact of fortified wine (various brands—I spotted Mogen David 20/20, a.k.a. Mad Dog, the football-stand brand of choice at my high school), a rusty chunk of angle iron, a wooden toggle button from someone's overcoat, a thoroughly weather-beaten (though full) package of Entenmann's chocolate chip cookies, a paint-can lid with a trace of pickle-colored pigment on it, one Vernor's bottle cap, three Pepsi bottle caps, a tangle of coaxial cable, a squashed teddy bear dressed in a train engineer's cap and overalls, a plastic five-gallon bucket empty (thank God) except for a dried crust of drywall joint compound, a plastic Kowalski kielbasa wrapper, and a striped men's dress shirt torn and twisted into a knot, as if an investment banker had fought the hounds of hell in this alley and escaped only with his skin.

I found all those things in the alley. But I didn't find the tooth.

20

At noon, back at home, I called Ciesla. He took my call sounding disgusted, as I'd expected. He was eating his usual lunch from the A&W down the street, munching his way around a burger.

"Yeah, Tom, did you question Bonnie yet? How did it go?"

He swallowed—a too-big swallow I could tell. He was eating angrily, as cops often do. If cops waited until they calmed down to eat, they'd all starve to death.

"Well, Lillian," he began heavily, "yeah, I think you're onto something. There's something stinking-suspicious about the Creighters. Fortunately for them, however, your adventures last night gave them all the time they needed to get their shit in one pile. And that pile's gone, yes, ma'am. Maybe we'll find it, and maybe we won't. I was about to call you up and thank you, because Porrocks 'n' I were getting bored around here with only the usual forty or fifty cases to—"

"OK, Tom—I'm sorry. I'm sorry, OK? I blew it, I fucked

up, I'm an absolute worthless moron piece of shit. But let's be fair. I turned you on to the right party, didn't I?"

"I don't know!" he shouted.

"Well, I did, goddamn it. I didn't *make up* that stuff."

"Why didn't you grab some of the evidence you said you saw?"

He had me there. When I yanked on that file drawer, the only thing on my mind was to use it as a tool to break the window. I saw the photos and papers, but my mind was so focused on getting out, and the time was so short... If I'd been less of an idiot, I'd have grabbed something.

"I don't know," I mumbled.

"I went over to the house after you called me."

"You did?"

"Yeah, I thought I'd better. It was dark. Nobody home. Then Porrocks and I went over at a normal hour, about nine this morning. Bonnie Creighter was home, she welcomed us in. The mother was sitting in the kitchen drinking coffee—"

"She was?"

"They showed us around the whole house. We didn't need a warrant. They were very cooperative. The place was spick-and-span—no nothing anywhere, no nothing. They were pretty casual—extremely casual."

"Did you check the file cabinets?"

"One had some stuff in it, family papers; the other was empty."

"That should tell you something."

Ciesla paused, as if counting silently.

I asked quickly, "What about the garage?"

"Empty. I found your peephole, though. Mrs. Creighter's car was in the driveway, a dark-blue Buick. You couldn't have mistaken it, could you?"

For a maroon Escort? I gave a pleading sigh.

"Funny, Bonnie Creighter called the station just before we showed up, reporting her car stolen."

"Huh!" I exclaimed. "Huh!"

"You wouldn't know anything about that, would you?"

"Huh, gee, Tom," I stammered.

"Just how did you get away last night, anyway?"

"Ran like hell." It was true, for about fifty feet. Ciesla made me wait until he'd taken another bite of burger.

"Lillian, don't you know you need evidence to convict? To even fucking *arrest*? It doesn't matter if you know who did it. The world is full of cops who know who did it. Now this lovely case may stay open forever, thanks to you."

I was past the point of wanting to drop down a chute to the molten core of the earth. "What are you going to do now?" I asked meekly.

"None of your goddamned business!" he yelled. "Do you hear me?" After a minute, he said, "I know you're trying to help, Lillian. But don't. All right? Don't."

"But what if they try to kill me?"

"That's your—" he caught himself. "I don't know." He sighed. "You've done me a few favors. Porrocks and I are paying you back by keeping a lid on this shit you've pulled. But there's no way you're going to get any kind of police protection. This ain't the movies. If you're afraid, leave town. Go hide out for a while. But I don't think they're going to do anything to you."

"Why not?"

"First of all, because I don't believe everything you've told me about last night." This was delivered pretty flatly. "It's just talk, and for all I know you made half of it up—

all of it. You need work, right? You want to sell an exciting story, right? I have no reason to think you're in any great danger."

"You think I'm lying!"

"You haven't been straight with me on this from the beginning. I don't know what to think."

The sound of a straw vacuuming the bottom of a drink cup came over the phone. "The second reason is, if these ladies really are the killers, they're so spooked of you they're going to stay the hell away from you. Killers are cowards. If you stay in this business long enough, you'll learn that. Now I'm warning you *again*. Keep your nose out of this or you're gonna get in bigger trouble than you ever thought possible. Don't call me anymore. I'm not obliged to talk to you."

Click.

Ciesla had acted that way with me once before, when I'd found a list of the salaries of all the detectives and deputies and printed it. He'd overreact sometimes, then get over it. I'd probably get him to work with me on this. After all, I was the one who knew a little territory here. But he had to stay mad for a while. In the meantime, I had no one to advise me.

I spent the next hour pacing, thinking, churning through possibilities. The whole mess was too dangerous to tell any of my friends about; the only one I wanted to talk to was Judy. But I realized that if I talked to her, she wouldn't just listen; she'd try to get involved, and if anything awful happened, well, it just couldn't be.

I needed to find a way to get at the Creighters. Maybe there was a back door into their weird creepy minds that would lead me to more evidence or that would break down their defenses, or both.

I kept wondering about the teeth. What did the Creighters want with Iris's teeth? Why would anybody want human teeth? There were strong overtones of necrophilia here: the morbid, the strange, the sickening.

I'd learned that journalism was essentially one big research project. You're a perpetual student, and as such, you continually have to ask for help. A great many things can be learned from books.

I'd learned, though, that an interview with an expert could take you further, faster than most any book. Of course, an expert could also derail you. But I was in a hurry.

I thought of the creepiest and most morbid people I'd ever met. It was a short list. Other than the Creighters and my great-aunt Alberta, there was Greg Wycoff. I shuddered just saying his name to myself. Greg Wycoff was a disgraced funeral director who'd worked for one of the biggest mortuaries in Detroit. He'd been the epicenter of a mesmerizingly juicy scandal right around the time I joined the *Eagle Eye*. It wasn't something that had really hit the media, but everybody seemed to know about it.

This fellow Wycoff was making a good living running the funeral home for the owners, a family that had built up two or three generations of good will in the community. I won't say the name because they're still in business. Wycoff built himself a still grander way of life by catering to a select club of necrophiles. It was actually a matchmaking business: He'd evaluate the corpses on hand against his client list, and set up "after-hours encounters." That was the story. The cops, who acted very wise about it, hinted that that was just the tip of the iceberg, though when pressed they didn't offer any details.

The owners of the funeral home never suspected anything. Wycoff got busted because the wife of one of his clients thought her husband was cheating on her. She hired a private investigator to tail him, and what a surprise *she* got. Can you imagine?

Yeah, Mrs. Thornside, your husband's been cheating on you, all right.

Oh, Mr. Sludge, I knew it. Who is she?

You might better ask, "Who was she?"

If the owners had figured it out, they would've handled it quietly themselves. I mean, my God. But the P.I. couldn't resist, he blabbed. So the owners were obliged to get the police involved.

The papers couldn't get anybody to corroborate; nobody would say a word to them. You could *taste* their chagrin; oh, man, they wanted that one so bad. Wycoff copped a plea on the package of charges they leveled on him, thus avoiding a trial and the gory details it would've yielded. I think he did some time in Jackson.

I ran into him once, about a year after I stopped hearing about him. I was covering a fund-raiser in Eagle for an independent gubernatorial candidate; Wycoff was standing next to the punch bowl talking about his philosophy of life, which he said came from the works of Cole Porter. I remember telling him he could use a dose of Dorothy Parker in there too, and he laughed hard.

Doing sick stuff to dead bodies—perhaps Greg Wycoff was a man I could learn from.

I called the mortuary he used to work for. The woman who answered the phone hung up before I got his whole name out. I went over there and found a driver buffing a hearse in the side parking lot.

"*Oh*, yeah," he said, snapping his rag at a yellow jacket that had lighted on the hood ornament. "He's gotten out of the business. Oh, yes, he's a changed man, I've heard." He gave me this huge sarcastic wink. He named a travel agency in Royal Oak and said Wycoff worked there now.

"He's a travel agent?"

"Well, he's gotta do something."

"Did you know him?"

"No." He looked crestfallen. "I started here just before he...left."

Greg Wycoff remembered me and readily agreed to meet me for coffee at Delia's on Woodward, a chrome-and-countertop diner that's been there so long there are dinosaur tracks in the parking lot. He looked as I remembered him, neat and trim with a confident air, like a football coach at a private prep school. He didn't seem the slightest bit surprised or insulted by my interest in his disgrace. A film of reserve veiled his eyes, yet deep in them I saw a barely concealed eagerness to dish.

After shaking hands we took a table at the back and ordered coffee. He ordered a BLT too.

"I really appreciate your meeting with me," I began as soon as Delia had brought our cups, steaming from the big Bunn shrine behind the counter. "Most reporters are liars, but for whatever it's worth, I give you my word that this talk will stay *entre nous*."

He cocked an appreciative eyebrow at the French term, which I'd thrown in with just the right shade of conspiratorial gravity. You never know what will ingratiate you with a source. Something very slight can do it.

"I come to you because you're—well, you're a man of certain experience."

He nodded in acknowledgment.

"Um, do you miss being a mortician?"

"Horribly. I miss it horribly."

"But you still have connections?"

"A few." He made a gesture as if to say, *It's all right, go ahead.*

"OK, here goes. I want to learn about people who mess with dead bodies."

He swirled cream into his coffee and squinted into it.

"I mean," I went on, "I guess there's more than one reason people want to get their hands on dead people. Right?"

He sipped his coffee and said, "Most people are in it for the sex. What's your angle, sweetheart?"

"I found out a secret about a recent murder."

"Something about the body?"

"Yes."

"I see. You've got an inside bit of information on something, and I can guess what it is, but I won't yet." He paused, then said, "Death is second only to sex in the fascination it holds for people. And when you combine them, you get the ultimate peak experience."

"Yeah?"

"Mm-hmm."

"Excuse me for being obtuse, but how do you—how does a person have sex with a body?"

"Oh! It's easy! Like falling off a log. First of all, if the body's been autopsied, you need some towels handy because there's going to be quite a lot of—"

"Stop! I'm sorry! I'll use my imagination. So most people are in it for the sex. What about the others?"

His sandwich came, and he lifted it to eye level to inspect it. Then he bit into it, showering crumbs down into his napkin. I gazed at the traffic on Woodward. A wino lurched past, open-mouthed.

Greg Wycoff swallowed and said, "Well, you know how there's a black market in Nazi artifacts, like crafts made from Jewish corpses?"

"No!"

"You've never heard of it?"

"No! God almighty! I mean, I've heard that the Nazis made lampshades out of people's skin and so on, but I guess—I would've thought all those things would be destroyed by now. Or buried, or something. I've never heard that there's a trading club for them."

He continued to eat as we talked, relishing his sandwich. "Well, in effect there is. These people have a sort of network, a deeply secret network. They don't betray one another. There's also a market for body parts in general. She puts just the right amount of mayonnaise on, doesn't she? I'm not talking about organs for black market transplants—now *that's* far-fetched! I'm talking about body parts harvested postmortem for use in things like death cult ceremonies—Satanism, I suppose—and plain old arts and crafts."

"Arts and crafts?"

"Fetish objects, you know. Ornaments. Some of them are quite beautiful." He adjusted the collar of his open-necked shirt, and I looked for a piece of jewelry. He saw me looking and held up his wrist. "See this?" He wore a beautiful braided bracelet that looked like fake elephant hair, you know, those thick fibers, but I knew instantly it was something human.

"My God."

"Assorted ligaments. They take dye very nicely. Honey, people have made art like this all over the world since the beginning of time. It's only modern culture that finds it offensive. Scratch the surface of white-bread America and you'll find an absolute *cavalcade* of unconformity! You want diversity? Most people don't know the meaning of the word!"

"But don't these people get found out eventually? I mean, what happens when they die and their relatives find the stuff?"

"Sometimes they don't know what it is. And if they do, they quietly get rid of it. What would *you* do if you found a tambourine made of human skin and knuckle bones in Grandpa's trunk? Call a press conference?"

A drop of tomato juice dribbled down his chin; he caught it with his napkin.

"So," I said, "there's some kind of underground market for stuff like this?"

"A very small and fragmented market, but there is one, yes. In fact, there's someone here in Detroit I'm thinking I should put you in touch with. Because I see your ears pricking up. This murder—you said there was something unusual about the body?"

I nodded.

"Like strategically missing body parts? A butcher job?"

"Sort of. Yes."

"Interesting."

Delia swooped by to refill our coffees. She was no spring chicken, but she moved like one. Wycoff said, "I like a good thriller, don't you?" He bobbled his head in excitement. "It's got to have an extraordinary plot! Like nothing you've ever heard, with plenty of twists and turns: a story that's almost over the top."

I had to smile. "So who's this person you should put me in touch with?"

"Someone who's trying to expand the market for death fetish artifacts."

"Oh?"

"A very industrious individual. Hmm. If you were in the *market* for an object—skin, bones, teeth—"

"Teeth?"

"Aha."

"Wait a minute, Greg. Where's your ethical code in all this? I mean, didn't they teach you anything in Jackson?"

He laughed. "Oh, they taught me plenty in Jackson." His eyes roved off to the side, and he inhaled deeply, with a satisfaction that made the hairs on my arms stand up. Then he said, "The way I see it, a body's a body. The dead don't give a shit, while the living have to live, you see. If you can't be happy without a corpse in your life now and then, well, should that by definition be bad? Should that damn you forever? As for body parts, well, doctors mine corpses for their natural resources all the time."

"But to kill for—"

"Heavens, no! Oh! That's where I draw the line. That's the psychopath line. No, no, no, no. Oh, no."

"Or to, like, *eat*—"

"No! No! That's beyond the pale, as far as I'm concerned."

I zeroed in on this person he mentioned. An artist, he said. An odd duck, to be sure, but very expert, some medical background, but no psycho. Made absolutely beautiful things.

"You've seen them?"

"Oh, yes," he said.

"Well, I've got to meet this guy. I think he could—"

"It's a woman."

"A woman?" My blood ran cold. "What's her name?"

"Clarabelle."

I looked at him.

"She calls herself Clara," he said, "and I add the belle. Just to tease. She's an odd duck, like I said, but she doesn't mind me. I rather like her."

"What's her last name?"

"Come to think of it, I don't *know*, dear. Not that I couldn't find out, if I wanted to. It's just that—well, who needs last names to have a good time?"

"Nobody."

"You got it, kiddo."

"What do these artworks look like?"

"It's hard to describe them. Think well, think Hieronymus Bosch meets the Sundance catalogue."

"Oh."

"You've got these amazing materials, other-worldly. You look at this thing and it doesn't *look* like a metatarsal or a gallstone, yet it reminds you of something, something deep within yourself. Clarabelle respects her materials. It's almost spiritual, the way she works. And it's very lucrative."

"It is?"

"Oh, my, yes."

The thing was, Wycoff told me, she wasn't very generous with her time. She was busy trying to make contacts in the Far East. She'd gotten the idea there's a bigger market over there. Could I buy something to make it worth her while to meet me?

I sipped my coffee. *I don't think so.*

I pictured a hollow-eyed ghoul all in black, with black lipstick, listening to eerie, disharmonic music, sawing away at a thighbone or something, while a pot of sinew boiled on the stove. If she'd recently gotten hold of some fresh teeth, I could maybe nail the Creighters.

"I don't have a whole lot of time here, Greg," I explained.

He decided to invite her over to his place that night. "I'll think of something to get her to stop by. I might have to fib about you a little."

"Don't tell her my name."

"Oh, heavens, no! Actually, I think the two of you just might hit it off." He polished off the last of his BLT and let me pay.

21

Greg Wycoff's house was a long, low brick job in Harper Woods. Three kids were playing monkey in the middle with a beach ball on the front lawn next door by streetlight. I smelled fresh-cut grass.

He answered my ring holding a frosty cocktail. "Come in, precious!"

A dachshund yapped at my ankles. "Oh, stop it, Roscoe," he said in a light, encouraging tone. "Stop it at once!" The dog yapped louder.

"Is she here?" I said.

"Yes," he said, nodding toward the rear of the home. "We're in the ruckus room."

"The what?"

"Well, I can't call it the family room. With no family and all, can I?" Then he whispered, "I told her you're an expert on the Far East—you know, an expert on the markets for rhinoceros horn and all that. She got very excited."

A change had come over him since lunchtime. His face and neck were flushed, his eyes were bright, his manner festive. He was wearing a lime-green Lycra T-shirt and black jeans.

"Great," I said.

"Wait, let me get you something." He stopped me in the kitchen, drawing me over to the counter. Beyond an archway I saw the back of someone's head sticking up from an armchair. The head didn't move. I noted a rough brick fireplace, natural-wood wainscoting, Japanese fishing floats. Classy.

"What are you drinking?" I asked.

"Mai Tais. I've been on a Mai Tai craze for four months now. A friend of mine had a luau. In Pontiac. These things are marvelous."

"Do you have any Scotch?"

"No, dear."

"I'll try a Mai Tai then. What's in them?"

"Oh, a little of this, a little of that. Rich and fruity."

"I see."

I heard a grunt from the person in the chair. Something about that grunt held my attention for the briefest second, then I was distracted by Wycoff's energetic mixology.

Making Mai Tais is labor-intensive, but he had it down to a science. Shloop went the ice, swish went the rum and syrups, squish went the cut lime, spat went the pineapple garnish.

"I should have mint, but I don't, precious. Sorry, here, drink up."

It wasn't bad. The raw lime juice saved it from being cloying. "Thanks. Hey, I know where you could get steady work mixing these things." I kept talking as we walked into the ruckus room. "A neat little lesbian bar."

"Oh, you flatter me."

"It's called—"

"Lillian, meet Clarabelle!"

I rounded into the conversation area, and there she was: garish print dress, monumental head, hulking figure, delicate pudgy hands holding her own Mai Tai. Her eyes were fixed on me in disbelief.

"The Snapdragon," I whispered, staggering slightly.

It was Mrs. Creighter.

"What is it, dollies?" Greg said, then guessed, "Oh, you already know each other!"

"That's one way to put it," I said brightly. *You murderous bitch*.

"I believe we've met," she said, making an effort to collect herself. Her boxy straw purse was sitting on the floor next to the chair.

I set down my drink but remained standing.

"I'm going to nail you," I said.

"What are you talking about?" she said, trying to look puzzled, but there was blood in her eyes. Blood and panic.

Wycoff didn't see it. He was quaffing his fourth or fifth Mai Tai, by the looks of him, holding it in two hands and gulping like a thirsty preschooler.

"Where are the others?" I demanded. "Did you harvest their teeth too? For what?"

She stared at me with that same cold, fake-puzzled look. Then her lips began to move silently.

Our host finally picked up the vibes. "Lillian, what's wrong? I thought you two would get on famously. Clarabelle needs information, and you need information. And *I* need a Miltown! Hah!"

I said, "You've given me plenty of information, Greg." I

grabbed Mrs. Creighter's purse and dumped its contents out on the floor. "Where's your stuff? Huh? Your little art pieces?"

Greg shrieked, "Lillian! Precious! You're being very naughty!" He hadn't expected to have to really function this evening and was caught off-guard.

"She's crazy," Mrs. Creighter volunteered, not moving from her chair.

I knelt and pawed through the contents of the purse but saw nothing I wanted. The dog Roscoe got into the spirit, yapping and running in circles.

"Greg, this woman doesn't share your moral code," I said, straightening up.

"She's crazy," Mrs. Creighter repeated, but she wasn't talking to Wycoff. "You can see it, can't you? Yes. Why are you sending me this trial? I know that, but—" Her eyes were fixed in the middle distance. "What should I do? I will follow."

"*What?*" Wycoff clutched his Mai Tai as if it were the only solid object in the room.

I told him, "She's not talking to you."

She went on, "I can't do anything right this minute, all by myself. You can see that."

Wycoff sobbed, "Will someone please tell me what's going on?"

"She's frightening me," Mrs. Creighter said to him.

"Good," I said.

"Time for all good bunnies to please, please go home," said Wycoff helplessly.

22

Silly me. I'd thought perhaps Mrs. Creighter was doing business with the doyenne of—what did Wycoff call it?—forensic art? But as it turned out, she *was* the doyenne of forensic art.

All right, I thought, *she's a talented weirdo with strange ambitions—who wants to kill me.* She wouldn't have done it in front of Wycoff, unless she wanted him dead too, which she wouldn't, as he was useful to her.

I beat it out of Wycoff's fast, then spent another restless night at home with my plank against the door. I tried to read myself to sleep on some Kay Boyle short stories, but all the wartime details made me queasy, so I switched over to Flannery O'Connor. Good old savage religion. The stories made me laugh, but they didn't anesthetize me. When dawn broke I brewed coffee and sat and thought.

I wondered anew what happened to Mr. Creighter: How did he die? Was he buried somewhere? Mrs. Creighter said he'd been dead for six years. Should I even be thinking about him? What if he died under mysterious circumstances? But circumstances weren't what I needed to stop the Creighters; I needed evidence the police could tack to their foreheads.

I went over the events at the Creighter home again. My mind came to roost on the photos and papers I'd seen. What about the papers? Something in the back of my mind was trying to click. Those pages: the distinctive sans-serif typography, the playbill-sized paper, the blocks of fine print.

Suddenly I had it. They were pages from *The Triangle,* the only gay periodical in the area. Specifically, they were the classified pages, the reams of lonelyhearts ads placed by gay men and women from all over the metro area.

The Triangle was primarily a shopper: It carried display ads for all the bars, schedules of events like drag shows and charity dance-a-thons, as well as a smattering of whatever gay/lesbian news there was.

Without a doubt, the most important part of *The Triangle* was the personals section. Surely it was the most profitable part of the business. Every now and then I'd read them for cheap thrills. There were always tons of "male seeking male" ads and "saw you on the bus" ads, but usually the "women seeking women" took up the smallest portion of space.

I gave *The Triangle* excellent marks in the distribution department. It was free, and you could find it not only in the bars, but also in at least half the coffee shops, Laundromats, newsstands, and bookstores in the three counties of southeastern Michigan.

I riffled through my magazines and found a recent issue. The theme for the week was "Sluts and Nuts: A Coming-Out Guide for the Rest of Us." There were essays on the subject by queers of all sorts, in between display ads for bars. I flipped through to the personals.

Male lonelyhearts and female lonelyhearts, straight and gay, want the same thing: love and a chance to give it back. For some, intimacy means companionship for country walks, movies, and firelight kisses; for others, we're talking spanking, fisting, and bootlicking, which carry their own charms.

Bonnie had probably placed at least one regular classified ad, for the disc jockey opening that Iris wound up filling. And what else? Placed some personals? Answered some? Each ad referred callers to a voice-mail extension paid for by the person who placed it. The police could get a hold of phone records, but I couldn't.

I read the female-seeking-female ads thoroughly.

If the Midnight Five had been gay women, well, that would've been an easy thread for the police to try to follow. But what if—what if they weren't exactly gay? What about the dreaded "bi-curious" classification? It's a common path of entry to the gay/lesbian world. And somehow it's sort of a flashpoint for confirmed dykes. I can't begin to tell you how many lesbians I've known who, in the midst of their discussion groups, book groups, journal-writing groups, what have you, find reason to stand up and yell about what a phony thing it is to be bisexual. Criminy.

Me, I can understand it. Why not go to a wine-tasting before buying a case? Iris had all but described herself to me in that fashion.

I drummed my hands on the floor while poring over the ads. Todd watched me closely.

Bi-curious WF seeking friend. I am 28, shy, curvy, honest. Magic words to me are Frisbee, Jacuzzi, psychology, astrology. You are sophisticated, sexy, athletic, vegan, financially solvent, animal-loving. Let's get together for coffee and hugs, possibly lasting relationship. Sincere inquiries only.

Spicy WF tomato seeks Latina hot pepper. Could we make great salsa together? I love music, dancing, equality, mountain-biking. No head games or racists.

Bi-curious? Join me and my husband for spirited fun. He will watch only. Clean, healthy, and discreet.

Ugh. It was futile without more information.

Was my assumption of multiple Creighter murders correct in the first place? Maybe the photos were from sexual encounters. I'd not seen dead bodies; I'd seen women's faces. I began to see how valuable a skeptical mind like Ciesla's could be.

I found myself talking to Todd, bouncing ideas off him. The air got muggier. The horse chestnut tree outside my window stood perfectly still. My anxiety mounted. I wondered how long it would take Ciesla and Porrocks to crack the case through the narrowed channels I'd left to them.

I put down a meal for Todd and took off to the City-County building, where I requested Carl Creighter's death certificate. "Cause of death: cardiac arrest and multiple trauma." Hmm. I read it again. Cardiac arrest *and* multiple trauma? "Place of death: Highway 68, Taos County, New Mexico."

Then I popped over to the main branch of the Detroit Public Library and, now having the exact date, looked up the newspaper death notice on the microfilm.

For a minute, scanning down the columns I thought

there'd been a mistake, that the Creighter notice had run twice, but no, there were two Creighter notices that day: Carl Creighter and his daughter Veronica Creighter. Same date of death, same place. Private interment at Woodlawn Cemetery, Detroit.

I scanned through the A sections of the prior days' papers but found nothing more, no story about the deaths. The DPL didn't have film for any New Mexico paper.

So Bonnie's father and sister bought it in a car wreck, possibly triggered by Mr. Creighter's coronary. Woodlawn was more or less on my way back to Eagle, so I stopped in, asked for the coordinates, and found the graves.

A hot moist breeze kicked up and rustled the shrubbery while moody purple clouds swept overhead.

Why did I stop in? I just had a feeling. When you're desperate to figure something out, you don't just dig for stuff you think'll be important. You dig for tidbits too. Because you never know which tidbit might turn out to be the one.

I don't know what I was expecting, but I was amazed by what I found: a marker the size and style of the Vatican. White marble to hell and gone. The main feature was a statue of an angel with a life-size lamb at its feet. On second look it wasn't an angel; it was St. Francis, the animal-loving saint. A stone sparrow nestled in the crook of his arm, a stone mouse nibbled his sandal strap, and his expression was one of sad benevolence. Above the names two biblical quotations were inscribed:

FOR SOME ARE ALREADY TURNED ASIDE AFTER SATAN.

WHEREFORE WE LABOUR, THAT, WHETHER PRESENT OR ABSENT WE MAY BE ACCEPTED OF HIM.

I wrote down the inscriptions in my notebook, then slowly walked back to the Caprice and drove home.

My apartment was quiet as usual, but I could tell some noise had occurred in my absence: Todd's ears were quivering, and there were three hang-ups on the old answering machine. We nibbled carrots and cookies together in the big orange chair, both of us a bit edgy.

At about three o'clock the phone rang, and I let the machine get it. The speaker crackled, "Lillian, Ricky Rosenthal. I don't know if you've heard, but Minerva LeBlanc is in town, looking into the midnight disappearances, and I thought—"

I picked up. "I'm here, Ricky. Minerva LeBlanc is in Detroit? Minerva LeBlanc?"

"Yeah. Hi." Ricky's voice was high-pitched but unhurried. Under his direction, the *Motor City Journal* ran like a sewing machine. "One of my city people bumped into her at police headquarters. She said she was doing research on the midnight disappearances. Trying to decide if they're worth doing a book on. I thought you'd be interested to know that. You might want to compare notes."

"My God, I can't believe it. She's only, like, the most fantastic crime writer in the universe. She's—oh, my God. I've read everything she's ever written."

"Really."

"Wow!" I was practically dancing in place. "I've always wanted to meet her! Do you know where I can get a hold of her—do you know where she's staying?"

"Uh-uh. But somebody here says she always travels first-class, which figures. She's gotta be so filthy rich from all those books—"

"I'll try the hotels. Ricky, if you hear of another sighting of her, would you please let me know?"

"Sure."

I hung up all in a dazzle. Minerva LeBlanc: The name tripped off the tongue with elegance and style. She'd made her first enormous splash about ten years earlier, with the book *Inside Johnny Florida,* a true account of one of the most gruesome slaughters in history. Surely you've read it, surely you know the story:

Johnny Florida started out as the mousy little son of law-abiding Hungarian immigrants, an extended clan that lived together in a big house in Queens, New York. As a young man he dropped his real name—his normal wimpy name, whatever the hell it was—and started calling himself Johnny Florida. He felt the name conveyed the kind of man he was, or fantasized being: hip, energetic, in control. But the kid was not very bright.

One day he decided it'd be in his best interest to take over the family business, which was a hot-sausage pushcart in lower Manhattan. His father and uncles declared they weren't ready to retire. There was a commotion; afterward, the house in Queens was very quiet.

Johnny Florida developed his own recipe for sausage, which he served from his pushcart. It was months before the murders were discovered and the skeins of sausages hanging from the basement beams analyzed.

Minerva LeBlanc, a trainee in a New York brokerage house, had eaten regularly from Johnny Florida's pushcart, and she'd become fond of the swaggering little dude. After the story broke, she quit her job and wrote a book about Johnny, his crimes and his trial, using information from dozens of exclusive interviews he granted her from the nut-house they put him in.

Inside Johnny Florida was a smash best-seller, a hit

movie, and a springboard for Minerva to scrutinize other sensational crimes. Since then, she'd written half a dozen more books about the bizarre, incomprehensible worlds of psychotic killers. Her research on open cases actually helped the police catch some of them. All her books rode the best-seller charts for months. I'd read and reread all of them, thrilling to her snappy descriptions and trenchant insights. Now here she was in Detroit, treading, perhaps, the very same pavement I was.

The Midnight Five were either the most puzzling string of missing persons the state had ever seen, or nothing at all. As any cop will tell you, people disappear every day; they walk away from their lives for a million different reasons, leaving things hanging in varying degrees.

Five women had disappeared overnight, one every few months, starting about two years ago. The first couple of them no one connected; then as the count rose, the police started to wonder. But there were no signs of criminal activity, no signs of struggle in their homes, no abductions witnessed, no nothing except that they didn't show up for work the next morning, or their tennis date, or whatever. I couldn't remember much about the women, except that they'd come came from different spots around metro Detroit and seemed to have nothing in common.

Iris could be the sixth. But unlike the others she turned up dead.

I got out the phone book and started calling the top hotels. The Townsend in Birmingham, the Westin downtown. My fifth call was to the Ritz-Carlton in Dearborn, and whaddaya know, Minerva was registered. Out right now, evidently; I left a message.

Now my little rush of adrenaline was over. I resumed

brooding, pacing, sitting, drumming my fingers. *What if she doesn't call back? What if the Creighters come for me? Or Lou? Or Bucky, for that matter.*

I was too paranoid to keep hanging around home. I put on my better blue jeans, an unfrayed madras-plaid blouse, and my penny loafers. I combed a little gel through my hair. I put my notebook and Iris's photograph (which I'd never given back to Porrocks) in my little leather bag and drove over to the Ritz.

Leaving the Caprice in the self-park lot, I walked up the drive. It was awkward because there was no sidewalk between the parking and the lobby. The architectural message was, *You should use the valet, you two-bit hick.* The valet looked at me politely.

I called her room from the lobby; she was still out, so I sat down to wait. What a lobby. The floral arrangements alone must've stripped about three acres of rain forest.

I waited, doodling in my notebook, looking up every few minutes. Just as the sun broke under the cloud cover and turned golden, clarifying the air outside and in, in walked a slim, simply dressed woman lugging a soft leather briefcase, looking a little tired, and a little troubled.

She was thinking. Boy, I could see her mind working as she moved. She stopped and spoke briefly to the concierge, then turned toward the corridor to the elevators. I bounced up and approached, my heart in my mouth.

23

"Ms. LeBlanc?" She turned. I could see her inner monologue shutting off. She looked me over with a businesslike expression, poised to deliver either a quick brush-off or half a minute's worth of attention.

"Uh, my name is Lillian Byrd. I'm a local reporter here, and I've been a terrific fan of yours for years, ever since *Inside Johnny Florida,* and—" Her face relaxed into a semi-condescending meeting-a-fan expression. I noticed searching eyes, thin lips, and a shortish jaw that almost gave her an overbite. She reached into her briefcase and drew out a pen. "And—and I don't want your autograph—I mean, I'd love to have your autograph, of course, but that's not why I stopped you, I—it's that I'm investigating the murder that might be the latest Midnight Five disappearance—six!—and I thought we maybe could talk, because I heard you're working on the Midnight Five, but maybe you aren't, in which case, uh." Am I a smoothie or what?

She put the pen away. Her expression now was identical to my seventh-grade gym teacher's when she had to grade me doing a routine on the balance beam or parallel bars. A determined suppression of laughter mixed with the cringing expectation of seeing me hurt myself badly any second.

I was gratified that she didn't just walk away. She looked around—we weren't alone in the corridor; there was a bit of pre-dinner traffic—and said, "Let's go into the lounge."

Wowie. We took a table in a corner. Here we had British hunt-club atmosphere; we sank up to our waists in manly-smelling leather chairs. The barman came right over.

"I'll have a lemonade, please," said Minerva LeBlanc. I held up two fingers.

"Certainly," said the barman.

"How did you know I was in town and that I was staying here?"

I told her. "And, you see, I thought it might be worthwhile to compare notes. I know a few things about this recent murder, and I have some pretty good suspicions. In fact, the killers got their hands on me the other night, but I got away—" I started blurting out everything in reverse order, then stopped. "*Are* you looking into the midnight disappearances?"

"Yes." She got that gym-teacher look again.

Our drinks came, frosty and pretty, and she picked up hers and chugged half of it. "Mmm!" The drink perked her up. She sat there across from me, a receptive, composed presence.

"Let me back up," I said. "First of all, thank you for taking a little time to talk. The reason I came here is, I feel like I'm stirring a pretty deep bean pot here, and I'd really appreciate it if you'd listen to my story and tell me what you think. I mean, do you have a little time?"

She nodded, getting out her notebook. She flipped it open and showed me a short page of notes. "I've been poking around for two days, and this is all I've got to show for it. The midnight disappearances: I don't know, maybe they'd make a good nonbook." She gave a short laugh. "I can't get a handle on them at all. Nobody knows anything, and the police can't pull out all the stops because so far there's no crime to investigate."

"Exactly. See, I'm not sure this murder I referred to is related to these missing women, but if it is, a whole lot of questions could be answered from it."

A cluster of pointy-toed guys came in and threw themselves into chairs in the opposite corner of the lounge. They were talking fancy business loudly. One shouted, "The only thing wrong with the deal's the goddamn Canadian taxes!" The barman glared at them and took his time getting over there.

Minerva took another long sip of lemonade. "Tell me about this murder."

So I did, starting from seeing the Polaroid under Ciesla's desk lamp (I got it out to show her), back to my unsuccessful attempt to pick up Iris at the Snapdragon, to my weird interviews with Bonnie Creighter and Gerald Macklin to the nightmare on Salem Street, to my even weirder encounters with Greg Wycoff and Mrs. Creighter again.

She asked a lot of questions as I went. "Wait, who is this Emerald guy again?...Did you believe everything the husband told you?...Are there any other men involved in this? What do you know about this Lester Patchell? Which direction did the drag marks come to his barn—from the road?"

"I believe Porrocks said from the road. I'm sure they would've noticed if they went toward the house."

"Right, right." Her eyes were shining; I could tell she was starting to have fun. Well, that was Minerva LeBlanc: A good grisly dish got her blood up. She nodded and watched me intently as I talked.

I watched her back. Her clothes were simple but clearly expensive: beautiful cocoa-silk slacks; leather basket-weave slip-ons, solid and elegant; a short-sleeved knitted jersey of perhaps linen-cotton in a seashell pink. It fit her like a second skin. Her hair was brown and straight like mine; she wore hers a little longer and swingier.

I'd gazed at her photo so many times, you know, those photos on the dust jackets. I'd study the pictures intently, trying to tell from the look in her eyes everything about her: What did she like to do on Sundays? Who was her favorite author? What was her favorite movie? Was she really a nice person deep inside?

Now, seeing her in real life, talking to her—well, there was a lot to take in.

She made a note now and then. When I got to the part about being apprehended by the Creighters, she said, "Oh, my God...oh, no! Oh, wow...*wow*. Whoa! How did you—oh. Wow."

The Wycoff stuff *really* got her going. "This is exactly the kind of...oh, my God. You're not making this up...I'd have given anything to be there. Wow."

When I finished, she peered searchingly into her lemonade for a while, then scanned the landscape of the lounge. After another minute she looked at me and said, "We've got lots more to talk about." Her eyes were bright and quick, steered by a pair of sleek rack-and-pinion eyebrows. Boy, was she pumped. I was pretty stoked myself to finally be talking to somebody besides Todd, who took everything I said seriously.

"The thought occurs to me," I said, "that Ciesla and Porrocks might be in a little over their heads too."

"That's very possible."

"I mean, how many murders do they handle? Hardly any." In fact, I had no idea whether Ciesla and Porrocks had ever been in charge of a murder investigation.

"Nothing," she said, "about this Iris Macklin situation adds up to anything they teach in police school."

"Yeah?"

She looked at her watch. I was surprised to notice it was an ordinary Timex; it didn't fit in with the rest of her ensemble.

"No wonder I'm hungry," she said with a crooked smile. "That French toast and coffee was ten hours ago."

"Didn't you have any lunch?"

"Forgot."

"Well—wanna eat?"

She smiled so big I almost fell back.

She signed for the lemonades, and we hoisted ourselves from the bottomless club chairs.

"I'll wait for you in the lobby," I said.

"No, come on up."

Cowabunga. As we rode the elevator I asked, "Where is everybody?"

"Where is who?"

"Well, don't you have, like, an entourage?" I'd pictured her like a movie star or a sports idol: Where was the companion, the personal trainer, the driver, the bodyguard?

She looked at me. "Hah! An entourage!" We were eye to

eye. I straightened my spine to become a trifle taller. "No," she said, "I generally travel alone."

I followed her down the corridor on her floor. As we passed a mirror I gave myself a little wink sideways.

It wasn't *a* room; it was a suite of rooms. You could imagine Queen Elizabeth and Prince Philip giving a pajama party for thirty of their closest friends. Pass the gin.

She freshened up while I gawked at the furnishings and tried to figure out where they hid the TV. Then I heard her voice in the bedroom, talking on the phone, but I couldn't make out anything.

In a few minutes we were on our way down to the lobby again.

"You know this town pretty well?" she asked. She'd ditched the briefcase for a lovely small shoulder bag, which she held tucked close to her side. I tried to do X-ray vision to see if she'd tossed a toothbrush in.

"Lived here all my life. I'd be glad to drive. I take it you don't want to eat here?"

"No, it's great food, but I'd like something...unusual. What do you suggest?"

"What do you feel like?"

"Spicy."

"Mexican spicy or Asian spicy?"

"Which would take us to the more interesting part of town?"

"Mexican."

"Let's go."

There was an easy feeling between us.

I shepherded her past the valet to the Caprice.

"Police secondhand!" she exclaimed.

"Yep." I felt suaver than suave.

Evening was coming, and it was going to stay warm.

"The air-conditioning's been shot for a few years," I said as we peeled out to I-94, "but the window cranks still work." The night air blasted in on us.

"Moreover," I said, picking up where I'd left off quizzing her, "I guess I'm a little surprised that you're doing your own research. Humping it around from police station to police station, copying records, reading microfilm in the library—you could pay somebody to do that." Traffic was moving smoothly; I jockeyed the Caprice into the middle lane.

"But I couldn't pay them to do my thinking for me." She had to shout a little over the expressway noise. "The serendipity of investigation. You know how you go into a library or a bookstore and browse? You notice one thing, it leads to another, which leads to another. The world is my library. That's how I feel. Would I have met you and heard your fantastic story if I were sitting in my brownstone in New York talking to my researcher by cell phone and fax?"

I was incredibly impressed.

"How long are you in town for?"

"Depends. I've been looking for a new subject for a book for about—oh, three months now. Something has to grab me, really grab me. I've been to half a dozen places around the country, poking around, talking to people. I like to get hold of something before everybody else does. Well, that's needless to say. I'm getting involved earlier and earlier in cases. If I decide to stay a while, I'll stay a while. If not, I'll go."

"Do people hassle you for sticking your nose into things? Cops? Victims' families?"

"Victims' families don't mind me. *Suspects'* families don't mind me. They fall all over themselves trying to tell me their stories." I nodded. "Some cops love me," she went on, "and some hate me. I really try not to get in their way. I respect them, but sometimes it's hard. You see something, you get a hunch, you make a connection—you want to check it out."

"Exactly. See that church over there?" We were now on the Jeffries freeway, looping over to the Fisher.

"Uh-huh?"

"There's a statue of the Virgin on top of it, with her hands folded. It looks like she's about to take a swan dive right into the expressway. See? People call that church Our Lady of Perpetual Suicide."

She liked that.

I said, "That's how I feel right now. I'm worried that I'm flirting with suicide, getting mixed up in this police business."

"Well, you're in it."

"Yeah. And that's not all. I'll tell you more when we get inside."

We were soon cruising the surface streets in the shadow of the mighty Ambassador Bridge. It was a lively area populated mostly by immigrants—legal and otherwise—from Mexico and points south. The particular neighborhood I'd landed us in wasn't the worst neighborhood in town, but it was far from the best. The working poor tried to keep up their wood-frame houses while the drug lords squatted in empty factories or rat-infested apartments.

Funny as it sounds, I'd never felt unsafe in the neighborhood. Maybe because I grew up in one similar. You learn a few rules, you get along.

"The place we're going doesn't look like much, but they give you the best enchiladas you'll ever eat."

I paralleled the Caprice under a streetlight between a twenty-year-old pickup and a dented new Lincoln.

We got out, locked and slammed, and I indicated the way. We had to walk two blocks, making two right turns.

As we approached the first corner, we saw a man and a woman arguing—what looked like a pimp and his hooker. The hooker appeared Mexican; the pimp was black. Their voices were angry and plaintive. An emaciated thing, the woman stood with her back against the lamppost, her arms folded, her breasts flat under a tight bandeau top.

He loomed over her, scolding, rubbing his knuckles, his breath huffing in her face. As we came closer I heard him repeating the same sentence, with varying inflections: "What I tell you? *What* I tell you? What I *tell* you?" He wore a white vest and a large pearl earring.

Instinctively, Minerva and I veered away from them, our path taking us closer to the building on the corner, a darkened grocery store. I became aware that the street was momentarily empty of traffic. Minerva dropped back slightly, a half-pace.

As we pulled even with the couple, I had a sudden terrible feeling. The pimp turned smartly toward us, stepped into our path, locked eyes with me, and said, "Give it up, bitch."

He was looking at my leather bag. I was looking at the knife in his fist, held point up, like a military sword.

24

I stopped and went into reverse, bumping into Minerva, who clamped my shoulder with her hand and pressed down. I froze, and she released my shoulder.

We all stood there just like that for no more than three seconds, but my memory of it is indelible: the murky street light floating down, the angry contemptuous face of the pimp, the disinterested posture of the hooker off to the side, the gathering darkness beyond. Someone was practicing electric guitar in a house nearby, a wailing blues lick.

After those seconds passed, I became aware of a sudden complete turnaround in the situation. The pimp lowered his knife. He said, "Whoa, now. Whoa, now" in a soothing voice. But his eyes were wide with fear. Then he smiled! "We're just friends here, right?"

The hooker slipped off the lamppost; I heard her heels clicking on the pavement, crossing the street. She was moving away with more alacrity than I would have guessed possible.

The pimp backed away a few steps, then turned and ran. He ran like an athlete, back straight, arms pumping. His white vest grew smaller and smaller in the darkness.

Finally, I turned and saw the revolver in Minerva's hand. She was standing slightly behind me and to the side; she must have drawn the gun the instant she saw the knife. I'd no more than glimpsed it when she shoved it back inside the demure little shoulder bag she'd been holding so close to her side. It went into some kind of special quick-draw pocket.

I stood there staring at her.

She squinted down the street, then blew out a big pent-up breath. A few cars whizzed by.

"I owe you my life," I said.

She shook her head. "He would've just taken our purses."

"You can't be sure."

She smiled.

"Holy ever-loving shit," I mumbled. My stomach was quivering.

"This is why," she said, holding up her wrist, "I wear a Timex instead of a Rolex. I don't like to tempt anybody on the street. They don't expect me to be carrying one of these. Let's go eat."

"You—you don't want to get out of here?" I half-hoped she'd want to hightail it back to the Ritz.

"No," she said simply. "Let's go where we're going. Come on."

As we walked, she patted her purse and remarked, "You ought to get yourself one of these and learn to use it. Especially if you're going to freelance around this town."

"Well," I said, "I once knew a police academy dropout who insisted that unless you've been through police training, having a gun will do you more harm than good."

"That's bullshit." She kicked a twisted piece of automobile trim from her path. "Too many women believe that. Why are women such idiots about guns? Any woman can learn to use a gun safely. Sure, you can still get hurt, but your chances are a hell of a lot better with a gun than without. You just experienced it, and don't let anybody tell you otherwise. Why let the scumbags push you around?"

We walked through a gust of shouting and laughter from the doorway of a little cantina.

"Why indeed. Hey, how did you get that gun through airport security, anyway? Are you that much of a VIP?"

"I didn't. I drove."

"Oh. What do you drive?"

"Dodge pickup."

"Really?"

We approached the restaurant, a shabby building festooned with neon beer and soft-drink signs.

"What's this place called?"

I opened the door. "People just call it the Great Enchilada Place by the Bridge. Everyone knows what you mean. There're other restaurants around here, more popular with the gringos, but they're all a lot fancier: They have names on the outside!" We laughed together.

The proprietor, a wiry little guy in a straw cowboy hat, cheerfully showed us to a table against the back wall. If the neighborhood was a bit the worse for wear, this joint wasn't. It looked exactly the same year after year. The lights were neither too bright nor too dim. Clean floor, clean tables and chairs. Little paper menus. The walls were dotted with gaudy tin picture frames housing religious images: the Sacred Heart, the Virgin of Guadelupe, the Nativity. They looked like a cheerful version of the Stations of the Cross.

There was a sprinkling of patrons this evening—a few families, some couples, all talking in Spanish. We were the only same-sex couple, but no one took notice of us.

But the very best thing about the place—and here you will know that I am a masochist at heart, perverse and impure—was the jukebox. It wasn't one of those gorgeous old Wurlitzers, it was a cheap one, packed to the top not with Tex-Mex, Latin pop, or even Top Forty.

It contained *only* the absolute worst hits of the 1970s. Only the absolute worst. Songs that are, for me, existential torture. Listening to them is an experience I crave only a few times a year, the way some people crave jumping into Lake Superior in the winter, or having thin nails slowly driven into their external sex organs, or holding their hands over candle flames, or exposing themselves to swarms of mosquitoes.

The moment we walked in, Helen Reddy's "You and Me Against the World" came pouring into our ears like warm baby oil.

After we ordered a couple of Coronas, Minerva said, "When you tell your friends about our little encounter back there, will you be uncomfortable saying he was black?"

I looked at her. In fact, I'd already begun rehearsing the tale and worrying over whether to edit the pimp's race in or out. "How did you know?"

"I can tell you're not knee-jerk PC, but you fight it."

I laughed in embarrassment. Minerva went back to studying her menu, and I reflected on my friends and myself. If in telling the story I conscientiously omitted the assailant's race, it would prove that I was color-blind. Yet every one of my friends, black and white, would wonder. Because, of course, no one is really color-blind.

Moreover, my friends know me well enough to know that if my assailant were white, I'd certainly make a point of saying so, in my usual offhanded way: "So this slimy-looking white guy pulls this knife…" Yet if I left it out, they wouldn't know for sure. And no one would have the guts to come right out and *ask*. For even to wonder out loud would be considered bad form, nay, *racist*.

When the waitress came back, we both ordered enchilada combo plates, then started in on the chips and salsa.

"This one's the hot one," I indicated.

"I'll be the judge of that." Minerva's energy level was rising moment by moment, as if the attempted robbery had been a kind of tonic. Her eyes—well, they twinkled. They really did.

She scooped up some salsa and crunched, then swallowed and reached for her beer.

"Oh, yes," she said after a pause. Then she grabbed her head as if stricken by an embolism. "Oh, Gawd, is this a terrible song. I'd forgotten it, but it's all coming back." We were hearing "Seasons in the Sun." Terry Jacks.

"This song," I said, "is like a tumor in your brain."

"It's exquisitely painful." She had one of those clear, expressive voices that doesn't need excess inflection to get its meaning across.

"Yes."

We looked at each other for a moment.

"All right," she said, breaking the spell. "Let's talk business. First of all, what connections, if any, can we make between this Iris Macklin and the five other women?"

"Well, I don't think any right now—"

Minerva interrupted and ticked off on her fingers, "You start with the basics. They're all women, they're all from the same general area, and they all disappeared at night. They went somewhere and didn't come back. What else?"

"Well, I think we have to try and see if there's a gay connection. What do you know about the five? Any lesbians in the bunch?" I'd read newspaper accounts of the disappearances (none were from Eagle), but couldn't remember anything specific.

"Mm." She flipped open her notebook and read off names, addresses, and a few facts: "Sixty-one years old, three grown children, grandkids, twenty-fifth wedding anniversary, no outside career, she liked to garden... This one was an art student at Wayne State, twenty-three, avant-garde, lots of friends... Two of them were businesswomen in their thirties, one a marketing executive for GM. She was married. The other ran a pet shop. A boyfriend was mentioned... The fifth one lived with her widowed father and brothers in Poletown—do you know where that is? Uneducated, she acted as the housemother, and they supported her. She'd just turned forty. All these women were white. I looked at photos and body stats; none seemed to resemble any other in any way: height, weight, hair color, hairstyle, glasses..."

She paused to take another corn chip. "Totally varied backgrounds. None of them seemed to have lived a lesbian lifestyle. No female roommates, no lesbian erotica lying around—you can be sure the police would've noted *that*."

"Huh, yeah."

"The fact that there's no physical resemblance tends to counterindicate a serial killer. Those guys, they look for types."

"What do you mean?"

"Well, they're all really badly fucked up, inadequate guys.

Something sends them over the edge: They lose their job, or their girlfriend leaves, or their mother dies, or a waitress insults them. Then they go out and find women who look like their boss or girlfriend or mother or the waitress. It's wrapped up in sexual inadequacy, which is why there's often sexual assault postmortem. They kill, then they explore."

I shuddered, thinking of the Creighters.

"Now, this detective Ciesla: He didn't believe what happened to you over there?"

"He said he didn't. I don't know what he really thinks."

"He's handling this badly. He should be taking you and those two psychos seriously. He should be jumping all over this."

"I think so too. But the Creighters don't fit the serial killer mold, though, huh?"

"First of all they're women. Second of all there are two of them. It's incredibly rare for two serial killers to work in concert. It's such a classically individual crime. Plus there was no sexual assault on Iris, was there? No. The thing about the teeth, I'm not sure that's the key. I mean, yes, the mother is twisted. She's involved in deep sickness with this body-part commerce. But I'm wondering..."

The waitress delivered our plates. They were piled high around the perimeter with beans and rice, a little shredded lettuce and tomato; then in the center there was the beautifully browned, cheesy flatland of the enchiladas.

"Oh, mmm, these look good," Minerva breathed. "Oh, smell them."

The waitress smiled. She wore deep-purple lipstick and fluffy hair. "Everything is good here!" she declared, then whirled away, snapping her fingers to "Rich Girl." Hall and Oates.

"It's disgusting how my mind is anticipating the lyrics," Minerva said, then dug into her enchiladas. "Ohmm. Mmm. Mmm!" Her mmm's started in her mouth and descended toward her diaphragm.

"It's old Mexico on a plate."

"Olé."

"The gringas eat." I doused my enchiladas with hot salsa.

The rest of our conversation occurred between bites of food, sighs of pleasure, and swigs of the tasty beer. A string of weepy ballads accompanied our meal: "Billy, Don't Be a Hero," "Leaving On a Jet Plane," "Daddy, Don't You Walk So Fast," "All By Myself."

"We could spend a lot of time trying to make connections between the first five disappearances, plus Iris," Minerva said. "That could amount to some pretty interesting work. I'm not sure the police are being as sharing of their information with each other as they could, not because they're uncooperative, but because there's so little to go on."

"Do you know whether any of the families have hired private investigators?"

"I don't, but I bet some have."

"I wonder who they are."

"Unless they turn up something big, you'll never know. I'd like to talk to the friends and relatives just to try to get a feel for these women. But like I said, it could take a lot of time. I think that should be our plan B."

Our! She said "our"! Then she talked about serials being harder to solve than crimes of passion, the spur-of-the-moment-type crimes.

"Most murders, they happen, then the murderer has to decide how to cover it up. Or *whether* to cover it up. It's usually impossible to accomplish an airtight coverup and alibi after the fact with no advance planning.

"But serials are usually carefully planned, with fewer screw-ups that lead to arrest. The best way to crack the string is to solve one. And you're always better off working on the most recent one. So. As fascinating as the Midnight Five are, I think the real pay dirt's going to be found in the case of Iris Macklin."

I listened to her avidly, my fork moving slowly. She ate with a steady rhythm, two bites of food, then a paragraph of explication.

"The way I see it," she said, "is the Creighters have moved from stage one killing to stage two. Stage one encompasses the original killings, then stage two is the killing to cover up the killings: the killing of witnesses. You represent a stage-two victim for them. Stage two, of course, leads to stage three, and a wider spiral of witnesses to eliminate.

"Once a killer attracts suspicion, it's almost impossible to continue killing without getting caught. It's very likely that if the Creighters get their hands on you again, you'll be their last victim. Even Ciesla'd be able to solve that one. It'll all unravel after you. So the trick's going to be catching them first."

"You really think I'm in danger? Ciesla said—"

"It depends on their plans. If they're planning to casually get out of town and disappear, maybe try to set up shop somewhere else in the future, then no. They'll never bother you. But if they want to stay and brazen it out, you could be on their radar screen. The more time that goes by, the safer you'll be. It could be an uncomfortable wait, though."

"It is already. Minerva, I feel terrible, having essentially blown the police investigation. I feel I need to do something for Iris. I have to. Not to mention save my own ass. As much of a craven loser as I might be, I just don't want to sit around and wait."

"Well, I'm willing to work with you on this."

"You are?"

We talked about everything, pondered over everything. I told her about the lonelyhearts ads from *The Triangle*. How could we find out if the Midnight Five placed or answered ads?

"There's no way I'm gonna get access to those files," I said. "For all I know they don't even keep records. It's a more or less shoestring operation."

"Where's the office?"

"In a storefront on Gratiot somewhere, near downtown."

"We'll pay them a visit, and I'll show you how to get what you want."

"Yeah?"

"Does Bonnie have a girlfriend?" Minerva wondered.

"I don't know. Maybe that's significant. She has this reputation for being a very private person. She lives with her mother. Maybe she's sexually frustrated."

"Maybe."

After a while we fell silent and just ate. Eventually Minerva said, "I just don't get two women acting as a killing team."

"Well," I said, "maybe killing isn't their main goal. Maybe death is a by-product."

She looked at me and blinked. "Oh. Now that's thinking outside the box. Think some more."

"I guess I'm trying not to jump to conclusions. I mean, I'm as sure as anything that the Creighters killed Iris. But what if the death was somehow unintended—"

"A bullet to the back of the head was unintended?"

"I don't know, I just mean—I don't know what I mean. Maybe there was some heavy S/M going on—"

"And Iris forgot the safe word?"

It was horrible, I feel horrible telling you this, but we just laughed. We did. We sat there and laughed for about a minute. People looked over, smiling.

I can't describe how much better it made me feel. I felt as if a compressed Superball of tension had floated away from inside me. My head felt clearer.

I thought the Snapdragon could hold a few secrets in its back rooms. "We'll have to get in there," Minerva agreed.

The very thought made my blood run cold, but, well, Minerva would bring her gun and best-selling know-how. What could go wrong? Hah.

I told her about my subsidiary troubles: Bucky and Lou. She listened with amusement to the Bucky story. "Serves 'im right! Ow! Yes!" she commented. "And what a prick that father was to fire you."

"The trait's known to run in families."

"So that's why you're freelancing now. Well, you've picked an interesting way to make a living."

"I'll say."

She grew more serious when I recounted my experiences with Lou. She questioned me closely as to what Lou had done and said so far.

"Lillian, of any of your problems, this is far and away the most perilous."

"You're kidding."

"No. You could be in real danger from Lou. She escalated from accosting you at the bar to calling you, to coming over and scaring the hell out of you. You haven't seen the last of her. Has she sent you any letters?"

"No. This all started—Christ, what? Just a couple weeks ago."

"She will. That'll be next. This might turn into a serious stalking situation."

"Well, I don't know what to do except keep discouraging her. I'm not going to worry about it."

The more time I spent in Minerva's company, the more comfortable I felt. The good honest food helped too. It felt solid in my stomach. We can solve this together, I thought as we finished our meal. We *will* solve it. Minerva snatched the tab and refused to let me pitch in.

We stepped back into the night, chased by the nasal tones of Jim Croce singing the class song of at least fifty percent of high school graduates in the 1970s, "Time in a Bottle."

I wasn't the slightest bit nervous stepping back out on the mean streets. Something about just being with Minerva made me feel confident and optimistic. A dog was barking madly a few blocks over; I imagined a cat balancing on a fence just above its nose.

As we approached the Caprice, though, I noticed something way wrong. Then Minerva noticed it too.

"Oh, Lordy," she said. "The Neanderthals have been here."

I looked the car over carefully. "No," I corrected, "just Bucky."

25

If I hadn't remembered the exact spot where we'd left the Caprice, I wouldn't have recognized it. It was practically obliterated.

Red paint had been splashed on it Jackson Pollock style, dribbled and flung as if in an artistic fever. Much of the paint was concentrated on the windshield and driver's door. I guessed it was supposed to look like blood.

Then there was a slew of scratched-in messages; it appeared that something like a large screwdriver had been used after the paint was thrown. "Fuck you bitch," "Fuck," "Cunt," "Bitch," "Suck me bitch." The scratches went deep, through all the paint layers down to the metal.

"How do you know Bucky did this?" Minerva asked.

"I recognize the scrawl." Bucky had a distinctive way of making his lowercase *b*'s, with a little tail going to the left. I noticed that in one place he'd first gouged "bith," then crowded in the *c* after doing some proofreading. He got it right as he worked around the car.

"That bastard," Minerva said, touching my arm. "Your beautiful car."

For a moment I fought back tears. To me, it *had* been a beautiful car. I'd taken such good care of it. But the tears stayed inside when I realized how insignificant this vandalism was in the context of the mayhem I was trying to find my way to the heart of.

"You know," I said, "he didn't even have the wit to write 'I am a bitch.' Well, I can get it cleaned up and repaired. I'm glad he didn't break the windows. While he, on the other hand, will never be able to transform himself into the kind of guy he wants to be."

I could imagine somebody coming along and looking quizzically at Bucky while he was at it. "Teaching a bitch a lesson," he would've growled, and the dude would've grunted in approval and moved on.

I went back to the restaurant, bought a beer, and begged some paper towels. Using the beer as a solvent I managed to wipe the worst of the still tacky paint from the windows and door handles. Minerva tried to help, but I waved her away. I didn't want to see her fine clothes ruined. I only got a little paint on my jeans.

Neither of us brought up the most frightening aspect of the whole thing: the fact that Bucky had to have followed me, then us, since that afternoon. I hadn't noticed anything suspicious anywhere. I tried to act offhanded with Minerva, but I felt deeply unsettled.

We drove off. We were silent for a while, then Minerva commented, "He probably feels even with you now."

"I hope so. I hope he's got enough sense not to try anything more. He's not going to do a serial harassment on me without getting caught."

I wondered whether Lou and the Creighters were following me too. Maybe they'd all bump into each other and start up a club.

People in other cars gaped at the Caprice, their noses wrinkling as though they were smelling something bad. "I'm sorry to put you through this." I looked sideways at Minerva. She was calm and collected, already refocusing on catching the Creighters.

"It's all right," she said. "Looks like the games are over for the night. So which way to the *Triangle* offices?"

"You mean right now?" My watch said eight-thirty.

"Sure, somebody's got to be working late."

She was right about that. The gay-bar lifestyle is an after-dark lifestyle, and its support systems don't keep regular hours either: There were after-hours hair salons, drag emporia, and, of course, porn shops. It wasn't unreasonable to imagine some bleary-eyed editor standing there stripping down page after page of classified copy.

Minerva used her cell phone to call information, then *The Triangle*. "Hi, can I stop in and place an ad? I know I could, but I'm right in the neighborhood. Thanks, see you."

She was poetry itself at the front counter. Tony Corkindale, one of the owners, was there, looking tired. She introduced herself; he knew who she was.

Tony was a moonfaced guy, not handsome, but with a forthright gaze and an aura of common sense. He and one business partner and one full-time employee worked hard to meet the media needs of Detroit's gay community. I introduced myself and stepped to the side, letting Minerva handle this interview.

"You don't want to place an ad, do you?" Tony said, smiling slightly.

"No. I'm investigating a murder, and so are the police. Only they're slow and I'm fast." Her tone was respectful. "And they're very heavy-handed. And I'm not. How would you feel about the police coming in here and seizing all your records on classified ads from the beginning of time?"

The implications of that thought made Tony Corkindale interlace his fingers as if to keep his hands from making fists.

"Please come around the counter and sit down," he said.

I was amazed. All Minerva did was talk straight, offer her help and intelligence, and get what she wanted.

Tony had been using a PC and spreadsheet software to keep track of his ads, so all he had to do was sort by phone number. The Snap's number (with Bonnie's name) came up twice for DJ ads, but her home number came up eight times. The payment name she'd used was R.T. Hayes. The ad copy was the same all eight times:

> **Scared? Me too.** If you're interested in loving women, let's explore together. Your secret's safe with me. Is mine with you?

"How perfect," Minerva commented.

None of the home numbers of the Midnight Five (Minerva had them in her notebook) came up in Tony's files.

So, we got more information, and *The Triangle* got a heads-up on an impending invasion of privacy. When and if the cops ever came around, he'd be prepared.

"Now," said Minerva as I set the Caprice on a western course from downtown, "we pack it in for the night." I wanted to keep chattering about the business afoot, but she held up her hand. "No. Stop. We need to turn it off for a while."

She was right.

"I'll take you back to your hotel, then."

"And we'll have another beer. Or something."

"OK, but..." I licked my lips. "Um, see, if I'm going to be gone much longer I need to check Todd's water and give him something to eat. My rabbit. Um."

She laughed and said she'd love to meet Todd. "We'll just hang out at your place. And in the morning we'll plan what's next."

All righty.

My neighborhood was quiet. The lower flat was dark; I pictured Mr. McVittie in his bed dreaming of assorted chocolate creams, large-breasted lady lifeguards, and ever-lasting agility.

I saw a long white envelope sticking out of my mailbox. I'd taken in my mail before I went out, so someone must have hand-delivered it. My name was on the front in block printing.

Once I'd shown Minerva up the stairs, turned on some lights, and introduced her to Todd, I opened it.

"I can't believe it," I murmured.

"Lou, right?" She was sitting on the couch with Todd in her lap. They liked each other right away. He was rubbing his chin on her knees; I felt a green stab of envy.

Leaning against the archway to the dining room, I read the two-page letter silently. It was done in painfully precise printing in black ballpoint on swirly pink paper.

Dear Lillian,

I don't know if you understand how much I love you. I do. I love you wider than my arms can reach!! As much as all the stars in the heavens!!

More powerful than a locomotive!! That's how my heart feels when I think of your heart!! But I am so sad that you have not given me one chance. Yet, anyway!! Here is what happens when we are together.

I come to your home in my real car (a brand-new black Mustang with quad-stereo) and I have flowers and a big bottle of wine and you say those are my favorite flowers!! I would love some wine!! Thank you!!

So we drink some wine and talk on your balcony while the sun goes down and the music is anything by K.D. Lang. We are so mellow. I have written some poems and you say those are the nicest poems I have ever heard. Then you say I would like to go out to dinner. I say let's go!! We take off in my Mustang and I drive us Downtown to a very special restaurant that has red roses on the table and no-one cares that we are gay!! I hold all doors open for you.

We eat surf-and-turf and strawberry cake with strawberries in the frosting and only one more glass of wine.

I am the designated driver!!

We go to the Snap Dragon and dance three dances, two fast and one Slow Dance. Is everyone ever jealouse!! You dance with no-one but me.

Then, my dearest Lillian, we go home to my home and I have prepared a special bath with scented oils and candles. The stereo is playing the tape I have made especially for you. You enjoy the songs very much. I have a very good stereo system,

I am very good with electronics. You see this!! The dogs are in the basement.

You take my hand and we have that first kiss. My heart is more powerful than a locomotive!! Then: You finally admit that you love me!! We partake of my bed and it is the most beautiful, exciting, mellow experience we have ever had.

Everytime I think of this night I know my life will change forever and I will make you the happiest womon in the world.

My Lillian, I have to show you how special we can be together. I must. Don't keep me waiting!! I can't stand much more!! You may call me at any time. I will see you soon.

Love, Lou.

I held out the letter. "This is the most pathetic thing I've ever seen."

Minerva took the letter and read it. She laughed only once, then folded it up. "It's no laughing matter, really. This is what I was talking about. Lillian, this is serious."

"Well, what am I supposed to do, put out a contract on her? How serious can it be? She's desperate. Fine. But I can't imagine she'd ever try to hurt me." As I spoke I edged casually over to the door and braced the two-by-four under the knob. Minerva pretended not to notice.

"Neither can she. But if she works herself up enough, she definitely could. And not even know what she was doing. This is how those things go."

"I don't believe it."

"Well. Put it away and don't think about it anymore for now. We're safe tonight."

"Now, that's a good suggestion." I glanced at her bag. "I hope that hunk of iron doesn't come in handy."

"Don't worry."

I put on some soft music, good music to make love by: Chet Baker crooning Cole Porter, Sarah Walker swinging with Gershwin, Morgana King going to town on Johnny Mercer. I glanced around the apartment: It didn't look bad. There was Minerva looking well-fed and expectant on my turquoise leather couch, bathed in golden light from one bulb of my pole lamp, which was turned strategically upward to bounce softly off the corner of the ceiling. My chock-full bookcases looked sophisticated, I thought. No TV in sight, and just a little green glow from the stereo components, stacked neatly in an odd, rounded metal case Mr. McVittie had given me. He said it was from a radar room in a ship.

"Would you like some Scotch? That's all I've got."

"Sounds good. I'd just like to sip a little." She sat petting Todd while I fixed the drinks in the kitchen. "What are your favorite flowers, anyway?" she called softly.

I paused in my pouring and smiled. "I guess sunflowers. Kind of plebeian, huh? But I love them. What are yours?"

Her voice came back low and mischievous, "I'm very fond of tiger lilies."

I almost dropped the whisky bottle.

Then she said, "Do you play this? Is it a mandolin?"

"Yes. Yes. Would you like to hear something?"

"Oh, yes."

I liked to hear her say that word.

I popped out from the kitchen, paused Chet Baker, and played "Wildwood Flower" for obvious reasons, then "Old Joe Clark," chiefly because I'd learned an impressive version of it from a record. Then I piled it on with "Ashokan Farewell." She listened with such an intense expression that I became a little unnerved. I put up the mandolin and restarted the music on the stereo.

A bar of bittersweet chocolate lurked somewhere in my pantry; I found it and broke it into small pieces and put them on a plate with some fresh orange segments.

"A little dessert," I offered as I brought out the tray, "in keeping with the evening. Chocolate was a very important commodity in the New World."

"And the famous Mayan orange groves." She turned from my bookcases where she'd been inspecting titles.

"Yes, the famous floating orange groves of the Mayan empire, where maidens learned the sensuous arts of harvesting and marmalade-making."

We laughed, in spite of the horrors out there in the night. We kept laughing through more dumb talk and chocolate- and orange-nibbling, until we left off nibbling the treats and started in on each other. The smell and taste of Minerva LeBlanc was more nourishing than any food I could imagine. If only food *could* be as great as sex.

You know how that first time is usually a bit awkward? Not like in books, where they always just jump on each other like champions, nobody fumbles, nobody messes up, everybody gets a medal—"our bodies fused together as one"—that kind of nonsense.

Speaking for myself, I can't help worrying whether *she's* worried about how I'll react to her body, her looks, her desires. Then: Will I have the stamina, the imagination she requires? Is she anxious about orgasms? All of that and more, you know?

With Minerva, though, there was no awkwardness. No

frightened egos, no negotiating. Although she'd been the one in control on the street, I found myself enjoying the lead in the bedroom.

I always try to set myself a challenge when making love: Which part of her body would she least expect me to dwell on? You can't imagine the sexual tension that creates. Well, perhaps you can. She's expecting you to *move on,* get to the good parts, you know, but you just settle right there and linger and linger, and eventually, if she's got a normal nervous system, she experiences a sort of breakthrough, you can feel it because a spark runs through her and she just sinks down under you, and you know you really have her. Because now she's sensitized, she's really feeling, and when you do get to the good parts—well, hold onto your Stroh's, fans.

Minerva LeBlanc, I'm pleased to report, liked my style.

26

In my dream I was swimming in a tropical sea just beyond a crashing surf line, surrounded by colorful non-threatening fish and mollusks. My heart was peaceful. I rolled onto my back and floated beneath a luminous green sky dotted by fluffy pink clouds.

Suddenly a burglar alarm began ringing somewhere onshore, then an outrigger canoe came surging across the waves toward me. Bonnie and her mother were paddling like mad, and Bucky, seated in the stern, was shouting something unintelligible over their heads. He was bare-chested and looked like a boiled pig. Lou, in her overalls and plaid shirt, rose from the prow and took aim at me with a rusty harpoon. I jerked upright with a start, my heart drumming in my throat.

It was dark, and the phone was ringing. I stumbled naked into the dining room to get it.

"Lillian. Aunt Rosalie." Her voice was low and urgent. "Are you getting up? It's four-thirty."

My tongue was thick. "Aunt Rosalie? What—um— why—it's still night."

"Oh, honey, don't you remember? Uncle Guff? Today's his last day."

A sledgehammer of regret rammed into my chest as I came fully awake and remembered what I'd forgotten.

My Uncle Guff and Aunt Rosalie had more or less finished the job of rearing me after my parents died when I was twelve. They got me at the dawning of a difficult adolescence, just as I was blossoming from an average, slightly rebellious kid into an ornery, pissed-off teenager. To this day I wince at some of the things I did and said to those kind people. They had no children of their own. I loved them and knew they loved me, though gallons of sodium pentothal couldn't have gotten any of us to admit it.

As an adult I tried to make it up to them by calling and visiting and being extra nice. About once a month we three would go bowling or shopping or fishing. Every few years I'd accompany them on a vacation in their boxcar-size motor home. They enjoyed having me around: someone to talk to who remembered the old days almost like they did.

Uncle Guff was my father's brother. He'd made a living as a mill worker at Great Lakes Steel for decades, and he was preparing to retire. About two months ago when we were out on the south end of Belle Isle trying to get the perch to bite, Aunt Rosalie had told me when Uncle Guff's last day at the mill would be, while he kept his eyes on his bobber.

The special day was today, and I had promised to go and

commemorate it with a photograph of him arriving at the plant for the very last six A.M. shift of his life.

"You have such a good camera," Aunt Rosalie had said. Now she was saying, "Lillian? Are you there?"

"Ohhh," I said into the phone.

"I'm so glad I called," she whispered. "He's in the bathroom now. If you'd forgotten to be there, he never would have said anything, but I know how terrible he'd feel. I'm fixing him ham and eggs."

"Oh, God, Aunt Rosalie, thank you for reminding me. I'm—I'm—*yes,* I'll absolutely be there. In fact, I'm on my way. Yes. Absolutely."

I hung up, mumbling, "Oh, God, oh, God."

Of course she knew I'd forgotten; I couldn't fake it with her. Nothing would have cut any ice, not even, "Gee, Auntie, I've been mixed up in a murder investigation where I almost got killed, and normal responsibilities have been slipping my mind." No. I'd shown her, conclusively, that even in a once-in-a-lifetime situation I was not to be counted on. This for me would be yet another shameful thing to wince about once or twice a week for the rest of my life.

But I had a chance for redemption. I'd go and set myself up for the best triumphant-workingman picture any shutterbug ever took.

I grabbed a roll of Plus-X and my Canon and set them next to my keys, then returned to the bedroom.

Minerva had been undisturbed by the phone call. She lay on my thin futon sleeping deeply, her body a perfect sculpture beneath the soft folds of the sheet.

I employed my patented "kiss-awake" method, and she stirred. I briefly explained my mission and urged her to go back to sleep. "It isn't even five o'clock yet. I'll be back by seven, I think. I'll pick up some doughnuts. Do you like crullers?"

"Mm-hmm," she sighed. "This is a great bed." I was amazed; she turned onto her stomach and appeared to try to burrow deeper into the futon, which I regarded as little better than a stale pancake. It rested right on the floor. It was a low-tech bedroom.

Her skin felt cool, so I drew my light summer blanket up to her neck and tucked it around her. Todd was sleeping in his bed in the corner.

I threw on some clothes and gave her one more kiss on the back of the head, which stuck out from the blanket like a satiny coconut, then hurried out.

The street was empty. I fired up my besmirched Caprice and headed for the Downriver steel town of Ecorse.

Whenever I asked Uncle Guff to tell me about his work at Great Lakes, he invariably answered with a three-sentence resume: "I started in the flues." Long pause, and a look into the far distance, lower lip between the teeth. Work in the flues, everyone knows, was dirty and dangerous. "Then I pulled ingots for a long time...real long time." The gaze shifted nearer, into the middle distance, the mouth relaxed, and a series of nods would begin. "Now, why, obviously, I'm a crane operator." And the shoulders would square up, and he would meet anyone's eye with the confidence of a man whose place was high above the factory floor, who was entrusted with other men's lives and took pride in it.

When I was little I thought he was involved in the production of soft drinks, as I would hear about "the coke works" and "pouring slag." I thought it would be exciting to mix big batches of Coke and pour off the resulting slag. Slag sounded like something I would force my enemies to drink, while I'd refresh myself with only the purest-quality Coke, iced down, of course, and fizzier than the kind found in restaurants and stores.

I cruised down West Jefferson alongside the Detroit River, silvery ribbon of maritime commerce, and made it to the main gate with ten minutes to spare.

The steel mill's distinctive silhouette loomed like a saw-toothed mountain range over the riverside neighborhoods. Six miles of shoreline—that's how big the place is. The docks front the water, then the mill buildings back up to them, then there are the rail yards, sort of all over the place. To get to their jobs in the mill, the workers have to climb up to a covered catwalk then cross over a thick braid of railroad tracks.

I hung around the Quonset hut next to the catwalk looking for good angles. Men and women were coming to work, walking past the guard in ones and twos; I knew that as the clock neared six A.M., the influx of workers would become a thick stream. I watched for Uncle Guff's red suspenders and knew he'd be watching for me.

I decided to set up for a few different shots. I peered through my viewfinder, mentally noting light-meter readings and fooling with my shutter speeds and stops. I became absorbed with the problem of exactly matching up the mill's roofline with the rising sun. The light meter didn't like it.

After a minute I heard the scuff of a shoe on pavement just behind me; I turned, and there was Uncle Guff looking the other way, as if he'd merely come over to inspect a weather-beaten fence post.

"Uncle Guff!" I gave him a big hug and a kiss, and he looked down and tried not to smile.

He was a trim man with thin lips and squared-off teeth, and bright blue eyes behind heavy safety glasses. He had on his usual work outfit of clean blue jeans, blue work shirt, and red suspenders. The suspenders were his only overt statement of individuality. The other employees favored heavy leather belts. One lean hand was wrapped around the handle of his dented black lunchbox. He held it up and said, "I'm gonna throw this here in the river after lunch."

I punched his arm. "All right!"

We got down to business. I positioned him and started shooting. He stood calmly, ignoring the curious looks of the other workers, his expression serious. Working quickly, I took shots in front of the door to the catwalk stairs, through the fence with the old administration building in the background, from a low angle showing the mill in the background, and a few close-ups. I got one glorious smile out of him when I called, "Think about clocking out this afternoon!"

"That's enough," he said.

I promised to get prints to him and Aunt Rosalie in a few days, and he turned and merged with the stream of workers going in. It was five minutes to six.

I smiled all the way back to Eagle, thinking how happy he'd be at the end of the day. In retirement he'd go fishing more often, work in his garage shop, and take Aunt Rosalie on more trips in the motor home. He liked to fish wherever he went. Aunt Rosalie told me how he once dropped a line off the stern of the Staten Island Ferry when they were in New York for some wedding. He snagged a big dead turtle, and the deckhands hollered at him.

I stopped at the Dunkin' Donuts on Woodward and picked up half a dozen crullers plus two large coffees. I love their crullers: The dough is very nice and eggy, and not as sweet as the other varieties.

As I drove on home, I felt my confidence and optimism grow. Sure, I was in a fix, but I had Minerva LeBlanc on my side now. Together we'd get the goods on the Creighters, save my butt, and give her another book to write.

What's more, I was falling in love. I thought Minerva the most intelligent, sexy, creative, fun person I'd ever met. I pictured us together in a variety of exciting situations, some involving armed confrontations with steely-eyed thugs, others featuring gourmet room-service trays and thick terry bathrobes.

I parked the Caprice in my usual spot in front of the house. It felt good to be up and about so early. The birds were twittering; the neighborhood was coming alive. As I carried my camera and the doughnut go-tray up the porch steps and into the vestibule, I noticed Mr. McVittie's front door standing open. That was unusual.

The two flats shared a common front door into a vestibule; the McVitties' front door opened to the left off the vestibule, and my stairs led upward to the right. In the summer the McVitties' window air-conditioning unit was usually on, which called for all doors and windows to be shut. I listened for the hum of the air conditioner.

Then I heard him calling my name from inside. I set my stuff on the stairs and went in.

The flat was furnished in high '70s style, lots of avocado and gold, heavily worn shag carpeting, and plenty of antiquing and swags.

"Lillian? Lillian!" he called. I followed his voice to the dining room.

He was standing there in his pants and undershirt, barefooted, talking to the ceiling, staring at something up there. "Lillian?"

"Mr. McVittie!"

He turned and gave me a bewildered look. "There's something. I can't see so good."

I looked up and saw a stain on the ceiling about the size of a dinner plate. It was wet and very red. And it appeared to be spreading.

The McVitties' dining room was directly beneath my bedroom.

27

I tore out of the McVittie flat and rushed upstairs to mine. I couldn't have moved any faster, yet I dreaded the moment I was hastening toward.

I stopped at the doorway to the bedroom, seeing already the inconceivable, impossible, horrible reality.

Minerva LeBlanc lay just as I had left her, facedown in my bed, the back of her head the only exposed part of her. There was so very much blood.

She'd been bludgeoned. A flap of her scalp hung off to one side, the right side of her head; I saw mashed tissue there, bone and brains, oozing blood.

I'm not up to the task of describing how much blood there was. It had soaked through the futon, the carpet, and the flooring, which I knew to be old and cracked. The air in the room was heavy with that warm-sharp smell that women know so well.

She was surely dead, I thought, but in the next second I

heard a ragged sound and realized she was still breathing.

I dived to her side, my mind racing. Mr. McVittie had followed me upstairs and was frozen in the doorway as I had been.

"Call an ambulance!" I shouted, "and the police! Nine-one-one, Mr. McVittie! Oh, God, keep breathing."

Direct pressure, I knew, stops bleeding, but if I pressed on the back of her head, I'd be pushing skull fragments into her brain. I didn't dare touch her.

"Breathe, honey, breathe, breathe, breathe." I saw that her head was actually turned slightly to the side, away from the door. I lifted the blanket and bent down to look into her eyes, which were half-open. They looked completely empty. I couldn't tell whether her pupils were symmetrical. Her lips were parted; I could see her beautiful teeth. They were undisturbed.

I knelt with her. "Oh, breathe, Minerva, help is coming, help is coming. If you can hear me, honey, you'd better breathe. Breathe, goddamn it."

Someone had fallen upon her so suddenly and with such force that she'd had no chance to struggle.

I heard Mr. McVittie yelping into the phone.

The mind-shattering implications of what had occurred came rushing to me: I had discovered her, she was in my bed, I had been the last to see her, we had been seen together by many people.

Minerva's shoulder bag lay where she had placed it, on the floor near her clothes. Then I saw the weapon, tossed aside and spattered with blood: It was my two-by-four, which I'd handily left next to the front door. The doors. Someone had sneaked in here. My God, I must have left the doors unlocked in my hurry to meet Uncle Guff.

Mr. McVittie returned to the doorway, hugging himself. "They're coming. Oh, Lord!"

"Did you see or hear anything?" My voice was a rasp.

He shook his head and backed away from me, then turned and ran down the stairs. I heard his door slam.

Had someone watched the house all night, waiting for me to leave? Or had they simply shown up at five A.M., assuming I'd be home in bed?

I looked at Minerva again, and a spasm ran through me: It could have been me lying there.

She and I were the same general size and shape, the same hair color. Whoever attacked her might not only have thought they were attacking me; they might have thought they killed me.

Who would have wanted that? Bucky Rinkell, if he'd gone psycho? The Creighters wanted me dead, or were they so calculating as to suppose that if they killed someone in my home it could implicate me, perhaps get me arrested and convicted? Did they think I might flee?

Lou might have wanted to kill me or Minerva, or both of us. How many of these people had been watching me?

Holy hell.

Sirens.

The paramedics arrived first and sprang into action, pushing me out of the room. I was standing in the living room gripping my head when Tom Ciesla, Erma Porrocks, and four uniformed officers came in. The faces of Tom and Erma were hard.

In one sentence I told them the immediate facts, then watched them move through the flat to the bedroom doorway.

Ciesla stopped there and barked, "Is she dead?"

The paramedics, two of them, were yelling to each other, and one was yelling into a radio, while equipment was flying all over the place.

"I said, is she dead?" Ciesla shouted.

"No!" snapped the one in charge, a compact black woman with a shaved head. Somehow she was threading a tube into Minerva's mouth. "Imbecile," she muttered.

"Is she gonna die?"

"Yes! Shut up and get out of here."

"Then we've got a murder scene," Ciesla said. He started giving orders to the badges, who dispersed. One talked into his radio, requesting a photographer and lab people.

I indicated Minerva's purse, anticipating their request for her I.D. "The last I saw, she had a gun in there," I told them. I was acquainted with a couple of the cops. They stared at my knees. I looked down and saw them bloody.

The paramedics came through the living room with Minerva lying on her side, frighteningly still; then they were gone.

I didn't see Todd anywhere.

More cop cars pulled up, more cops came in, until it looked as if they'd been spread on with a knife.

Porrocks asked me a few questions. I told her who Minerva was and how my morning errand had taken me away from home.

"Where's your camera?"

I looked at her blankly, not remembering.

"Retrace your steps from the car," she prompted.

It took me a minute to do so in my mind. I pointed to the stairs; she followed me down to the landing. The camera and doughnut-and-coffee tray were gone. I turned and pounded on Mr. McVittie's door.

Porrocks called, "Police!"

Mr. McVittie opened the door and handed out the camera. His mouth was full of fresh cruller. He glared at me defensively.

"You'll want to talk to him too," I said as he shut the door.

Fortunately, he hadn't monkeyed with the camera. I handed it to Porrocks, knowing she'd want the film as evidence. "You'll be careful with the film?"

"You can count on that."

"Because it's an extremely important roll of film, the pictures in there. Not just as evidence. It's my family, you see."

She looked at me searchingly. "What do you think happened up there?"

"Oh, God, Erma." My chest felt empty. "I don't fucking know. Whoever did this could be any of three or four people I know."

"You have that many enemies?"

We went back upstairs, and Erma sent a junior detective down to interview Mr. McVittie. I got down on my hands and knees to look for Todd.

As soon as he saw my face at floor level, he wriggled out from behind a bookcase and into my arms. I held him tight. "Oh, Toddy."

His food and water dishes needed attention. I filled them, anticipating what was next.

"We want you to come to the station and tell us everything," Ciesla said. He'd been in the bedroom studying things. "We need to know every detail of where you went and what you did yesterday. And more before that."

"Sure, Tom. Where'd they take her, do you know?"

"Probably Beaumont Hospital."

I got my bag and keys, and went around to all the cops and told them to be careful of Todd. Some of them were taking notes and making diagrams; others were going through my stuff in the rest of the apartment using latex gloves. They wouldn't start going through my stuff in the bedroom until the photographer and lab people had come and gone.

Ciesla told me the police would probably do all the work they needed that day. I was grateful that he didn't assume I'd be under arrest before the day was out.

I followed Ciesla and Porrocks outside. Gaggles of neighbors had alighted at the property lines. The police were tying their yellow ribbons.

"Is that *your car*?" Ciesla asked, staring.

"Yeah. It went through the mill last night."

"You've got a lot to tell us."

28

Porrocks set a cup of coffee in front of me. "You look like hell."

"No shit."

"You want sugar or cream?"

"No."

The detectives' office smelled of floor wax and copier toner. One of the tubes in the overhead fluorescent fixture buzzed and flickered. My ankles were wrapped around the legs of the same chair I'd sat in a few days ago when I'd tricked Porrocks into leaving the room so I could steal a look at Iris Macklin's postmortem. The same chair Ciesla put me back into for my scolding afterward. I thought it was a hot seat then.

Now the two detectives were ready, Bic Stics poised, to try to make sense out of, most probably, yet another murder in their jurisdiction, yet another unpleasant surprise connected with a brainless reporter who should've gone and gotten a job somewhere else, anywhere else far, far away: the French Foreign Legion, the Alaska pipeline, an asbestos mine.

The cops wanted to know every goddamned thing I did and said, everything that'd happened to me since I'd seen Iris Macklin in the Snapdragon. I told them all over again about that, and stabbing Bucky, and Bucky in the darkroom, and snooping around the Creighter house, and talking to Greg Wycoff, and meeting Mrs. Creighter again, and Lou's attentions.

"You'll find a letter from her in my kitchen junk drawer."

Ciesla unwrapped a hunk of coffee cake he'd baked, and we shared that. I was hardly hungry, but thought I could use the energy.

It took hours and hours to go over everything. Every time I gave a fact, they had about six questions to go with it. Most of them I didn't know the answers to. For instance, I knew Lou's full name, Louise Deronio, but I didn't know exactly where she lived, or what her days off were, or whether she did in fact drive a brand-new black Mustang, or whether she had a history of mental or emotional instability. They asked about Mr. McVittie, who to them was as much of a suspect as anybody, but Jesus, I'd seen him standing there, uncomprehending, looking at that blood on his ceiling. Did Minerva LeBlanc talk about any enemies? They asked about *my* stability. Had I ever heard voices telling me what to do? Would I allow myself to be fingerprinted?

I wished for a simple solution to the troubles of the world: I wished for the police to arrest Bonnie, her mother, Bucky, and Lou, and put them all in jail forever. That way, no more bad things would ever happen again. How very simple.

I cried, I wrung my hands, I pounded Ciesla's desk, I spilled my coffee.

At different times other cops and even the chief, a hairy-eared dude I never liked, stuck their heads in with questions or handed notes to Ciesla and Porrocks.

The hours went by, and we didn't get word that Minerva had died. "They flew her to Ann Arbor," said Ciesla after reading one message. "They're operating, and if she lives, we're not going to be able to talk to her for forty-eight hours at least—if ever."

At one point midday he went out to talk to a few reporters in the downstairs lobby.

"All I told them was there was an attempted homicide in your apartment, and we're investigating. Reporters are gonna be bothering *you* now." He jabbed a finger at me. "As someone who gives a shit about you, I suggest you say very little."

"No problem on that. Did they ask if I was the victim?"

He laughed coldly. "They did, and I said no comment." All I could think was, it must have been a slow news day.

The questioning went on and on. In the early afternoon Porrocks sent out for sandwiches and Cokes. She and Ciesla tore hungrily at theirs.

I told them in painstaking detail about Uncle Guff's Last Day (I was starting to capitalize it in my mind). "The film will show I went there. The pictures will corroborate what I'm saying." We all understood, however, that the pictures couldn't prove I hadn't bludgeoned Minerva LeBlanc. Perhaps I'd done it before or after running down to Ecorse for my alibi.

I gave them Uncle Guff and Aunt Rosalie's address and phone number. "He'll tell you too. I don't suppose I'm gonna get the negatives back anytime soon."

Ciesla snorted.

Visions of Aunt Rosalie having a nervous breakdown floated through my mind. Some things just can't be helped. I accepted my fate.

Now this will either surprise you or not, depending on the opinion you've formed about my intellectual competence. I never once thought about getting a lawyer. I mean, not even the faintest concept of "lawyer" crossed my mind the whole day.

Why? I guess I just thought my job was to help the police find the truth. I totally trusted Ciesla and Porrocks. I had not attacked Minerva LeBlanc with the two-by-four. In the end, I was lucky Ciesla and Porrocks were who they were.

Ciesla said, "We've got a lot of work ahead of us." He drummed his fingers on his desk. He and Porrocks looked more puzzled and worried now than when they were first looking around my apartment. They looked tired too.

"Is someone trying to locate Minerva's next of kin?"

Porrocks answered, "The New York police have been notified, and they're handling it. We're not going to release her name to the media until that's done."

Ciesla looked at her and said, "Anything more?"

"No," said Porrocks.

"I can go?"

They nodded together.

I couldn't stand it anymore. "Erma, Tom, do you believe me? Do you believe everything I said?"

Porrocks's mouth was grim. "'Course we do. Lillian! Come on."

Ciesla just watched me, but I thought I saw belief in his eyes.

All he said was, "Don't do anything stupid."

"And of course," Porrocks chipped in lightly, "don't leave town. All right?"

29

By the time I started thinking about a lawyer, it was getting late. I decided I'd pick one out of the phone book on Monday.

Dusk was falling when I rounded the corner in my ridiculous hacked-up car and saw the hard lights of a TV crew in front of the house. I backed up and went away, driving over to a nearby elementary school parking lot. I sat there under a tree in the gathering darkness, glad to not be talking, glad to be aware of my own healthy heartbeat, and growing angrier by the minute at any and all of the goddamn people who were cutting down good women and making my life hell.

I began to fantasize about doing some murdering myself. Yes, I'd gone way beyond dictator fantasies to the dark, dark regions of Old Testament vengeance. I wanted a fucking necklace of *everybody's* teeth: the Creighters, Lou, Bucky. I wanted to see eyeballs pop. I wanted to see blood spurt from severed arteries. I wanted to see dogs feasting on entrails. I thought they were all guilty, and I hated and feared them all.

I prayed for Minerva, hauling out the Hail Mary and the Our Father, as I shamelessly do in my most desperate hours. If she lived, would she ever be the same? How could her brain function as it had, sharp and clear and cool, when bits of it were strewn across my percale pillowcase? *Oh, dear God, this is a big one. Thy will be done.*

A soft flash of heat lightning drew my eyes to the treetops. It was clouding up and smelled like rain. It'd been holding off for days, but now we were in for a storm. I blotted perspiration from my face with the sleeve of the Wayne State University T-shirt I'd thrown on that morning.

If whoever had attacked Minerva thought they were killing me, they might keep thinking that until the police released her name. How could they know otherwise? If the press had talked to Mr. McVittie, he could have told them the victim wasn't me, but I thought chances were good he'd be too freaked out to open his door to anybody.

I was glad Mrs. McVittie was up north looking after her sister and missing this whole gruesome show. She was a sweet old thing. I imagined Mr. McVittie up on a stepladder scrubbing at the ceiling. I wondered whether he'd eaten all six crullers and drunk both coffees.

I hadn't gotten to know any of my other neighbors yet. Maybe some of them knew who I was when I walked out with Ciesla and Porrocks, maybe not. I believed I had a chance to play dead, sort of, for a short period of time, maybe just overnight. Aunt Rosalie and Uncle Guff wasted little time watching television news; they listened to oldies radio. If they did hear something distressing, I trusted they'd have the sense to call the police and ask.

I formed a hazy plan of paying visits to all four of my tormentors that night. Was I thinking straight or what? I wanted to confront each of them and look into their eyes, in spite of my fear, and make them look into mine. Perhaps I could induce a fatal heart attack or two. At the least I might learn something more.

All right, this was not a rational, police-like plan. But at the moment it was all I had. It was my plan, goddamn it.

I checked my watch; an hour had passed. I went back to my corner and saw TV lights *still* burning in front of the house. I was about to turn away again when I noticed something disturbing. Stuff, a long mountain of stuff was piled up along the curb in front of the house, and the TV lights were trained on it. What the fuck?

I parked halfway down the block and walked up and couldn't believe it. The yellow police lines were gone. My stuff, all my furniture and books and clothes and food were piled up more or less neatly on the strip of grass between the sidewalk and curb, eviction-style. My turquoise couch. My photo albums. My golf clubs. My stereo. Where was Todd!

I turned around to find a TV camera in my face. Hank Lyman, a local reporter I'd met here and there, stuck his mike up and said, "And this is Lillian Byrd, the tenant at this address where the brutal attack took place, coming—"

I grabbed his arm holding the mike and stuck my hand in front of the camera lens. Hank's channel had the highest ratings in the city.

"Hank, don't. See, nobody knows I'm alive. I mean, I—there's some people I'd just as soon think I was dead— or pretty dead—right now. It's hard to explain. Would you, could you please not report that I wasn't the victim until tomorrow? Please? My safety could be at stake."

"Uh, Lillian," he said, forcing the mike back up to mouth level, "we're live here."

I reeled away from him; he went back to talking into the camera. A few bystanders were eyeing my belongings as if they were gold ingots. I couldn't tell what, if anything, was missing. Ciesla had told me I'd get a list of whatever the cops took as evidence.

I asked one of the bystanders, "Did the police bring this stuff out here?"

He shook his head and pointed. "That guy in there."

Mr. McVittie's flat was dark, but I knew better. I tried my key to the vestibule, but he'd installed a chain latch. I pounded and shouted. A light went on. He came and pulled the door in to the chain stop. His face was red; the little bastard had humped that whole truckload of shit piece by piece down a flight of stairs and out to the curb.

"Goddamn it!" I yelled. "Why did you do this? Where's my rabbit!"

He held up a finger, went away, and came back carrying Todd by the nape. He slipped him out to me.

"Why did you do this! You're not supposed to do this! It was a crime scene! The police might have to come back!"

"They said they was done!" he screamed through the crack.

"Why did you do this!"

"I have a right! You ruined my propitty!"

I stomped back to the curb and dumped out a cardboard carton of stuff and found some newspapers. Todd sat quietly in the grass while I did this. He was an amazingly calm rabbit. Hank Lyman's cameraman came over, tape rolling.

"We're not live now," Hank assured me.

"Goddamn media parasites," I muttered.

Hank giggled snottily. "That's very ironic, Lillian. Miz big-time weekly reporter."

"Fuck you," I snarled.

I put a thick layer of newspapers into the bottom of the box and added Todd, then carried it to my car, set it in the passenger seat, and cranked down the windows an inch.

As I trudged back to my stuff a fat drop of rain hit my forehead. I looked up to see a black roiling sky underlit by the glow of the city. The wind started to whip. Another drop hit my ear. By the time I felt the third drop, Hank and his crew were hurrying to their truck.

The vultures were reluctantly moving off, watching me over their shoulders. As the rain spattered down I rooted through the piles for important things: my box of checks, my passport, my mandolin, Todd's water dish. My good loafers. A half-bottle of Dewar's, bag of bunny chow, a couple of carrots. My books would have to wait. I stuffed my pockets and took an armload, including fresh jeans and a couple of blouses, back to the Caprice. Todd was scrabbling anxiously until he heard my voice.

"Hang on, Toddy. We'll be all right." As I walked back to my stuff, the sky opened up in earnest. Sheets of rain, torrents of thrumming rain all but obliterated the glow from the street light nearby.

I stood there alone in the night, straining my eyes toward the dark mass of my worldly goods, hearing more than seeing them getting ruined. A roll of thunder shook the air, then a blast of lightning revealed the sorry sodden lot of property my life had amounted to so far.

I turned and splashed back to the lacerated Caprice, soaked through and disgusted. To hell with the whole god-damned mess.

I felt a cold sense of purpose building in my heart. *Thy will be done. Yeah. And I'm the one to do it.*

30

The Caprice had a good defogger system; I fired it up and let it idle for a few minutes while I more or less scraped the water off myself. In addition to my Wayne State T-shirt, I was wearing blue jeans and my Chuck Taylors. All that cotton must've held a quart of rainwater.

I decided to find a cheap motel as a temporary base of operations. Todd could stay with me overnight, but I might have to give him to somebody for a while, maybe my animal-loving friend Billie, who'd offered to look after him if I ever went on vacation.

We took off to the north Woodward corridor. I hung over the steering wheel, brooding. The thunderstorm had swept over, and it felt like a new one was coming. I abandoned the idea of barging in on my enemies. For all I knew, they were all after me again, having seen me babbling on the tube. I peered into the rearview mirror: an array of rainy headlights. I turned east on Eleven Mile into Madison

Heights, then cut down John R into Hazel Park. My clothes were drying out, and I felt a little warmer.

Around the racetrack in Hazel Park, there are dozens of motels. I pulled into the first one on the right, the Acapulco. I requested a room around back, "where it'll be quiet." Then I asked the clerk for a couple of extra towels, which he grudgingly produced. I intended to make them into a little bed for Todd.

The amount of exotic glamour the Acapulco possessed was in inverse proportion to its name. I needn't get into it. I cut up a carrot top for Todd and gave him some water. He seemed satisfied.

I stripped off my clothes and took a hot shower, then put on the clean things I'd grabbed. That was better. I was glad I had the Dewar's. I set the bottle on the night-stand and went out to the car to rummage in the glove compartment.

Most times when you go looking for a forgotten pack of cigarettes you don't find them, but this time I did. Half a pack of Camel Filters jammed sideways between a Mel Farr Ford ice scraper and my sunglasses case, which I'd mis-placed months ago.

They tasted a little rough for being stale, but not bad. I smoked and sipped the whisky, sitting on the floor near Todd, my back against the bed. The whisky felt warm and good.

The thought of Bonnie and Mrs. Creighter going free after murdering Iris, trying to murder me, and maybe mur-dering Minerva LeBlanc wasn't something I was going to be able to live with. I had to obtain justice or—I squinted and tried to hold back the thought, but there it was—die trying. More immediately, if I didn't put a stop to the Creighters, they were going to put a stop to me.

One thing was clear: The Creighters weren't going to pop into the police station and confess. And I also knew there would be, had to be, more evidence at the Snapdragon. Hadn't Mrs. Creighter referred to "the place," and hadn't Bonnie said something about having to wait until closing?

Much as the idea made me sweat, I was going to have to check out the Snapdragon.

I got out my notebook and pen and wrote down everything that had happened so far, then read it over. Then I just fiddled around with the pen, scribbling stray thoughts. When I stopped thinking about the Creighters and the Snapdragon, my mind fell quiet for a while.

Then my hand wrote "Judy." Everlasting hell. I am awful. Here I was, still half in shock from having a one-night stand butchered out from under me, and I start hankering for Old Faithful. How utterly abominable.

But I wanted her. I was sore in body and spirit. I wanted her, more than ever, to comfort me, help me, hold me. To pity this poor misbegotten fuck-up. Yeah, that's what I was reduced to: craving pity.

I wanted Judy so much I could smell her, taste her. The more I tried not to think about her, the more vivid she grew in my mind, there in sort of a cloud before me in her soft green wrapper. The deeper grew, oh, you know, that place beneath your heart that opens and roils like Kilauea.

Todd had gotten settled into the towel nest I made for him. He hunkered alertly, sniffing the smoky air of the motel room with its overtaste of industrial-strength air sweetener. I got him back into the box; he looked at me with something approaching annoyance. I left the lights on, locked the door, and fired up the Caprice.

With Todd in his box on the seat beside me, I took Ten

Mile across town instead of the expressway; it was a less conspicuous route. The night felt menacing. Other cars pressed too close. I tried to watch every single car and face.

Judy's car was in its regular parking space.

I stood in the doorway with Todd's box under my arm. I rang but got no response. Rang again. Judy had insisted I keep my keys to the place, to the point of developing a hysterical rise in her voice when I tried to give them back a few months ago. I let myself into the building, padded down the corridors, then knocked softly.

"Hey, 'sme." When my key touched the lock, the door opened. Someone else was on the other side, wearing Judy's green wrapper.

"Hello," said she.

I knew the voice, I knew the face: Sharon Wurtz, a hard-mouthed opportunist ever ready to hold the hand of a woman going through a breakup. That was her method. Some women move in on the fresh chicken—women new to the community, oh, those dewy divorcées!—and some move in on the newly vulnerable lonelyhearts. Not that they rent billboards proclaiming their specialty. You just realize it after you've been in the community a while, after watching people and getting to know how they handle themselves.

So Judy was probably in the bathroom, or worse to imagine, lying frozen under the sheets in the bedroom listening for my voice. I stood there like Peter Pan, the full force of the moment hitting me like a wrecking ball, so that for an instant blackness rose in front of my eyes. I fought it down. Sharon's expression was sympathetic, which was worse than a mean smile.

If I'd stood there for an hour, I don't know whether I'd have been able to formulate a sentence. She said hello again. Todd moved in his box, and her eyes tried to see over the top. I pivoted and walked away down the corridor.

31

Judy's arm finally got tired from carrying that torch. I stalked out to the car. Whoa-ho, that was right between the eyes. And I asked for it. How I ever asked for it. Mm.

Todd and I got back in the car. He was unconcerned. I was grateful for that. More and more I saw how animals could be great human substitutes. People who keep fucking up—my God, where would we be without pets? If *I* kept fucking up, probably the only person I'd have to talk to in the whole world would be Todd. But you know, in a sense I was relieved. There's a certain tension inherent in spinning out a relationship like that. Moreover, I realized that deep down I'd been rooting for Judy all along.

I peeled out of the parking lot and headed back east on Ten Mile. I rolled down the windows and gulped the damp night air, which was warming up again after the rain, into the heavy hot stickiness typical of Detroit during a July heat wave.

My mind was overcrowded, my emotions overtaxed. Grief, guilt, shame, all those god-awful feelings were coursing through me. It was useless to try to keep them straight. As I drove I didn't even speak to Todd. I think he fell asleep. It'd been a long day for him.

My mind wandered. Maybe there's not much difference between a hero and a fool. A fine dividing line perhaps, a narrow gray area between heroism and foolishness. What's the difference? Luck? Just luck? Success versus failure, perhaps. Given identical situations, identical tests, even identical intentions, is the only difference between hero and fool the outcome?

It was about two in the morning. I stopped at a gas station pay phone and called Billie's number in Ferndale. I always figured I'd use an animal kennel place to spare her the trouble of looking after Todd, but at two A.M. I didn't have much choice.

She was home and had just gone to bed. She waitressed part-time at a couple of short-order places. Last I knew, she was housemother to three cats, a dog, and two tiny orphaned squirrels.

"Yeah," Billie said, "come on the hell over. Fine. I just got a hedgehog. The squirrels grew up, they're gone. I've got a pen we can use." She left the question of why I needed to find a port for Todd at two in the morning in the ozone for the moment.

Next I called the university hospital in Ann Arbor and asked about Minerva. All they would do was acknowledge that she was there. Still alive, then.

Billie was in her late fifties and had a Lucy Ricardo hairdo and an independent spirit. She found a way to go on year after year waiting tables and taking the odd cook's job, never wanting to do anything more shit-eating than that.

"Now, you might think waiting tables is about as shit-eating a job there is," she remarked to me once over a meat loaf special, "but it's got an ace in the hole other jobs don't. And that's quitting."

"Tell me," I said.

She obliged. "Quitting a waitressing job is the biggest power trip in the world. First of all, you always do it when it's busy, because that's when the pressure's the worst and it's really gotten to you. So you pick your moment." She tucked a bright copper strand behind her ear.

"Of course, the manager or owner has got to be a sumbitch, or you wouldn't do it, and you wouldn't to it to a woman if you can help it. You gotta hang on until you've got a full section, then you throw down your apron and you deliver just one line, or two lines."

She tossed her head. "I've had it. You want this job? You want *this* job? A boss is gonna know what's coming the second you put down that tray and reach your hands behind your back. He's gonna come right over and try and stop you. He'll be mad at first, ooh! Then he'll plead. Finally he'll grovel. But you've got that apron off, you're talking loud right in the middle of the place, and all of a sudden you've got your purse and you're out the door, and they're all sitting there looking at that apron on the floor. That's power, kid."

I asked how many jobs she'd left like that. "Only two. And I've been waitressing for thirty years. But—see—how can I put it? The thing is, you know you can always do it. That's what keeps you going. Plus, I've coached a lot. There's lots of young people who think waiting tables is lower than whale shit. It's not. You don't like how a guy talks to you, you give him the cold shoulder. He's got no complaint against you, and he can't think of a reason not to tip a little, but he doesn't come back too quick. Mission accomplished. Some fancy bitch screeches you're too slow? Same thing. Or you spill a glass of ice water in her lap. So sorry! You like a customer, you treat 'em right. They come back, and they tip OK. Yep, I'll waitress till the day I die, if my legs last. And they'll be lucky to have me."

So that's Billie on the half-shell. "Come in, Toots," she said, opening the door on her sleepy menagerie. Lumps of fur lay draped around the living room, stirring a little. A shrouded birdcage loomed in a corner. I noticed what appeared to be a giant pine cone lolling on the floor.

"The hedgehog. That's Doris. Don't step on her." A houseful of animals will always smell different than one without, but Billie was a fairly good housekeeper; I detected only a low-level muskiness. Todd made no protest when I put him in a large wire cage Billie dragged up from the basement. Not that he had a choice. He was a pretty dignified rabbit.

"So what's the latest?" She said it casually, but her eyes searched my face. Evidently she hadn't ingested any news today.

"I just need a place for Todd for a while. Maybe for a few days, I don't know. Maybe only tonight. Maybe forever. Want a rabbit, lady?" I grinned, but I suppose I looked a little unhealthy.

"You're not moving too good," she observed.

"OK," I said, "I'll level with you as much as I can. I'm going to do something sort of dangerous after I leave here. I've gotten mixed up in something. In fact, I'm slightly homeless at the moment. I've got a motel room, but if something weird happens, I want to make sure Todd's OK."

"Can you be a little more specific?" She sat down and put her feet up on a hassock. Her calves were big and knotty, but her feet looked dainty in their pink scuffs. "There's beer in the icebox. Want one?"

"No, thanks." I told her about how I lost my job.

"Excellent," she said. "That was excellent. They are pigs. Buttheads."

"So I'm freelancing now, and this bears on what I'm up to tonight. I'm—I'm investigating something. By the way, the police are sort of clued in to what I'm doing. Not that I have their full approval," I muttered. Under Billie's bullshit-proof gaze my resolve wavered a little, but I gathered myself.

"If I don't call you by morning, please get in touch with the Eagle police, Lieutenant Ciesla, and tell him I'm missing. OK?" I wrote his name on a scrap of paper and laid it on the coffee table.

"I don't like this a bit, baby. I get the distinct impression you don't know what you're doing. What if I call up this Ciesla as soon as you leave?"

"And tell him what? Even if you get him on the phone at this hour, he won't do anything. Take my word for it." We sat a while in silence. "A woman's got to do what she's got to do," I said.

"What is this, a miniseries?"

I waved goodbye to Todd and opened the door.

Billie jumped up. "Goddamn it. Well, you're a big girl, girl. Just don't leave me any permanent rabbits."

"Right. See ya. And thanks, Billie."

As soon as I got to the car, my hands started to shake. I realized my stomach was way too empty, so I drove over to the White Castle on Woodward and swung into the drive-through. My belly jumped with hunger. Three cheeseburgers, small fries, large Coke.

I pointed the Caprice north again to hit Coolidge and scarfed down the food. My stomach settled right away. My watch said two-thirty, so I took it easy behind the wheel, on my way to the Meijer Thrifty Acres in Troy. If you have any sense, you hate the Meijer's experience, but I gotta admit, it's the best place to buy burglar tools in the middle of the night. For one, it's open, and two, nobody really notices anybody else.

Meijer's is practically a suburb unto itself, sprawling blandly out to the weedy edges of undeveloped land zoned commercial. On the way in I stopped at a pay phone to make a brief call.

I woke Kevin, the waiter, and cashed in a favor. He was all right. I said, "All you have to say is yes or no. The doors at the Snap are on alarm, right?"

"Yes. Shit."

"Don't worry. I could have found out myself if I'd wanted to stop in for a drink tonight. There's a contact on the door-frame, right?"

"Right."

"And it isn't silent, right? A bell rings?"

"Right."

"Anything else on the system that you know of? Office door?"

"No."

"Motion detectors or anything?"

"No. God no. The rats'd be setting them off all night." I could hear him beating his hand on his forehead as he did when distressed.

"Do you know Bonnie's code numbers, the numbers she punches into the keypad? Or Sandra's?"

"Uh-uh."

"OK. Thanks. You got a wrong number call tonight. You never talked to me. Thanks, Kevin."

"Shit."

I sauntered into the blinding white wash of light, found the hardware department and stood before the selection of pry bars. One with a thin-bladed hook seemed best. I picked up a small cold chisel and a hammer too.

I made my way toward the front of the store, trying to decide whether to buy anything else. The aisles near the cashiers were clogged with pool-toy displays and barbecue supplies. I saw a menacing-looking water pistol and briefly imagined filling it with drain cleaner or something, just to have one more weapon on me besides the pry bar. Nah, well.

The few other people in line were buying beer or small quantities of groceries. The cashier gave me a bit of a look. I fingered the pry bar and said, "Locked my keys in the car."

"Oh."

As she was handing me my change, I felt a peculiar sensation on the back of my neck. I looked over my shoulder. Standing there one check stand over, also receiving change as she stared intently at me, was Lou. Goddamn.

Her expression was a mixture of delight and awe.

I collected my stuff and headed for the doors at a run. But Lou could move. By the time I reached the parking lot she was on me like a duck on a june bug.

"Hey!" she cried, seizing my elbow and spinning me toward her. Her eyes were wild. "Hey! Oh, happy night!" She handled me all over as if I'd been a missing tot. "Thank God you're all right!"

I shrugged her hands off and tried to twist away, but she grabbed me in a bear hug from behind. "Lillian, *wait!*"

I couldn't get a breath to yell.

"Will you wait just a second?" Her raspy voice abraded my eardrums. I nodded, and she let me go. I turned to face her.

She was shook up big time. "When I saw the news on TV, I didn't know what to think. I was so scared for you! I went over to your house, but you were gone. I couldn't sleep! What time is it? I came here to buy some ice cream and some cards"—she opened her bag, and I glimpsed a couple Häagen-Dasz containers and a slim second bag—"I was going to write to you some more in these cards." She pulled out a few greeting cards featuring big-eyed children.

"Cute, huh?" She looked at me with frightening tenderness. "Did you get my letter?"

"Yes."

"Well, did you read it?"

"Lou, I have to go."

"What are you doing here? What did you buy? What's that stuff for?"

"None of your business." I looked into her eyes trying to see the kind of demented malice she'd have needed for the attack on Minerva.

"Lou, did you come to my home this morning?"

Her salt-and-pepper ponytail swayed behind her head. "No, darling. Did you want me to?"

"No!"

"Who was that woman in your apartment? The one they told about?"

"No one you know." I just couldn't read her. "I'm going now. Let me go, all right, Lou? You've got to get over this. Get hold of yourself."

To my surprise she didn't argue. She merely stepped aside and said, "All right." I thought I saw a sly expression.

As I wrenched the Caprice out of the parking lot, I saw her walking unhurriedly toward a cluster of cars. I didn't wait to see which one was hers.

I aimed south once again. Checking my mirrors over and over, I looked for Lou, looked for anybody on my tail. As far as I could tell, I was alone again.

The clock struck three. A safe hour for dirty work just about anywhere. I made one pass by the Snapdragon parking lot at a good clip, then came back. No cars, no Emerald, no red Fiero, nobody. I turned into the neighborhood beyond the back alley and parked on the street a few blocks down. No car followed me.

I kept a crummy black nylon windbreaker stuffed under the front seat, along with a pair of work gloves that I used when pumping my gas at the greasy budget stations I patronized. I pulled them out, put on the windbreaker, and shoved the gloves into the front pocket. The chisel went in one back jeans pocket, my pocketknife and flashlight in the other. The hammer I slid down the front of my jeans, its claw hooking over my belt. Keys in my front jeans pocket. The pry bar fit up the right sleeve of the windbreaker. I got an old blanket out of the trunk and rolled it under my arm. I was fabulously ready.

I set off toward the alley, looking over my shoulder as I went. I could have cut through backyards, but the danger outweighed any benefits of concealment: too many ultra-alert homeowners whose houses have been broken into two or three or ten times.

The most dangerous neighborhoods to go sneaking through are the ones fighting decay. Why? On posh streets the houses have expensive locks, good perimeter security, and complacent residents. In neighborhoods gone far to ruin, with burned-out houses everywhere and drug boys on the corners, people barely give a shit who's cutting through their backyards. But the hopeful streets, so many of them in Detroit, they've got the tough homeowners.

A German shepherd skulked in the backyard of one of the houses on my way. He kept silent until I was exactly abreast of him, then exploded into a screaming mass of fur and teeth, lunging at the fence, grabbing the top pipe with his paws. His head reached well over it. Gnashing his jaws, he looked as if he'd dearly love a meal of soft human throat.

32

"Down, you motherfucker." Climbing back into my skin, I veered around him and glanced over my shoulder at the house. No light.

I tried to make noise with my feet as I walked into the alley, to scatter the rats and bugs. The main light came from the only functional light fixture for a block, which, unfortunately, was a bulb right over the back door of the Snapdragon. It was encased in a cage of steel and Plexiglas.

Skirting the pool of light, I inspected the back of the building. There were a couple of ground-level basement windows, but they were barred. Painted over, too, so I couldn't see in. Ankle-high debris crowded up along the wall. I grabbed the bars on each window and shook them. Some ox of a guy might have been able to tear one loose with a pry bar, but not me. The door was heavy steel, with a flange covering the bolt area. It was a tougher one than the front door.

I continued down the alley in the darkness. At one point when I stopped to get my bearings and listen, something heavy ran across my foot. I jumped straight up and fought not to come down again. A rat the size of a raccoon disappeared behind some cans.

Everything was quiet. Coming around to the front of the building, I had a clear view of traffic from both directions. Livernois was a big five-lane avenue, so when cars went by at that hour, they were moving. I was pretty well-exposed, but I could also see anyone approaching. I preferred it this way to a tighter space where somebody could come upon me at any moment.

I lurked just at the corner of the little wooden entry hut, which was tacked onto the side of the building adjoining the parking lot. The door to the hut was locked, of course. It was a crude affair with a heavy hasp and padlock. The hut was made of thick lumber painted dark green. Bolt cutters would have been the thing to bring.

The weakest point on the whole job looked like the hinges, so I took one final look around, put my blanket down, slipped my pry bar out, and donned my work gloves. I eased one edge of the bar into the space between door and jamb; the hinges didn't fit very tightly. I worked the bar back and forth, rocking it with my weight. The wood started to splinter, the one-way screws anchoring the hinges starting to give. I'd never broken into a place, but I'd opened plenty of wooden packing cases when I had a summer job in receiving at GM Truck & Coach in Pontiac.

A tiny sound came from over my shoulder between the creakings of the wood. At the same instant I inhaled and almost keeled over from an overwhelming cloud of alcohol vapor. I turned and brushed noses with a wino who was rocking in time with me, hovering his head over my shoulder.

Other than his breath, he smelled exactly like the rancid alley. For all I knew I almost fell over him in there. I gave him a fierce look, and he stepped back. He was doubtless much younger than the sixty he looked. His chin glinted with silvery stubble and a little drool. A quilted winter jacket hung from his narrow shoulders. He had to be hot in it—I'd started to sweat in my windbreaker as soon as I put it on—but God knows he was probably afraid to take it off and forget it somewhere.

His hands were empty. He looked down at my blanket. I put my foot on it. I got out two dollars, packed into my left front pocket for just such a contingency, and handed it to him. He took the money without speaking and moved away down Livernois.

I kept rocking and working the bar. Finally, the top hinge came loose, and I was able to force enough of a slot to squeeze through. I pulled the door back into place behind me so at least from a distance it would look normal.

The rest was easy. I grasped the knob of the inner door with my left hand, wound up with the pry bar in my right, and bashed it into the one-way window set into the door. The glass wasn't plate glass; it was some kind of reinforced stuff, but it broke anyway. A small hole with crumbly edges opened up. I chipped at it until I got most of it broken away. The door was a heavy one, but the window was the weak link. Just big enough for me to get through.

I folded the blanket over the jagged edge and ducked through headfirst. I walked on my hands along the floor until I could get my feet through, the gloves protecting my hands from the sharp debris. Why didn't I just reach in and open the door from the inside? The alarm system. I'd remembered seeing a sticker on the door, which prompted my call to Kevin.

Most systems are alike: contacts on the doors that set off the alarm if broken, the same on windows that can be opened. Nobody uses that silver tape anymore to detect breaking glass. I'd held on to the knob before I broke the glass, because I didn't want the door to rattle and possibly disturb the contacts.

Using my flashlight I found the keypad in a nook behind the bar. Its red light glowed steadily. So I was inside, but as far as the alarm system was concerned, the perimeter was secure. I felt pleased with myself.

My small cone of light made shadows jump all over the place. The empty bar felt like the antechamber of a tomb. The tables and chairs were neatly spaced, each table with an ashtray, a candle pot, and a card with the snack menu on it, stuck on edge between them. Dead quiet.

I remembered Kevin mentioning rats. Well, I couldn't worry about goddamn rats. I figured as long as I couldn't hear anything moving, I'd be glad enough. The building's walls were cinder block, no windows except for the two basement ones. I poked around behind the bar looking for anything unusual. I crossed the room, stopped for a minute, then slowly edged into the back hall. I stuck my head and flashlight into the restrooms, nothing. Then I opened the door marked PRIVATE.

I was so tense, my spine felt as if it would snap in half if I made a sudden move. I felt for the light switch. Bright fluorescent photons filled up the room. Typical manager's office. Beige metal desk, office chair, phone, a straight chair. A small safe next to the desk covered with papers, invoices, a coffee mug, a copy of *People* magazine. Delivery schedules posted on the wall. I opened the desk drawers. Just junk: cigarettes, hand lotion, paper clips. A file cabinet in the corner. I opened every drawer, looked into every folder. Nothing, just paperwork: utility bills, payroll records, tax records. Most everything was in the same handwriting, Bonnie's I supposed, a boxy combination of cursive and printing. Office supplies. The safe was locked.

Dread rose in my chest and sent tentacles through my body. I shut off the light, closed the office door, and continued down to the end of the hallway. The back door was there, beyond that the alley. The stairwell yawned off to my right. I crept to the bottom. Another door there. I grasped the knob, locked. The door was pretty heavy, another metal one.

I got out the chisel and hammer and went to work. The metal-on-metal blows rang in the concrete-block stairwell. I punched through the lock core, not knowing whether that would do it, but the knob clicked and I was in the basement, looking.

It was dusty, nearly empty, and smelled like stale beer. There were several light switches on a box mounted on the rough cinder block, and I flipped them all.

The basement was smaller than I'd expected, split into two narrow spaces, one of them merely a passageway that led to a compact area where the beer kegs and pop canisters stood, their plastic lines leading upward, then disappearing through the ceiling to the bar.

One side wall appeared shiny, and I realized it was the steel door of a walk-in cooler. Of course, every bar of any size has a walk-in. I moved down the passage and stood before it. No lock on it. Images of dead bodies stacked like wood zoomed, unbidden, through my mind. Or else they were hanging there draped in plastic shrouds, their mouths gaping and bloody and toothless.

I grasped the chrome latch and heaved. Cold air flowed out around my ankles as the gasketed door moved in a smooth arc. Inside, I saw a more or less orderly arrangement of beverages and perishable food supplies. I felt relieved and chagrined all at once. Where the hell did these people commit their horrors?

I turned back. The other room looked unused. There were a few cardboard cartons piled up, which proved to be empty. Most everything looked pretty dusty and undisturbed.

Except—something didn't add up. As I scanned the basement again I realized there was only one window. But out in the alley I knew I saw two basement windows. There were more boxes stacked at the far end, stacked up pretty high against the wall, higher than my head. It was a dim cul-de-sac down there with a string dangling from a bare bulb. I could just make out the white string in the darkness. I felt my way over and twitched it.

The yellow light from the bulb showed that the boxes were sealed with tape and labeled things like BANK CARDS, REG JOURNAL TAPES, etc. I touched the boxes, nudged them some. While they seemed heavy enough to be full of paperwork, they were oddly balanced.

I boosted one down, tore off the tape and looked inside. There was just crumpled-up newspaper on top of a few inches of old magazines. I took down another, and another— all the same. Then I noticed the point of the whole exercise. The boxes were stacked up against a door, a low wooden door about chest high set right into the cinder blocks. I couldn't imagine any reason why the staff would have had occasion, or even the curiosity, to poke around those boxes. I shoved them aside and found another padlock.

As I worked on this one I kept expecting the booby trap to go off, you know, a volley of poison arrows or a falling anvil, but eventually the lock broke and the door swung open.

33

Maybe there was an automatic light switch connected to the door, or maybe my hand found the switch by itself. I was in a room about the size of my apartment. Any connection to reality ended at that doorway. I knew I'd found headquarters.

The place was furnished sparsely and lined with patterned wallpaper. In the center of the room stood a large round display case; in fact, it was a pie case like you see in diners, lit up with fluorescent tubes. It glowed in an eerie, radioactive way. I approached and looked. Inside was an array of tiny off-white things, stuck on little clear pedestals. I looked closer, not opening it. They were teeth, of course. I counted twenty-two of them, engraved or inscribed somehow with tiny spots or symbols in black. They looked familiar, like mine, only nicer.

A cardboard tray on a lower shelf contained more teeth, unadorned. The air smelled musty and dead.

There was another significant thing in the room: a hospital gurney, complete with straps and white sheets, set at an angle near a couple of metal cabinets, as if it were a piece of occasional furniture. The linens were tucked in neatly around the edges. A crummy couch covered in tattered brown corduroy sat against one wall, looking as if it'd been dragged in from the alley.

I opened the cabinets. They contained an array of dental instruments: picks and burrs and those big pliers they use for the old one-two. God almighty. Some stainless steel basins. I took out a basin and carried it around with me in case I needed to throw up.

There was a small table in a corner, tricked out like an altar, with a cross and plastic flowers and a string of tiny multicolored Christmas lights framing everything. A collage of Polaroid snapshots was taped to the wall around it. Faces of women posed in this very room.

Lots of pictures but not many different faces. Ten or a dozen. All were alive when the photos were taken. There was Iris. She looked all right. I mean, she was just looking into the camera with a serious expression. Not terrified. She was sitting on the couch. The gurney wasn't visible in the picture.

Then I recognized the wallpaper: It was made up of small Bible pages, set edge to edge like tiles, plastered from floor to ceiling, all the way around the room. My eye focused on, "Therefore snares are around thee, and sudden fear troubleth thee." Right on.

I followed the pages for a while, realizing they were in order from left to right, in columns of six. Genesis began right of the door, and Revelations finished off to the left. I was literally standing inside the Word. Then I remembered noticing the same odd wallpaper in the Creighter living room. I'd just glanced at it but noticed it had an unusual rectangular pattern, just like this.

I stared into space for a few moments, trying to make sense of everything. Of anything. I couldn't.

Then I noticed a black notebook, the kind with a nice sewn binding and hard covers, propped on the altar table. I opened it and found it blank except for the first page.

On that page were written a few simple columns in what looked like the same handwriting I'd seen in the upstairs office, and at that moment a big chunk of the puzzle slammed into place.

The columns were labeled: Subject, Age, Date, Method, Result. Under "Subject" there were merely the letters of the alphabet. My eyes skipped to the "Method" column, where I read on the first line for Subject A, "Psalms." Under "Result" was the word "Unsuccessful."

The method for Subject B had been "Deuteronomy." The result was the same, but indicated by ditto marks, as if the writer hadn't been eager to write out the word "Unsuccessful" again.

Different books of the Bible marched down the page under "Method," and the ditto marks went on unvaryingly through the most recent entry: Subject N. The date for N was last Sunday, and N's age was thirty-four.

The rest of the dates fit. I was looking at the shorthand chronicle of a deprogramming retreat founded around the time that the first of the Midnight Five had disappeared. Iris Macklin's entry meant there'd been fourteen subjects. The Midnight Five were here. The blank lines beneath Subject N and the blankness of the rest of the pages in the notebook sickened me more than anything I'd seen so far.

I closed the notebook.

Back to the pie case. For once something wasn't locked. I unlatched the door panel, and a blast of chemical smell came out. Carefully I reached in and took out a little pedestal with its tooth.

I couldn't easily make out the marking on it; it looked like a dark beetle. I noticed a magnifying glass on a shelf inside the case. I held the glass and the tooth up to the light. The tooth was an incisor. Painted in gorgeous—I have to tell you—detail was a copy of one of Raphael's Madonnas. I couldn't tell you the name of it; I skipped too much of art history class to know. This tooth had everything—the expression, the hair, the background, the proportion.

I rubbed my finger over it and realized it was actually an engraving, a shallow engraving. Like scrimshaw. I shook my head. Can you believe it? Human-tooth scrimshaw.

I pictured Mrs. Creighter, a corpulent elf, sitting patiently at her workbench, smiling slightly perhaps, as her pudgy nimble hands created these delicate masterpieces.

I took a quick look at the rest of them, then checked my watch: three-forty. I'd been there a very long time for a break-in.

The other teeth sported a variety of religious art. Thirteen of them were arranged in a row in a special holder. With a start I realized I was looking at DaVinci's *The Last Supper,* one face per tooth. Jesus, with extra halo, was in the center. All the teeth were front-type ones. I remembered Iris's molars were left intact.

I found another little tray, or dish, filled with small bones, in the bottom of the case. A round bone caught my attention. It was convex like a shield, and it rang a bell in my mind. Bonnie's amulet, yes. Her amulet wasn't some faux Native-American charm—it was somebody's kneecap.

Nicely smoothed, to be sure, stained mahogany and set with little chips of human teeth.

I left everything as I found it and looked around for a phone. I'd call Ciesla, then exit and keep watch until he showed. Clutching my burglar's tools, I started back up the steps. I allowed myself a deep breath and pictured Ciesla's face when he got a load of all this.

I swung around the corner from the top step, moving fast now into the hallway. But something was wrong—the lights were on in the bar. And Mrs. Creighter was planted there, feet apart, aiming her gun at me. And as I skidded to a stop on my heels, as I'd thought only characters in cartoons could do, she shot me.

34

Knowing what I know now about how easy it is to score a solid hit with a handgun at close range, I'm a little surprised at what happened. At the last microsecond my body began to react, and I must have twisted some way. Mrs. Creighter probably thought I was diving for the floor, so she jerked the barrel of the gun down as she pulled the trigger. *Cak!* The report was sharp and very short. She missed, then fired again. The bullet struck my right thigh in an explosion of hot force. My leg flew out from under me, and I hit the deck.

I screamed, not so much from pain as panic. Mrs. Creighter rushed over to me. As I writhed on the floor she looked down and yelled something, but I couldn't hear her: My ears were ringing from the shots, which had been amplified in the narrow bare hallway. I felt a deep burning in my thigh. I cursed a torrent, getting a little hysterical as blood welled up between my fingers. "You bitch from hell, you piece of shit, you shit..."

"Shut up," Mrs. Creighter said. Towering over me, she looked like a Macy's balloon. Bonnie appeared next to her, holding a drink and a cigarette. Evidently the two had come in quietly while I was down the basement, fixed themselves a couple of drinks, and discussed strategy while waiting for me to come up. Bonnie kicked away my pry bar and hammer.

"Come on, let's go," Mrs. Creighter said. "Get up, come on."

"Ma, don't touch her!" Bonnie cried. "Why did you shoot her? Now I have to—we have to—"

Mrs. Creighter stood over me grinning violently, appearing not to hear.

Bonnie let out a desperate sound, almost a sob. "Wait a minute then." She set her drink down on the floor. Grunting heavily, they dragged me by the arms down the hall to the stairwell.

I tried to resist, clutching the doorframe. As we tottered on the brink, Mrs. Creighter let go of my arm, and I pitched forward. To avoid flying down behind me, Bonnie let go too. I felt space open below me and thought, what the hell. I relaxed and just sort of bounced all the way to the bottom, turning one somersault, I think. My back slammed against the door at the bottom. Mrs. Creighter clattered down after me.

"You ripped up our locks," she said, pushing open the door and stepping over me. Bonnie, having retrieved her drink, clumped down to join us.

"Come on, get up," said Mrs. Creighter, nudging me with her foot. "We're not going to hurt you anymore."

Hah. I pushed myself into a sitting position, my legs stuck out in front of me. The pain in my thigh was hot and fierce. I'd thought you got a kind of grace period after getting shot, you know, when you don't feel pain. Well, I didn't get one.

Mrs. Creighter went over to one of the metal cabinets and took out a white towel from a stack in there. She spread it on the couch and said, "Come on, sit over here. Come on."

Bonnie said, "Oh, Lord." She eyed me the same way she had before, with that dreamy, almost submissive look. Yes, that was it. My stomach turned.

Mrs. Creighter pointed the gun at me again. "Get up."

Putting weight on my right leg made me see stars. I hopped over to the couch and flopped down on it. Bonnie brought another towel and tried to dab my jeans with it. "Are you all right?"

As she bent over me her amulet swayed forward and touched my nose. I jerked back and snatched the towel from her. "Get away from me."

There was only a tiny dark hole in my blue jeans. I pressed the towel against it. The wound was bleeding, I could feel it, but it wasn't gushing. Just flowing steadily. The gun was the same .22 auto, so I counted myself lucky that the slug was little and probably just lodged in the muscle somewhere. It sure felt big, though.

"Take that jacket off," Mrs. Creighter ordered. I did and threw it on the floor. She picked it up and felt the limp pocket, then seated herself on the other end of the couch at my feet. Bonnie hopped up onto the gurney nearby, biting her lips. The three of us sat there for a few moments without speaking, catching our breaths. The initial pain in my leg began to subside, replaced by a deep, dull throbbing. My situation wasn't a good one.

I watched Bonnie. There was something about her, a duality, some ambivalence that gave me hope. All along Mrs. Creighter had been the more murderously hysterical of the two. They were a perversion of the mother-daughter unit, all right. How deep did murder run in each of them? They were both sweating, their foreheads identically sheened with perspiration.

Bonnie seemed somehow stronger than her mother, yet emotionally vulnerable. She appeared confused. I had to find a way to take advantage of her.

As we sat there, Mrs. Creighter appeared to go into sort of a trance. I remembered a passage in one of Minerva LeBlanc's books that said the few people who've survived serial-killer situations report that the murderers' faces appear totally expressionless, devoid of any feeling or awareness. Mrs. Creighter's face was like that now.

But Bonnie's face was boiling. Emotions seemed to be surging through her: excitement, repugnance, guilt, love, loathing. She startled her mother and me by breaking the silence.

"Ma, I—" She stopped.

Mrs. Creighter slowly looked over at her, through her. At the same moment, she put her hand on my foot. I flinched.

"Ma, I don't want this one dead. This one's different." Bonnie was fighting something—it was all over her face. "This is screwed up, this is all screwed up now."

Mrs. Creighter said, in a voice as expressionless as her face, "Nothing's screwed up. Everything's well in hand." Her face was embryo-like, with a pushed-up nose and a small, curving chin. She was the most grotesque human being I had ever seen.

I took a deep breath of the dank, close air. I didn't have time to waste. Everybody knows you're not supposed to try to push crazy people around, lest they go off on you, but these two had already gone off on me. I was scared, angry, and bleeding, and I had the feeling that Bonnie, though ostensibly in control of the situation, could be manipulated.

"Bonnie," I said, in a tone that was firm but warm, "let's cut the crap." She looked at me in surprise. "I know you have feelings for me," I suggested. "That's the reason you haven't grabbed that gun and finished me off. Am I right?"

Her lips parted, then closed in a faint smile.

"You're a very misunderstood person," I went on. "That's frustrating, isn't it?"

"It is, it is!" Tears of self-pity sprang to her eyes.

I saw my opening and forced myself to take it. "I bet you can't guess my secret."

"Lillian?"

"I have feelings for you too, Bonnie."

"You feel something special for me?"

"Something very special." That was true, all right.

I thought Mrs. Creighter wasn't listening from the depths of her trance, or murderous reverie, or whatever the hell it was. But she was.

"My little girl isn't right," she said. "She's made mistakes in her life. But here is where we find redemption. We all find it here."

"Ma, be quiet."

"Don't make another mistake."

"Ma, be quiet. She knew what was going on. She could see it. I have to think."

"She's a fraud." Mrs. Creighter lifted her eyes and addressed God—her God, anyway. "It's all right. We're going to go on just like before. In praise. In glory. We need nothing else." She fondled the gun in her lap like a darning egg.

Without warning, Bonnie hopped off the gurney and

grabbed a roll of adhesive tape from an open shelf. Quiet fragments of words poured from her lips; after a few seconds they coalesced into "No one's going to leave me, no one's going to leave me."

I thought she was about to bind me up, but no. Before her mother could react, she stripped off an arm's length of tape and wound it around her mother's wrists, flipping the gun away as she did so. It clattered on the floor. Mrs. Creighter gasped. Then she bent and extended a second length down around her mother's legs, which stuck out like hams from the hem of her flowered dress.

It took her all of five seconds to neutralize the old girl.

Her mother yelled, "Don't go speaking in tongues on me!" Bonnie slapped one last wad of tape over her mouth.

Then she grabbed up the gun, which I knew I couldn't have gotten to first anyway.

Mrs. Creighter looked down wonderingly at her bonds.

"I don't want you shooting her again," said Bonnie.

I relaxed fractionally. "Thank you so much."

Mrs. Creighter grunted and pulled at the tape.

Then inspiration struck. Mustering an extremely sincere smile, I said, "Look, Bonnie, this might be premature, but we could run away together. You know? And be rid of all of this. What do you say?" I extended my open hand. "You've had a lot on your shoulders. I want to take care of you. I'll handle everything so you can relax."

Ding. Before my eyes Bonnie turned from an impenetrable psycho into a pathetic little girl. Her body language completely changed. I saw the tight carriage of a grown-up melt into the uneven, trusting movements of a child.

She hopped back up onto the gurney, then hopped down again and sat on the floor next to the coffee table, looking up at me. She held the gun with both hands, as if it were too heavy for just one.

I said reassuringly, "There really aren't any secrets, are there?"

She shook her head, smiling in relief.

From there we covered quite a bit of ground. With the malevolent force of her mother temporarily neutralized, Bonnie began to talk as if she were a dam somebody had just blown a hole through. She spoke rapidly, without pause, using odd repetitions and fragments. I had to listen closely to follow her.

"In the beginning I was little, and I knew I was different. I was different, but I didn't know how, and then it was that we had no choice about the proper way to worship, but then…"

The deal was, Bonnie told me, that her father had been a charismatic preacher in some fiery sect I'd never heard of, and he'd held complete and dysfunctional sway over the whole family. After a stint as a teenage missionary, Bonnie escaped and took up a swingin' lifestyle, insofar as a stunted weirdo like her *could* swing. She had a few gay experiences, then decided that was *it* for her, the key to life.

She deluded herself into thinking she could normalize relations with her family, and made the mistake of coming out to them while they were all together in an automobile en route to a family reunion at some relative's house out West.

Mr. Creighter had a heart attack at the wheel, Bonnie went on, sending the car into a ravine. Bonnie's sister Veronica was killed instantly, but Bonnie and Mrs. Creighter were thrown clear. While unconscious, they experienced a sequence of religious visions involving winged lizards, talking cacti, smoldering crankcase oil, and each other.

Bonnie landed in a private mental institution for a time, then got it together enough to set up housekeeping with her mother back at the old homestead.

Because God told her to, she bought the bar with all the money they had. God instructed her to do a great many other things from then on, and she did them all, with the avid help of her mother. Over time, it seemed, Mrs. Creighter took on more of a leadership role.

From time to time during this monologue, Mrs. Creighter grunted and yanked on her bonds. She was pouring sweat. The bosom of her dress was soggy. As for me, my thigh was hurting worse, and I saw more blood oozing from beneath the towel, darkening my jeans. My head felt light. I tried to make ESP contact with Billie, telling her to call Ciesla. *Wake up and call the police now,* I telegraphed.

35

Bonnie talked for perhaps an hour solid. I learned that for her, there was nothing contradictory in building up a business that catered to gay women and killing off a small percentage of them in the name of God. Owning the bar obviously fed Bonnie's need to be near women, her need to feed herself sexually.

The Midnight Five, as I'd guessed, fell into the category of curious, nervous women who had responded to her blind ads and had come to the bar once, perhaps after hours. I pictured others creeping in during business hours, tentative and scared, looking not very approachable. I'd seen such women occasionally at the Snap. They'd sit in a corner with a drink, not calling attention to themselves, rarely talking to anyone, but watching the room with hungry, shame-filled eyes.

I could see Bonnie lying in wait for such women and discreetly pouncing, with no one the wiser. Someone who came to the bar publicly just once, especially a bar as busy as the Snapdragon, well, who'd remember her?

Bonnie seemed to think such women could be turned away from the terrible path of sin they were about to take. I'd heard of the Bible being used as a weapon before, but it remained unclear to me exactly how Bonnie put it to use. I got the sense that the murders were supposed to be some kind of sacrifice or atonement.

I learned that Iris had been special to Bonnie because she seemed to actually like Bonnie. So Bonnie broke her rule of only preying on women unknown to others at the bar. It'd been simple carelessness in disposing of the body that set the ball rolling for me to start asking questions.

I gathered that the mother had always been a little cracked, but being married had held her together. The family tragedy had set her loose and put a cherry firmly on top of her psycho sundae. She seemed to get a deep satisfaction out of helping her daughter. As she saw it, Bonnie was earnestly cleansing herself of evil, here in this basement, and she wanted the show to go on and on.

Bonnie, I thought, was about to begin telling me about her mother's ghastly hobby, when her speech slowed. Her words began to jell into complete sentences; her frantic cadence dropped.

She looked me in the eye and said, "Certain things were not my fault." Then she fell silent.

Something had happened to the Creighters after the psychological jolts they'd received. Mother and daughter shared a certain number of genes and a certain outlook. I guess it was natural for events to affect them similarly and for them to act in tandem. They'd convinced themselves that their actions were moral and just, if not by the standards of earthly justice, then divine.

I saw a glint of reason gradually take hold in Bonnie's eyes; I knew it to be fundamentally false, but at least it was something. Her psychotic break couldn't last forever.

As if reading my mind, she said, "Someone should stop us."

I started to say, "That's just what—" but we were both startled by Mrs. Creighter leaping to her feet, free of her tape.

While Bonnie had been talking, she'd remained quiet except for the occasional grunt, but she'd been silently working free. I saw that her perspiration had acted as a lubricant, helping her slip out of the tape. Now she ripped off her gag—a small piece of her lip came off with it, leaving a bloody spot—and shrieked, "The word of God doesn't sit still! Listen to God!"

It was go time. "Shut up!" I screamed at her. I edged forward on the couch. "Bonnie, look, you're not crazy. You've convinced yourself that you're doing God's work, when all along you've only been serving your own appetites. You indulged yourself, then tried to make up for it by destroying people just like yourself."

I pointed to her mother. "*She's* the crazy one! My God, have you ever met that Wycoff, her necrophiliac boyfriend? You've been protecting her, catering to her, dancing to her tune this whole time because of *guilt*?"

"A little guilt is a good thing," said Mrs. Creighter. "Pay attention to me."

"Shut the fuck up! Shut up!" I said, "Don't listen to her, Bonnie, listen to me. I'm probably God anyway." Bonnie stared at me, listening, trying to piece it together; she was trying. "Bonnie, lay down this stupid burden you've been carrying. Lay it down. You can't change anything about your father and sister. *You're* not crazy. You'd like to be, though—it'd let you off the hook. Well, hell. Be a woman. Be a real woman now and end this."

Bonnie opened her mouth and hoarsely said, "Yes."

Mrs. Creighter lunged for the gun. Bonnie wasn't ready for her, and the old girl came up with it.

"I know the devil now!" Mrs. Creighter cried as she pointed the gun at me. I closed my eyes and rolled off the couch. Nothing happened.

When I opened my eyes, she had the gun aimed at her daughter. She paused. Then she turned it to her own temple.

Bonnie leaped at her mother, but Mrs. Creighter moved incredibly fast. She circled the couch holding the gun out of Bonnie's reach. Then she reached down, pointed the gun in my direction, and fired.

There was a flash, and my head slammed against the floor. The next thing, I was hearing their voices, high and panicky, above my head. I must have fainted.

Unbelievably, the bullet didn't hit me. I think it singed my hair. Bonnie and Mrs. Creighter were upstairs, screaming.

I struggled to my feet, my leg flashing with pain. I limped over to the window, remembering when I got there that it was barred. The voices upstairs rose to a crescendo. Two shots and a ricochet: *Cak! Ca-ring!* An instant of silence, then a shriek from Bonnie and an ugly torrent of gibberish from her mother.

I dragged the gurney over to the wall, since the window was above my head. I climbed up and wrapped my blood-soaked towel around my fist. I pounded, and the glass shattered. I bashed at the bars, but they were solid.

"Hey!" I hollered, reaching out through the bars, shoving my hand through alley scum, dead leaves, oily muck. "Hey!" I prayed for some prostitute or junkie, anybody, to be passing through. I listened. "Help!" Nothing. I turned back toward the room. Silence. "Hey! Help!" I hollered again. The hollering made my head pound.

"What? Who's there? Who's that?" a husky voice came to my ear through the jagged hole. "What the—who's there? Bonnie, is that you?" Footsteps tromped to the window, and I saw work shoes, then denim-clad knees, then a pair of brown elbows. Carefully the person put his face to the ground and turned it sideways. It was Emerald, the parking attendant. He looked into my eyes with his own kind, anxious ones.

"No, it's not Bonnie. It's Lillian Byrd. Remember me? I can't get out. Please help me." I felt dizzy and had to cling tighter to the bars to keep from swaying.

"Lillian Byrd, what are you doing down there? What's going on?"

"Insanity! Terrible! You've got to call the police. They shot me."

"The police shot you?"

"No! Bonnie and her mother have me cornered down here. The mother's got a gun. They killed that DJ. They killed the Midnight Five and then some."

"I always knew she wasn't sound," Emerald said. "Sweet Jesus! My house just got robbed, and I was looking to see if they dropped any of our stuff back here. I live across the fence, three blocks down. I almost caught 'em."

Another shot. "Emerald, go! Tell them they're shooting right now. She's gonna come down here again."

"Dear Jesus! Here, take this." He reached under his shirt and pulled out a snub-nosed revolver, and handed it butt-first through the window. "Shoot the bitch if she comes at you. Just aim it and shoot. OK, OK." He took off down the alley.

I hopped down from the gurney. It was quiet now upstairs. I turned the gun over in my hands. It sure settled my gut to have it. Someone descended the steps. Mrs. Creighter pushed through the door.

Her hair was wild, and blood dripped from her mouth. The gun dangled from her hand. Her eyes swept the room, then she saw me.

She smiled. "Well now, dearie—" she began, then stopped when I waved Emerald's gun.

"Stay where you are," I commanded. "The police are on their way. Don't do anything."

"Hah!" she said. "You found that! Bonnie must've had it hidden somewhere. It's not loaded."

"The police are coming."

She sank to her knees, then arranged herself cross-legged on the floor, as Bonnie had done. She seemed to forget about me. Gazing off into some distant reality, she looked like a circus freak: proud of herself in a weird way, yet sad at the same time. All of her up front. She sat like that for a while, and I waited, tight with fear.

My ears strained to hear police sirens. *Come on, Emerald.* I tried to lock eyes with Mrs. Creighter to get a look inside her, but it was impossible.

"A tooth for a tooth," she mumbled.

"And if he knocks out the tooth of his slave, he shall let him go free for his tooth's sake." I'd done a little Bible study in my day.

Without warning she lifted her gun and fired in my direction: *Ca-ring!* I threw myself behind the couch, which jerked as the bullet hit it. I smelled singed cloth. I feared the next shot would go through. As the movies had taught me, I popped my head around the side, fast, and shot back, once, twice.

The noise from all this was indescribable. Emerald must have put a pretty hot charge in his gun because my whole arm bucked skyward when I pulled the trigger. Mrs. Creighter didn't move. Neither of us had hit the other.

As I peeped over the couch she again lifted her gun, this time in both hands, took serious aim, and fired. The bullet whizzed through the couch, just missing my ribs, and ricocheted off the wall. I heard the tinkle of her ejected cartridge as it skittered to the floor.

I was too terrified to stick my whole head out again to aim, so I just blindly poked the gun barrel over the top of the couch and fired three more times.

This is a very lousy way to defend yourself.

I didn't hit Mrs. Creighter, and she still had more ammunition. She fired once more into the couch; the bullet tore through, caromed off the wall, and stung me in the butt. The spent bullet just bounced off my jeans. Tendrils of sharp gun smoke curled into my nostrils.

As I cowered in my hiding place I heard her rise and advance in my direction. I pulled my trigger again. *Click.* Empty. Oh, yes.

My back was against the Bible-plastered death-chamber wall, and the angel of chaos was bearing down on me. I turned to the wall seeking grace. "Whoso diggeth a pit shall fall therein" read the passage before my eyes. Right.

Suddenly there was a terrific crash upstairs, followed by pounding footfalls, a hesitation, then somebody big and determined rushing down the stairs.

I poked my head up to see the door blast open and Lou barrel into the room, carrying some long strange weapon. I don't know about Mrs. Creighter, but I was expecting a cop.

Mrs. Creighter instantly turned on her, snarling, but her

voice strangled in her throat as Lou rammed her dogcatcher noose over her head and jerked it tight. The heavy wire noose disappeared into the folds of her neck.

Lou accomplished this in a second. "Stay there!" she yelled to me. Mrs. Creighter's gun went off, then dropped from her hand. It was her last round; the slide was stuck open. She pawed the air, then grasped the noose's metal pole as if she were impaled on it, went down to her knees, then collapsed onto her side, her eyes bulging.

Lou loosened the noose slightly, planted her foot on Mrs. Creighter's waist, and announced in a tough voice, "You're not goin' nowhere, lady."

As I was trying to grasp what had just happened, a bolt of white light shot into the room from behind me: a police flashlight. Moments later I was under arrest for possession of an unregistered handgun.

36

During the turbulent ten minutes that followed, I lay on the floor waiting for the paramedics, attempting to synopsize the night for the police. Lou stood to the side, listening and chiming in.

Owing to her obsession, she had set up her own surveillance on me, at first to satisfy her own compulsion, then later to keep track of my dangerous blundering as well. Being an electronics buff (I remembered mention of it in her letter), she got hold of a homing collar used on wild animals and secretly attached it to the Caprice's undercarriage.

She had to work during the days, but at night she tracked my whereabouts from her home, using some kind of radio receiver. She decided to rendezvous with me at Meijer's to see what I was up to so late in the evening. She'd had me totally fooled.

Later, when she realized my car was near the Snapdragon, she followed, sensing catastrophe. She brought along the weapon she knew best, her animal noose. So intent was she on getting to the Snap that she ran a red light a few miles away and clipped a newspaper delivery van. No one was hurt, but her front axle was bent, so she abandoned the car and hustled the rest of the way on foot, equipped with her noose and a nearly delusional sense of invulnerability.

"Thank you, Lou," I said, grasping her hand.

"You're welcome. Lillian?"

"Yes."

"Don't worry anymore. About me. You know what I mean?" We talked around the stolid presence of the cops.

"Double thank you."

She appeared exhausted yet clear-eyed, as if she'd been through a catharsis. She wasn't fidgeting.

The ambulance guys insisted on strapping me to a stretcher and carrying me upstairs. To tell the truth, I felt pretty used up. Bonnie wasn't dead, though she looked it. She lay in a lump on the dance floor, her eyes glassy while another pair of ambulance guys worked on her. Her mother's aim had been better on her, and she'd got one in the gut. I asked why they didn't just throw her into the ambulance and get her over to the hospital, and they said they needed to stabilize her first. I was stable enough.

They took Mrs. Creighter away in a police car, but I suspected she'd get into a hospital at some point.

Emerald was standing outside, along with the wino I'd given the two dollars. They formed the crowd for this event. I told the ambulance guys to hold it. Emerald said it was sure lucky his house had gotten broken into that night. If he hadn't had occasion to go out looking for his stuff... And you know, I did find—I actually did find my wife's purse in that Dumpster!" he said. "No money in it, to be sure."

The police were obliged to confiscate his gun and inform me that although I was going to the hospital, I was under arrest for having the gun, for which neither Emerald nor I could produce documentation. "It is *my* gun," Emerald shouted at the officers. "It is a five-shot Smith & Wesson Chief's Special, and I have the serial number memorized. You ever try to get a handgun permit in this city?"

"But she had ahold of it," a cop said.

"It's OK, Emerald," I said.

They took me to Receiving Hospital, the best place to go in the city if you've got a bullet in you. They must handle a thousand cases a year. Ciesla and Porrocks showed up. The doctors let them into my cubicle after they'd gotten an IV going.

A Detroit cop had shackled my ankle to the gurney. Ciesla persuaded him to come in and take it off. The doctors and nurses left me to wait for the X-ray guy. A non-life-threatening gunshot wound at Receiving is low priority, given the cornucopia of drastic medical emergencies generated by the city twenty-four hours a day.

Ciesla took my hand, bless him. I didn't have anything to say. "Decency makes me thank you," he said. "I know you were trying to do the right thing. But you should have been killed."

"I know."

"You're so stupid."

"I know!"

He asked for the details and made notes while I talked. Porrocks hovered, patting my arm. A nurse came in and gave me a shot for the pain, which was getting worse now that I was finally relaxing. I felt the effects of the injection immediately.

"Tell me," I asked her in my throatiest voice, "will I make it?"

"Oh, certainly." She was apple-cheeked and efficient and talked with a Scots accent. "You'll need a bit of surgery, no doubt."

"Will I be able to do pirouettes after this?"

"I should think so, of course."

I tapped an imaginary cigar and wiggled my eyebrows. "That's funny, I never could do pirouettes before!"

She clearly wanted to throttle me with the IV line, but I got a good pair of laughs out of Ciesla and Porrocks. It was a relief to hear them laugh. Then an orderly came and pushed me down to X-ray and back.

Ciesla said the handgun charge would probably be dropped. Then a surgeon walked in, examined my leg, making it hurt horribly, and said they would indeed have to operate to get the slug out. Porrocks promised to call Billie for me, then the cops bid me adieu.

They only kept me two days in the hospital. I learned from Ciesla that Bonnie had made it and was supposed to recover fully. He also told me that it wasn't Bonnie who'd come after me that morning and attacked Minerva; it'd been Mrs. Creighter, who presumably was losing patience with the cat-and-mouse routine.

Billie collected me and drove me to Aunt Rosalie and Uncle Guff's house; they were gracious enough to take me in. She brought Todd over the next day. I imagined he looked glad to see me. I certainly was glad to see him. I started working on my story for the *Motor City Journal* right away.

Minerva, I learned, had made it through two surgeries, during which the doctors had found more of her brain left than they'd expected. They put a plate in her head to replace the segment of pulverized skull, then she promptly lapsed into a coma. Her parents ordered her shipped back to some medical center on Long Island, where they lived. I didn't get to see her before she was taken away.

While Bonnie recovered from her wounds she and her mother were charged with the murder of Iris Macklin and the attempted murder of Minerva LeBlanc.

Judy called me once after she heard about my exploits. "You are not a person I can cope with in any way anymore," she said stiffly, after making sure I was all right.

Ciesla and Porrocks let me know pretty much the same thing, although Ciesla couldn't help bringing over some frozen spaghetti sauce and homemade chocolate chip cookies. Aunt Rosalie thanked him nicely but eyed the food suspiciously behind his back. I knew what she was thinking: *A man who cooks? Bad medicine.*

"Erma thinks we would have cracked this anyway," Tom said. "But I'm not so sure. If the two of them kept denying everything, they might have gotten away with it. In Iris Macklin's case we thought it was the husband. He wouldn't take a polygraph. I don't know why. I think Bonnie Creighter's going to tell us where the other bodies are. She's not too mentally tough anymore."

I never did learn exactly what went on in that basement, exactly how Colossians was inflicted on Subject E, for instance, and I suppose in retrospect that's for the best.

Evidently Mrs. Creighter's morbid business in forensic art was merely a sideline, the supply of teeth from the fresh corpses a happy coincidence. She'd held down a part-time job as a dental hygienist, where, coincidentally, they'd had a rash of thefts of equipment and supplies.

I wrote Minerva's parents a low-key letter, trying to help them understand their daughter's last hours before the attack (minus certain details), trying to express my sympathy and my grief, so small in proportion to theirs. No one knew whether Minerva would ever wake up. I suggested that I'd come to visit her soon.

As far as I could learn, she didn't leave behind a lover in New York. The parents wrote back telling me to keep away.

Within a few weeks my leg was practically back to normal and my story was finished. It ran as the cover piece in the *Journal,* titled "How Not to Catch the Crooks: My Adventures With Murder and Chaos in Detroit's Underbelly." Ricky Rosenthal loved it, the response was terrific, and he gave me an assignment to write a feature on life on the Detroit P.D.'s vice squad. My freelance career was underway.

When the story came out, Judy found it necessary to call again. She tracked me down in the new apartment I'd rented a few blocks away from the McVitties' duplex. I had a phone, a card table with two folding chairs, and a box of groceries. That was it. Todd and I rolled around the empty apartment like marbles in a coffee can. I'd spent a wad getting the Caprice repainted the same nice shade of evergreen. But I'd saved a hundred dollars out of my check from the *Journal* to go on a shopping spree at John King, the great used bookshop near Wayne State. I was working on a list of essential titles when Judy called.

"Our community," she told me huffily, "doesn't need this kind of crazy crap going on." As if *I'd* killed somebody.

"What community?"

"You know," her voice was scratchy with irritation, "the gay and lesbian community. This kind of publicity doesn't do us much good. You went and poked around in dangerous places. You got yourself shot, Lillian! That is not the kind of message women need to be hearing! Plus, everybody thinks queers are killers anyway, and this kind of stereotyping, well, it's just irresponsible."

"But Judy, I—you've missed the point. These women, the Creighters, I don't think you could call them gay, or even festive. They were maniacs."

"Oh." Sarcastic-like.

"And do you suppose true Christians go around killing people? Anyway, wouldn't you *want* to know about something like this? I can't help it if it was sensational." *Moreover,* I thought, *this is the stuff rent checks are made of.*

I didn't ask about Sharon Wurtz, and she didn't offer any information. I figured I'd see them around.

Lou called after reading my article. I suggested we meet for coffee, which we did, nice and normal, at Yokey-Dokey. I wanted to make sure she understood how grateful I was that she'd showed up when she did.

"Anybody woulda done it," she mumbled into her hazelnut latte.

"I don't think so."

"Well. So. Maybe we can just be friends? You know, friends?"

We shook on it.

I heard nothing from Ed or Bucky Rinkell. I guessed the Buckeroo thought he'd taught me the lesson I deserved.

Except he hadn't.

That loose end gnawed at me; something, like a little angel on my shoulder, told me I should tie it up. Whatever I did to him had to focus on his car, as he had focused on mine. He knew I doted on my car, and I knew he cherished his. Yes, he cherished his car as a surfer cherishes his board, as a porn star cherishes his penis, as a corporate vice president cherishes his corner office. It bolstered his identity. As long as he took care of it, it would take care of him. To other guys, their cars are babe magnets; to Bucky, his Camaro was a babe substitute.

No way could I simply trash his car, as he had mine, and get away with it. No, he'd know it was me, and I'd get it again some way. He'd never, ever let me have the last word. Fine.

Everybody knows the most beautiful paybacks are the self-inflicted ones. I thought and thought, and finally came up with a plan. All it would take was one more tiny bit of skullduggery. That, and the willingness to relinquish the moral high ground I'd been so firmly standing on from the beginning.

One fine day I cruised around to a couple of stores and obtained a pair of bolt cutters, a sheet of coarse sandpaper, a pair of coveralls, and a hard hat for good measure. I swung through downtown Eagle close enough to the *Eye* offices to glimpse Bucky's sparkling blue Camaro at the curb. It was resplendent. Really, it was. Then I drove to his apartment building.

Most of the tenants worked during the day, so the place was quiet. I parked around back, donned the coveralls and hard hat, and strode up to the main entrance. A minute after I pressed all the doorbells with my palms, the speaker crackled and a querulous voice said, "Yes?"

"Maintenance." I was ready to talk my way in, but whoever it was hit the buzzer instantly. Listening up the stairwell, I heard an apartment door open, then shut after a questioning pause.

I found Bucky's storage closet in the basement, having vaguely remembered the setup from the tour he'd given during his ill-fated cookout. I recognized the hibachi and the ice chest with its WLLZ bumper sticker.

The closets were wire-fenced cages with combination padlocks. After slicing off the lock with my bolt cutters I found Bucky's car-wash pail. It contained a sponge and bottles of Ivory Liquid, Windex, Armor-All, and a generic bug dissolver. Nestled in the bottom was the object of my quest: a can of top-of-the-line Turtle Wax. I pried it open with my knife. It was about half full.

I got out the sheet of coarse sandpaper and scraped a fair amount of grit into the wax. I pressed and stirred it into the top layer with my finger, then carefully smoothed it over with a wadded-up Kleenex and replaced the lid.

I put everything back the way it was, then messed up the rest of his stuff, as if a burglar had been looking for valuables. Then I beat it.

Have you ever looked at sandpaper under a microscope? It's fearsome. That's the way it looks to paint too.

A few weeks later I learned that Gerald Macklin got his promotion at Hastings Benevolex after all; his face popped out at me from the business section of the *Free Press* one morning. "Congratulations, buddy," I said to the head shot, then tore up the paper.

The day was the last cloudless, hot one of the year. I fired up the Caprice and drove around the metro area aimlessly, letting the gritty expressway wind blow through the windows, across my face.

For the hell of it, I cruised past the *Eye* offices. I had to look twice, but there it was: Bucky's Camaro, with a brand-new paint job. *Orange* metallic sparkle this time.

Even that didn't cheer me up, though, and I hit the expressways again. Eventually I pulled into a sprawling suburban cemetery, all flatness and tacky chapels. The sun was beating down, straight overhead.

The caretaker helped me find the rectangle of sod that covered Iris Macklin six feet down. There was no stone yet.

I stood there remembering my fleeting impression of her beauty and the senselessness of her loss. A shadow swept across the grass. Looking up I saw a hawk on the wing, cruising the updrafts, hunting for mice among the tombstones. I would remember Iris forever. It was all right that I knew next to nothing about her.

I thought about the Midnight Five and the rest of the dead women, their desperate last hours. It was time to quit thinking about them. I thought about Minerva LeBlanc, lying insensible in some clinic where no one could know how wonderful she had been.

I thought about people who can't handle what God gives them and decide to take it out on the rest of us.

Hunkering down, I plucked a stem of clover and chewed it. The hawk, a red-tail, dropped like a stone from the sky. In a minute it was up again, climbing, talons empty, starting all over.

About the Author

Randall Lamb

Elizabeth Sims is a book person through and through. A ten-year veteran of bookselling, she has also worked as a reporter and a photographer. Her short fiction and poetry have appeared in *Moving Out* and *The Smudge*, and her book reviews in the *Detroit Free Press*. A longtime resident of the Detroit area, she now lives in Northwestern Washington. Visit her Web site at www.elizabethsims.com.